SWEET SURRENDER

A SUGAR RUSH ROMANCE

NINA LANE

PUBLISHING

Sweet Surrender
A Sugar Rush Romance

Published by Snow Queen Publishing

This book is a work of fiction. All names, characters, locations, and incidents are products of the author's imagination, or have been used fictitiously. Any resemblance to actual persons living or dead, locales, or events is entirely coincidental.

Cover photography: Sara Eirew
Cover design: Perfect Pear Creative Covers

ISBN: 978-1-7360527-9-2

SWEET SURRENDER
NINA LANE

§◆

Efficient Kate Darling needs lessons in seduction, and hot bad
boy Tyler Stone is the perfect teacher. But falling in love isn't
part of the curriculum.

Warning!
Contains kitchen sex, disco music, classic cars, pancakes at 2:00
a.m., dirty movies, alphabetizing, and bad puns

The Sugar Rush books are sexy contemporary romances by New
York Times bestselling author Nina Lane. They can be read as
standalone novels or enjoyed as a series.

SWEET DREAMS
SWEET ESCAPE
SWEET SURRENDER
SWEET TIME
SWEET LIFE

CHAPTER 1

*P*erfect legs.

Long and shapely with toned calves and delicate ankles. Legs that curved in all the right places and could wrap around a man to pull him closer. Legs he wanted to touch, even though they were encased—*so wrongly*—in thick, industrial nylons. Even worse, they emerged from under an ugly, black skirt and extended down to a pair of flat, sensible shoes that were probably old-lady orthopedic.

But those *legs*. Good thing he was an expert on women's bodies, or he might have ignored her. As it was, he'd been struck by the beauty of her legs the second he stepped into the chaotic mess of the Sugar Rush Candy Company's library. She was standing on a ladder by a high bookshelf, her attention on a row of books and her legs right at his eye level.

He stopped behind her, his gaze following the line of her calves up to her ass. He couldn't make out any hint of its roundness under the straight skirt, but no way did a woman with legs like that have anything less than a perfect, heart-shaped ass.

"Need any help?" he asked, his voice unnaturally loud in the cavernous space.

She shrieked.

Tyler flinched.

The woman twisted around with a gasp, one hand grabbing for the shelf. A book thudded to the floor. She teetered. He caught sight of wide, startled eyes behind a pair of glasses just before he darted toward her. His arms shot out the instant she lost her balance on the ladder rung and pitched forward.

She landed in his arms, her feet hitting the floor and her body falling against his in a warm, sweet-smelling bundle that jolted something loose inside him.

Well, *damn.*

He hadn't expected her to be soft and apparently young, with full breasts that pillowed right up against his chest and—

"I'm so sorry." She gripped his T-shirt for balance, her gaze colliding with his, her face close enough that her breath brushed his lips. "I didn't hear you come in."

"I'm a ninja like that."

As pick-up lines went, it totally sucked, but all the blood was rushing from his brain and straight to his dick. He couldn't form a coherent thought. Every ounce of his awareness was focused on the feel of this woman in his arms.

Under any other circumstances, he'd hardly be surprised by his reaction, but the past six weeks had been such a fucking disaster that he'd smothered his sex drive under the weight of guilt and self-disgust.

Now he was unexpectedly holding a woman who smelled like a thousand good things and whose curvy, soft body fired his lust back to life. A woman who reminded him of everything he loved about the female species.

"Are you okay?" he asked.

"Yes." Her voice was warm and throaty, like she'd swallowed a butterscotch.

She pulled away from him, her breath expelling on a rush. Her breasts heaved under the formless shape of her suit jacket.

Tyler's heart was beating unusually fast. Her eyes met his, her shock fading as she straightened her glasses and tugged the lapels of her jacket together.

"I was...I was just looking for a book for Mr. Stone," she explained.

Mr. Stone. His pleasure dissipated. That meant either his eldest brother Luke or second-eldest brother Evan. The superheroes who'd saved Sugar Rush a dozen years ago and were now steering the company all over the world like a couple of candy-making caped crusaders.

She must be their Girl Friday. He was sure he'd never met her. He'd have remembered her.

She bent to pick up the book that had fallen to the floor. Her skirt tightened, displaying exactly what he'd suspected—a round, perfect ass that, like her legs, had no business being held prisoner by ugly fabric.

"Kate," he said, her name coming to him in a burst. "Luke's secretary."

"Executive assistant." She straightened, her eyebrows lifting.

"Tyler Stone." He extended a hand. "Family fuckup."

"Ah." Her fingers closed around his, sending warmth up his arm. "Yes, we've communicated via email about Sugar Rush events, as well as Luke and Polly's upcoming wedding. I've heard a lot about you."

"Hasn't everyone?"

"Your reputation does precede you." She tugged her hand from his when he would have held it for a minute longer than was appropriate just because he wanted to. She stepped back, holding the book against her chest. "What are you doing here?"

"Dying a little."

"I beg your pardon?"

He glanced around the wood-paneled room, the reality of his situation crashing back in on him. Before he'd been told about his punishment, he'd barely remembered there was a basement library at the corporate headquarters of the Sugar Rush Candy Company. He sure as hell hadn't known, or cared, that it was a fucking disaster.

With its coffered ceiling and mezzanine stretching across two walls, the library might have once been nice. But now books and ledgers haphazardly stuffed the floor-to-ceiling wooden shelves, memorabilia cluttered the cases, and open file cabinets overflowed with papers, maps, and photographs. A huge oak desk sat against one wall, the surface scattered with papers and an ancient computer. Everything was dusty, crumbling, yellowing, and old.

Except for Kate. Despite her granny clothing, she wasn't any older than his own twenty-seven. And she smelled damned good, like caramel or something. Only better.

Too bad she was a cliché with her severely cut suit, black-framed glasses, and her hair scraped back into a bun so tight it looked like it was stretching her eyebrows up. With her long legs and that perfume, she would've otherwise been appealing. If not almost hot.

He flopped down in the desk chair and put his feet on a low filing cabinet.

"I've been banished here by the king of the realm." He spread his arms wide to encompass his new home. "I got into some trouble recently. Well, I've been in trouble for a while, but this last one was a doozy. My father sentenced me to do penance down here in the dungeon."

He fully expected her to ask, "What kind of trouble?" because that was the only interesting part of his explanation.

Instead she asked, "What kind of work?"

"I'm supposed to whip the library into shape." Tyler scratched his head. "I guess the former librarian wasn't known for his organizational skills."

According to Evan, the Sugar Rush Library and Archives had been Fred's domain for close to forty-five years before he'd passed away two months ago. Since the library wasn't used regularly, Luke hadn't immediately advertised for a replacement.

Only when Evan's environmental team had started using the archives to research Sugar Rush's cocoa bean crops and sustainability issues had he informed Luke that they had a "situation" on their hands.

With Fred at the helm for so many years, no one had ever paid much attention to how the library was run or the fact that it was a mess. Fred could apparently produce a requested book or ledger in thirty seconds, and if the place looked more like an old bookshop from a horror movie than the library of a multi-million-dollar global candy company, the other employees neither minded nor cared.

Except for now, when the C-suite actually needed to *use* the damned archives and found themselves at a total loss without eagle-eyed Fred the Librarian.

And when Tyler's father and brothers needed to "teach him a lesson."

Why they thought he could actually get anything done here was beyond him. It wasn't as if he knew the first thing about libraries.

Then again, this was less about the actual library than it was a way for the Stones to pull Tyler into line. His father had tried to do that over the years with threats, arguments, and cutting him off financially, but the punishments had never stuck.

This was different, though. In the past he'd been caught for minor offenses—underage drinking, trespassing, a few lame attempts at vandalism. But he'd never done anything bad enough to mess with his family's reputation. He'd sure as hell never destroyed property or been arrested.

Until now.

Yeah, he'd fucked up royally. And he was lucky he hadn't been killed, as his father had reminded him multiple times.

Guilt stabbed him. He fiddled with a pen on the desk, aware of Kate watching him.

"So you're the new librarian." Her gaze skirted over him, taking in his torn jeans and white T-shirt. "Good, because we need one. Why are you starting on a Friday?"

"Just to get the lay of the land." Especially since he couldn't remember ever having set foot in the library, not even when he was a kid.

"Well, several projects need library resources at the moment," Kate said. "Mr. Evan Stone is compiling information about education initiatives. He's ready to offer scholarships for students to participate on the Cocoa Bean Team."

Tyler wasn't surprised Evan had recruited Luke's assistant to help launch the Cocoa Bean Team, the sustainability project he'd been setting up for the past six months. This coming summer, a group of Sugar Rush employees, volunteers, scientists, researchers, and students would join a farmers' collective in Venezuela to study and help with local infrastructures and cocoa bean crop production.

Tyler didn't really get the whole thing, though that was often the case with Sugar Rush projects, but the employees had been buzzing with excitement about it for a while now, and apparently the company was already getting tons of great publicity.

Yet another reason his colossal fuckup couldn't get into the press and screw up Evan's work and reputation. If it had been any one of his other brothers, Tyler might not have cared as much, but everyone—including him—had a soft spot for Evan, whose congenital heart defect and four surgeries had never prevented him from going after what he wanted. Including his girl Hannah, who was now living with him at his beachside cottage in apparently blissful happiness.

All of which meant Tyler had to suck it up and fix his mistake. Even if the toppling piles of books and crammed file cabinets felt like a mountain. Even if he had no idea where to start.

"Also, I'm compiling information about Sugar Rush's history of candy for the new revamp of the website, so I'm looking for vintage ads." Kate approached the desk, gesturing to the book she still held, which bore the title *The Origins of Candy*. "And I need data on the latest 'healthy chocolate' trends for Mr. Stone."

"Which Mr. Stone? Luke or Evan?"

"Mr. Spencer Stone."

Christ. Now she was working for his lab-nerd brother too?

"He's researching ways to diversify the nutritional composition of traditional chocolate." Kate placed a sheet of paper at his elbow. "And this is a starting list of books and documents I need for the Cocoa Bean Team. Once you find them, you can either bring them to Luke's office or call me and I'll come pick them up."

Tyler squinted at the paper—a neatly typed list of stuff including words like *strategic initiative*, *analyst's report*, and *risk assessment*.

He had no clue what any of that was, much less where to find it.

"Yeah, this isn't really my area of expertise," he hedged.

"Since this is your new job..." She peered over the tops of her glasses at him. "You'd better make it your area of expertise."

Well. She had a strict schoolmarm thing going on too. How much of that was an act?

He let his gaze wander over her body. The top button of her white shirt had come undone, revealing a tempting V of pale, creamy skin. Maybe she wore sexy lingerie under her starchy clothes and had a secret erotic side she rarely let other people see.

He tried to smother a sudden rush of intrigue. A woman had gotten him into this mess in the first place—heck, the female species had been getting him into messes since first grade because he could never say no to them—and he sure as hell didn't need one getting in his head now. Especially not one who, lush body aside, seemed to define the word *uptight*.

"You're a super-assistant, aren't you?" he asked. "Able to leap over scheduling conflicts in a single bound."

She looked unamused.

"The more I know about what's going on, the easier it is for me to do my job." Kate whipped a crisp white business card out of her breast pocket. "Here's my card. You can reach me either at my direct number or email. Let me know if you find any historic Sugar Rush advertisements."

She started toward the door. Tyler looked at her ass, which unfortunately was once again hidden behind the straight black curtain of her skirt. He picked up the business card. *Kate Darling, Executive Assistant, Sugar Rush Candy Company.*

A chuckle rumbled in his chest. She looked like a *Kate* for sure. A *Darling* not so much.

He tossed the card back on the desk and surveyed the mess of a library. His father had made it clear—organize the collections *to his standards,* pay off the boat damage, and then they would "have a discussion" about Tyler's future.

He had no choice. His father had cut off his access to his trust fund and allowance. He'd get paid for his work at the library—standard entry-level salary—which he'd use for basic living expenses and to pay Savannah's father back for the speedboat.

If he didn't, he risked prosecution. He wasn't so stupid not to realize he'd still gotten off easy, considering the alternative.

There was just one question left. How the fuck was he going to get this done?

He picked up Kate Darling's card again. Not only did she rule over his older brother's life of schedules and meetings, she was helping with both the Cocoa Bean Team, and Luke and Polly's upcoming wedding. And she was doing research about chocolate or whatever for Spencer. In other words, the woman got shit done, even to the high standards of his anal-retentive brothers.

So if anyone at Sugar Rush could help him with the damned library, it was a hyper-efficient assistant who knew about things like spreadsheets and databases. A woman who actually gave a damn that a book collection was in alphabetical order.

Relief filled Tyler's chest, easing the knot of tension that had been there since he'd first been handed his sentence.

Kate Darling was his key to finishing the job and getting the hell out of Sugar Rush. All he had to do was convince her to help him. An efficient little do-gooder like her?

No problem.

CHAPTER 2

"*H*e did *what?*" Kate couldn't keep the shock out of her voice, and she quickly tried to conceal it with a delicate cough.

Since her encounter with Tyler Stone less than two hours ago, she'd been wondering exactly what kind of trouble he'd gotten himself into. But she hadn't expected *this*.

"He could get charged with grand theft auto." CEO Luke Stone turned from the window of his office, which overlooked a majestic view of the California coastline—not that he appeared to care about the view. His mouth twisted with disgust. "In California, speed boats are included in the grand theft auto code."

"Was he...er, under the influence?" Kate set a stack of folders on his desk.

"Yeah, the influence of a rich, pretty socialite." Luke punched a few keys on his keyboard. "The boat belonged to her father. Worth a fortune. Tyler decided to take it on a joyride without asking permission and ended up crashing it into a channel marker. Lucky he wasn't killed."

Good lord. And here she thought Tyler had been caught lighting his flatulence on fire or something nonsensical like that.

She hadn't imagined he'd done something dangerous and beyond stupid.

"Was the girl in the boat with him?" she asked.

"No, she had the good sense to stay onshore." Luke heaved a sigh and sat back in his chair. "At least she was able to call the Coast Guard to go out and rescue the jackass."

"Will he have to go to court?" Kate asked.

"Unfortunately, no. My father was going to let him take the fall—court, fines, jail, whatever, but Evan convinced him not to. Last thing we need is shitty publicity, especially right when the company is finally getting so much good press. To have the media all over Tyler for being a dickwad rich kid...no."

"Sounds like he still has to pay, though."

"Yeah." Luke dragged a hand through his hair. "Savannah's father agreed not to press charges if Tyler makes regular payments for the boat damage. My father won't let him take the money from his trust fund, so he has to earn it legitimately. He misses a payment, and Dan Corrigan will prosecute."

"At least he gave him a chance," Kate ventured.

Luke nodded. "Even as a kid, Tyler thought life was one big game. He never took anything seriously. Not even school. He'd do stupid things to get attention, but always managed to charm his way out of punishment. Never changed."

Kate could easily see the rakish boy still in Tyler, but surely there was a reason he'd been like that. She hadn't been born efficient and methodical; she'd become that way at a young age because it had been the only way she could help her father. She supposed she hadn't changed much either.

"After our mother died, he got worse," Luke continued. "We've let him run wild for too long. Totally our fault."

Regret tightened his mouth. His eyes were creased with fatigue. He needed a green smoothie with extra protein and perhaps some mixed raw nuts.

"You did the right thing," Kate assured him, not just to humor him but because she believed it. Luke was right—Sugar Rush and the Stone family had endured a lot in recent years, and they couldn't let their young and impulse-challenged brother screw things up for them.

Not that Tyler had seemed the least bit interested in fixing his colossal mistake by organizing the library. He probably wouldn't even show up for work, much less find any useful books or articles for her.

He was hardly the librarian type anyway, with his big body that had felt like a solid wall of muscle when she'd fallen against him, her breasts crushing against his powerful chest and his arms closing around her like steel bands—

She cleared her throat. "So the library is his punishment?"

"In part. My father also froze his trust fund and assets." Luke turned back to his computer. "Time for him to grow up and live on what he makes from actually working."

"Excuse me for saying this, sir, but it doesn't appear that Tyler quite knows what he's supposed to do in the library."

"No one expects much from him," Luke admitted. "He just needs to make an effort and straighten things up. I've already sent out a call for applications for a new librarian. As soon as we hire one, he or she will take over the actual organization, and Tyler will have more direction."

"How long does he have to work there, then?"

"Until he pays off the boat damage. And proves he can get his shit together."

His voice had the implacable CEO quality Kate had come to recognize over the past two years—the one that laid down the law at board meetings and had fired uncooperative employees—but this time it was softened by a distinctly *troubled older brother* tone.

"As always, let me know if there's anything I can do to help," she said.

Luke nodded. "Thanks. Right now I need the latest budget reports, please."

"Of course."

She left his office and returned to her desk. Over the past two years, she'd invariably become involved in Luke's personal life by sheer virtue of being his assistant. She knew about their family history—the death of their mother in a car accident twelve years ago, the subsequent hospitalization of their younger sister, the scandal of Luke's paternity suit that had been proven false, the corporate vultures who had circled Sugar Rush before Luke pulled the company out of a hole and launched its global success.

The fact that he trusted her so much, to the point of confiding in her about family troubles, only strengthened her loyalty to both him and Sugar Rush.

Kate brought him the reports, then called down to the kitchen for the green protein smoothie and bowl of nuts—reiterating that there should be no hazelnuts since Mr. Stone didn't care for them.

The elevator at the end of the corridor swished open. A man strode toward her, his attention focused on a clipboard he held in one hand. Kate's pulse leapt into a nervous, happy rhythm.

Dressed in a tan, off-the-rack suit that fit his lean, slender body well, if not to tailored perfection, Miles Norwood was like a harvest—thick, curly, wheat-colored hair brushed away from his high forehead, bronzed skin, and beautiful brown eyes that Kate longed to see fix on her with warm pleasure. But in the few months since he'd been contracted as an independent data consultant at Sugar Rush, Miles had never looked at her with anything more than vague indifference.

"Hello, Kate."

She loved the sound of her name in his voice, soft and yet crisply professional. It was totally different from the way Tyler Stone had said her name. Tyler's *"Kate"* had been short and abrupt, like he was crunching into a piece of hard peppermint candy.

She shook her head, irritated at the unexpected thought of the youngest Stone brother.

"How may I help you, Miles?" she asked.

He scratched his chin and looked at the clipboard again. "I was running some new predictive analytics during my lunch break. I think they might help with operational efficiency of the gumdrop sector."

"Efficiency, hmm?" Kate smiled, even though Miles still wasn't looking at her. "Now you're speaking my language."

He frowned at his clipboard. She suppressed a sigh. She'd always attributed his indifference to the fact that his brilliant mind was filled with data crunching and analytics—of course, a man like him couldn't be bothered with the trivialities of small talk—but even the nerdiest of nerds at Sugar Rush made an effort to carry on a polite conversation with her while they waited to see Luke.

Still, it was a flaw she could overlook, given what she knew of him. An MIT graduate, Miles had started his own consulting company shortly after graduating and was now a highly in-demand data analyst who'd worked with numerous companies. Kate had been the one to scrutinize his track record and check his references before Luke hired him for a six-month contract at Sugar Rush.

She'd also harbored a crush on him for all the months he'd been working there, which had led to exactly nothing since he was dating a pretty girl named Melanie. Kate had seen the two of them from afar when Melanie came to Sugar Rush to join Miles for lunch. His sun-streaked hair glowed as he bent his head close to hers, wholly attentive and focused on her between bites of his salad.

In addition to her knowledge of his work and high regard at Sugar Rush, those personal glimpses had told Kate everything she needed to know about Miles Norwood. He was the type of man who concentrated his undivided attention on whatever task he needed to complete...or on whichever woman held his heart.

She let her gaze roam over his straight nose, beautiful mouth, and high cheekbones that put Adonis to shame. In appearance Miles was also the opposite of Tyler, who was big like his brothers and had strong, hard features that were more suited to an outdoorsman than a spoiled rich boy.

Tyler also had a tousled mess of dark hair that probably hadn't been trimmed in months. And that dusting of stubble on his jaw was a clear sign of disrespect to his family's company, not to mention that he wore faded jeans and a worn T-shirt to work.

And why the freaking frack was she thinking about Tyler again?

"...appointment?" Miles said.

Kate broke out of her daydream. Her cheeks grew hot. "I beg your pardon?"

Miles tilted his head toward Luke's closed door. "Is he available for a short appointment?"

"Er, let me find out." Kate hastened to bring up Luke's calendar on her computer, scanning his schedule which had uncharacteristically slipped from her steel-trap memory. "He has a call at eleven thirty, but..." she dropped her voice to a conspiratorial whisper, "...let me see if I can fit you in for a few minutes."

"Thank you, Kate."

Oh, he had such beautiful manners.

She hurried to check with Luke, who agreed to meet with Miles before his call with the head of the chocolate division in Switzerland. Kate relayed the information to Miles.

"Excellent." He pulled out his phone. "I expect my explanation to take about fifteen minutes."

"That will be fine." Kate waited while he typed something on his phone.

She liked his hands—they were long and well-shaped with

clean, neatly trimmed fingernails. The hands of a pianist or a... well, a data analyst.

She searched her brain frantically for something to say. "Er... so how is Melanie these days?"

Miles blinked, as if he were trying to traverse the jump in subjects. "Melanie? I assume she's well. I haven't seen her in a few weeks. She and I are no longer dating."

No longer dating? No longer dating!

"I see." Kate retained her bland expression while her heart did a spinning cartwheel. "I'm sorry."

Miles shrugged and took a step back. He didn't look terribly heartbroken by his admission, not that Kate would be able to tell if he was.

Would it be a breach of etiquette if she were to ask him out for coffee right now? Would that make her look desperate and overeager? Was it too soon after his breakup to make a move or was he fair game?

Kate bit her lip in frustration. Most women seemed to know this sort of stuff instinctively, but she had no romantic instincts where men were concerned. She could organize a fantasy football spreadsheet and prepare any kind of income tax form, but she'd always failed miserably at the dating game.

Before she could work up her courage to say something else, Luke stepped out of the office.

"Good to see you, Miles." He extended his hand. "Come on in."

Miles gave Kate another nod of thanks and went into the office with Luke.

Kate sighed. Not for the first time, she wished she'd been raised with *some* sort of female influence that could have at least provided her with a map for the dating maze.

Much as she loved her father and his fellow quarry workers, they hadn't exactly been able to guide her through the specific intricacies of being a girl. Heck, most of the time they hadn't even seemed to *know* she was a girl—she was cute, odd little Katie who organized her father's taxes, kept the house clean, and packed him a healthy lunch every day. She created spreadsheets for their poker matches, taught several of them how to use QuickBooks to streamline their personal accounts, and maintained a 4.2 high school GPA.

By the time she got to college, where all the other young women already knew about hair, clothes, makeup, and boys, Kate had fallen easily into her established role as the smart but plain mascot—well-liked, highly resourceful, and a definite peculiarity.

All of which was fine with her...until three successive relationships had crashed and burned with spectacular unexpectedness, shocking her into the realization that all her organizational skills and administrative proficiency were useless when it came to romance.

She pulled out her phone and did a search on the etiquette of asking a man out shortly after a breakup, ignoring a pang of guilt that she was doing personal research on company time. Her quick scan yielded few definitive answers and a bunch of "it depends" responses. But since Miles didn't appear, on the surface at least, to be too terribly heartbroken about the breakup, Kate decided it was okay to ask him out for coffee.

She glanced at the closed door of Luke's office. Her palms grew clammy at the thought of making a move. Unable to focus on work, she fidgeted with her old-fashioned Rolodex, reorganized her supply drawer, and ate two Whipped Creams and a Chocolate Crunchie.

Miles finally emerged at eleven twenty. Kate gauged his expression, relieved that he didn't appear to look disgruntled or stressed out.

"Do you need to schedule a follow-up?" she asked.

"No need. I'll be giving a report at the next board meeting."

"That's wonderful." Kate smiled, buoyed by Luke's positive response. Surely that would make Miles more receptive to her.

"I'll add you to the agenda. Will you be working on your report this afternoon?"

"Yes."

"I'm sure you'll need to take a break at some point," she remarked as casually as she could.

"Probably." Miles brushed a piece of lint off his sleeve.

"Like a coffee break," she added, fixing her gaze on his left shoulder.

"I usually drink coffee at my desk. As long as it's from a sustainable source, of course. I find Ecuadorian coffee especially smooth."

"Have you tried the café au laits from the Chocolate Café?" Kate asked, trying to think of the specialties at the other restaurants and cafés on the Sugar Rush campus. "Or the fruit smoothies at the Gumdrop Bistro? I'm rather a smoothie expert, if I do say so myself. I can direct you to the best combinations."

Miles started checking his phone. "Luke said the next board meeting is on Monday. What time?"

"Ten." She gripped a pencil with growing frustration. "Look, um, you wouldn't want to have a coffee, would you?"

"Don't they usually serve snacks and coffee at the meetings?" Miles gave her a distracted smile and typed something into his phone.

"I meant—"

"Thank you, Kate. You can send the agenda to my email. M Norwood at Data Analytics and Information Technology Consulting Services Incorporated dot com."

He turned and headed toward the elevators. Kate's heart plummeted. She sank down on her chair again.

A low whistle sounded behind her before a deep male voice remarked, "Lady, you have a terrible lack of game."

CHAPTER 3

$\mathcal{K}$ate whirled around. Tyler Stone approached her desk, shaking his head in apparent dismay. Her cheeks burned.

"It's very rude to eavesdrop," she muttered.

"Hey, you made a move in a public place." He came to a stop beside the desk. "Couldn't help overhearing. You have chocolate on your mouth."

She shot him a startled look. "What?"

"Here."

He flicked his finger over her lips, the touch inappropriately intimate in the middle of the office. Kate ignored a sudden rush of awareness elicited by the memory of how she'd felt locked in his arms. He held up his finger to display the large flake of chocolate that had apparently been clinging to her lip the whole time she'd been talking to Miles.

Perfect. She groaned and reached for a tissue to pat her mouth.

"Hey, if Norwood were the kind of guy who grabbed a chance when he saw one," Tyler remarked, "he'd have said, *'Chocolate on your lips? That means your kisses are extra sweet.'*"

Kate restrained herself from smiling. She didn't want to encourage his flirty attitude in the workplace, but she appreciated his attempt to make her feel better. She further consoled herself with the fact that Miles hadn't even really looked at her, so he probably hadn't noticed she couldn't eat a piece of chocolate neatly.

Tyler leaned his hip against the side of her desk and folded his arms, knocking over her leather pen holder with his elbow. Kate threw him a look and straightened the pens.

"May I help you?" she asked, infusing the question with her *executive assistant to the CEO* tone.

"Yeah." Amusement rose to his eyes. "You can direct me to the best fruit smoothie combination at the Gumdrop Bistro."

Kate flushed with new embarrassment. Now she was the girl with chocolate on her lips who couldn't ask a guy out without looking like a bumbling fool.

A teasing smile tugged at Tyler's mouth, lighting his brown eyes to the color of roasted chestnuts.

"I'm partial to the Tropical Twist myself," Kate admitted, her embarrassment shifting to the conspiratorial feeling of sharing a secret. "Though the Peachy Keen runs a close second."

"Old Miles doesn't seem like much of a smoothie guy." Tyler leaned closer to her. "Try asking him to dinner. You can gaze at each other over the candlelight and whisper sweet nothings about data analysis."

Had he read her mind? She recalled her daydream about having lunch with Miles in the courtyard. She'd imagined him leaning toward her exactly the way Tyler was doing right now, except that Tyler was quite a bit bigger than Miles and smelled like spice and peppermint rather than the floral-yet-masculine aftershave Miles wore. His body was also effectively boxing her into the L-shape of her desk, making her nervously claustrophobic rather than warm and cozy.

"What is it you need, Mr. Stone?" She pushed her chair as far away from him as she could get. "If you want to see your brother, he's on the phone with Switzerland."

"Poor Switzerland. But actually, I'm here for you." Tyler pulled a crumpled newspaper clipping from the pocket of his jeans. "Here's something I found in the library for the website."

Faintly surprised that he'd actually made an effort, Kate took the clipping from him. Dating to 1926, it was an ad featuring a new lollipop from Stone Confectioners, the name of the company before Luke changed it to Sugar Rush twelve years ago in a corporate overhaul and rebranding.

"This is an incredible piece of history." She gestured to the photo on the ad, which showed a man standing beside a truck labeled *Stone Confectioners: San Francisco.* "That's an old Ford Model T pickup, too. Classic vehicle."

"How do you know about classic cars?" He sounded faintly baffled.

"My father and his friends are into working on old cars." She shook her head with fond amusement. "Though sometimes instead of actually working, they stand around drinking beer and talking about the cars they had as teenagers."

"Kate?" The door to Luke's office opened, and he came out with a sheaf of papers. "All-company email about the annual report."

"Yes, sir." Kate rose to take the papers, which only put her in closer proximity to Tyler.

Luke paused, glancing from her to his brother lounging on her desk.

"Hey, bro," Tyler said. "How's Switzerland?"

"Swiss." Luke's eyes narrowed slightly. "What are you doing here?"

"Tyler just brought me some library materials I asked for," Kate explained quickly. "They're for the revamp of the website."

"Found them like that." Tyler snapped his fingers.

"Good," Luke replied mildly, turning to go back into his office. "Glad to know you're making an effort."

After the door closed, Tyler raised an eyebrow at Kate. "It's a start, right?"

She indicated the clipping. "Thanks for this. Where did you find it?"

"In one of the drawers."

"But you just shoved it in your pocket?" Kate shook her head. "You know, newspaper clippings should be protected by acid-free paper and handled with gloves to prevent damage. You can't just manhandle archival materials."

"Hey, you got a problem with this, take it up with Luke or my father." Tyler shrugged. "I never pretended to know a damned thing about libraries or archival materials or whatever."

Kate sighed. It certainly wasn't her business to get involved in a Stone family decision, but she couldn't help feeling a bit sorry for Tyler. He'd been put in a position where he had no idea what he was doing. Surely his father and brothers could have given him a job he could actually *do.*

"Is this all there is in the entire library?" she asked.

"Well, I haven't searched the *entire* library yet," Tyler replied defensively. "Not that I know much about where to look or what to look for."

Kate pushed back from her desk and stood. Her arm bumped against Tyler's. Goodness. He certainly had a hard set of biceps. Granite-like, even. Must be all that working out at a fancy gym instead of actually working to make a living.

She texted Luke that she'd be away from her desk for a short while, then grabbed her small briefcase filled with office supplies, skirted around Tyler, and headed for the elevators.

"Well, come along," she tossed over her shoulder.

"You've got a real commanding schoolmarm thing going on," he remarked, coming up alongside her. "You'd have been right at home as the headmistress of some Victorian girls' school."

"I imagine you're an expert on girls' schools, Victorian or otherwise," Kate replied dryly.

"I'm an expert on many things," he said with a wink, "Victorian or otherwise."

Hah. If only he knew how immune she was to typical male charm, having witnessed its effect on women. Though the hardworking quarry guys were light-years away from a spoiled trust fund baby like Tyler, they shared an appreciation for good times and believed in the power of their charm. And in their overly protective way, they'd warned her away from men like them— not that she would have succumbed to such superficiality anyway.

They entered the elevator, and she pressed the button for the lower level. The doors slid shut. Kate stared straight ahead to avoid having to make further conversation with Tyler.

Why was he standing so close to her? This elevator was big enough for a dozen people, and yet the air was warm with his body heat, and she could feel the brush of his granite-hard arm against hers, and her nose filled with the pepperminty scent of him—

The man certainly had a tendency to *loom*. She cleared her throat and glanced to her side, prepared to ask him to please step out of her personal space.

He was leaning against the wall on the other side of the elevator, a good four feet from her, his head bent as he scrolled on his phone.

Kate's heart gave a weird little thump. She'd never encountered a man whose presence had quite so profound an effect on her. Tyler had the physique of a quarry worker, if not the work ethic.

Broad in the shoulders, with long muscular legs and those arms that could easily heft an eighteen-pound double-edge rock hammer. Even his hands were big and wide— probably clumsy with delicate tasks but capable of controlling a power drill while it sank deep into a sheet of limestone.

Not that Tyler Stone knew anything about quarrying or power tools. If he'd gone to work for her father a decade ago, there'd have been no chance of him ending up spoiled or lazy—Edward Darling would have shown him exactly how to engage in hard, physical work.

Tyler looked up. His gaze met hers with a force that felt like metal striking stone. Creating sparks.

The doors slid open before Kate even realized the elevator had come to a stop. She pulled herself out of the haze that had descended over her and stepped toward the door. Miles Norwood stood in the corridor, holding a green smoothie with a pink straw.

"Miles." Kate forced a weak smile. "I see you went to the Gumdrop Bistro after all."

"I was feeling a bit peckish," he replied with a bland smile.

Behind her, Tyler muttered something that sounded vaguely like *"more like a bit prickish."* She shot him a frown, but he was back to scrolling on his phone.

Miles entered the elevator and pressed the button for the first floor. Kate's pulse sped up with both anxiety and frustration—she wanted to make another attempt to ask him out, but no way would she try again with Tyler here. She could practically hear him snorting with laughter.

Miles closed his lips around the smoothie straw. What would it feel like to have him kiss her? She hadn't been kissed in a very long time, and certainly not by someone as perfect as Miles Norwood.

"Have a nice day." He nodded a farewell and exited on the first floor.

Kate let out her breath. The doors closed behind him and the elevator continued its descent.

"Really?" Tyler asked dryly. "That stick in the mud gets you hot?"

She glowered at him, deciding to ignore the *hot* comment. "For your information, Miles is polite, brilliant, and dedicated to his work. You could take lessons from him."

"You could take lessons from me." He shot her a lopsided grin as the doors opened at the basement level.

"Lessons in what?" Too late, she thought she shouldn't have asked.

"In how to get a guy interested in you. Because you're failing miserably with Old Stick in the Mud. Not that he'd know a come-on if it kicked him in the balls."

"He had a girlfriend," Kate informed him. "They broke up recently."

"Ah, so that's why you're moving in. Was the girlfriend as prissy as he is?"

Ignoring the silly question, Kate headed down the basement corridor.

"I'll give you a tip." Tyler followed her. "You need to wear better clothes. No way should you be hiding that killer body under Grandma's suits."

Killer body? Seriously?

"And you have to show off those incredible legs of yours," he continued.

Kate's heart skipped a beat. He'd been looking at her legs? He'd *noticed* them?

How amaz...er, unprofessional.

"I know I'm not a fashion plate, but my clothes are perfectly suitable for work," she replied tartly, stopping at the closed library door. "Besides, how do you know what kind of body I have?"

"I've felt it." The deep tone of his voice indicated his approval.

A shiver tripped down her spine. She'd felt his body, too. His rock-solid, very male body whose muscles probably rippled and flexed with every movement...

She squashed that line of thought and turned the door handle. Locked. Behind her, Tyler moved closer—so close that she could feel the heat radiating off him.

"Not to mention," he remarked, his breath stirring the tendrils of hair at her nape, "you really need to let a guy see those curves. He'll imagine doing all sorts of good and dirty things to you."

Kate slanted him a narrow look, even though her skin warmed at the sexy, rumbling sound of his promise. Had *he* imagined that about her?

"I do not want anyone to imagine those kinds of things at work," she said.

"What about after hours?" He lifted an eyebrow.

She pulled in a breath and chose not to answer that question. His voice was getting her all hot and bothered, and he wasn't even the one she was interested in. Obviously her rather neglected libido was finally standing at attention. Her nipples definitely were. Thank heavens her suit jacket was buttoned over her breasts because Tyler was definitely the kind of man who would notice perky nips.

She slipped to the side to let him unlock the door. He didn't move. Instead his gaze roamed over her—not a quick assessment, but a slow, rolling look as if he were stripping her down and imagining her naked.

A glow flickered to life in Kate's belly, unfurling outward into her veins. If a man had ever looked at her like that before—and she couldn't recall one ever doing so—then she certainly hadn't responded like this.

Her heartbeat increased, even as warning signs flashed in her mind. She knew better. A party boy with a string of beautiful girlfriends and a total lack of responsibility was not her kind of man. At all.

"The door," she prompted, her voice oddly squeaky.

Tyler dug a key out of his pocket and handed it to her.

"Open up, Darling," he murmured.

Kate closed her hand around the key. She struggled a little to take a breath. Because he was talking about more than just the door.

CHAPTER 4

*T*yler didn't move when Kate edged in front of him again. A gentleman would have stepped back to allow her space, but he'd never pretended to be a gentleman.

Besides, he liked being close to her. Brought back all sorts of memories of closing his arms around her and not wanting to let go.

He let his gaze slip down to her ass. Ugly as her clothes were, he was starting to appreciate that they concealed the lush curves he'd felt pressing against him. It was like keeping a secret. One a douche like Norwood didn't know about.

Kate inserted the key into the lock. The smell of her hair drifted to his nose. Fresh, clean, just like he remembered from that morning. He lowered his head closer and inhaled, letting the scent of her sink into his blood. Nice.

Though he'd grown up with five brothers, he'd been with plenty of women in his twenty-seven years. As a result, he'd absorbed a lot of knowledge about feminine lotions, creams, and perfumes. No question that Kate Darling's scent didn't come from the low-level shelf at the drugstore.

She smelled…not expensive, but *plentiful*, like things growing and blooming. And with her round ass and full, plump breasts that he could still feel crushed against his chest...the scent of lushness suited her perfectly.

His dick twitched. She pushed open the door, and he stepped away from her. His physical reaction didn't surprise him, though he wasn't about to try and start anything with her.

A little flirting would be required to get what he needed from her, but he wouldn't take it any further than that. Aside from the fact that Luke wouldn't like him messing with his super-assistant, Kate had a cute, if sort of pathetic, crush on starched-shirt Miles.

And, douche-ness aside, Miles was exactly the kind of guy she should be with—efficient, organized, smug, and probably a vegetarian. They could sit around after work drinking sustainably sourced tea and discussing algorithms.

He followed her to the desk, grabbing the open bag of potato chips he'd left by the computer. She eyed him with disapproval. He extended the bag.

"Want some?"

"No, thank you." Kate sat down at the paper-strewn desk and flipped open her briefcase. She removed a legal pad and a fountain pen, then turned to boot up the computer. "This is the library computer?"

"What's wrong with it?" He crunched into a handful of potato chips.

"What's wrong with it?" Kate repeated in faint disbelief. "It's an ancient PC running Windows XP. What kind of database software is installed?"

"I have no idea what you're talking about."

She scanned through the computer files, bringing up standard applications like Word and Excel. "There isn't any kind of library automation system or even a cataloging database."

Again he was clueless.

"I don't get it," Kate continued. "How was Fred maintaining the system?"

"I think Fred *was* the system."

Kate studied the computer with a frown. "Does Luke know about this?"

"Doesn't Luke know about everything?"

"He can't possibly know about this or he'd have done something about it ages ago."

Like she was drawing a pistol at a Wild West shooting match, Kate unbuttoned her suit jacket and whisked her cell phone out of a leather holster.

A laugh rose in Tyler's throat—because a *cell phone holster*—but it faded when the button of her white shirt came undone between her breasts. His gaze snapped like a rubber band to the gap.

The folds of her shirt opened to expose a wall of white cotton, like a heavy-duty slip. Tyler couldn't prevent a rush of disappointment. From his experience, women who used high-end shampoos and lotions would not, under any circumstances, wear granny underwear. Apparently Kate Darling was different.

He glanced at her open briefcase, which was neatly organized with pens, pencils, notepads, all sizes of paper clips, tape, scissors, binders, and rubber bands. She was like a little organizational superhero.

He reached over and picked up a packet of Sugar Rush Chocolate Bon-Bons that was nestled in a corner of the briefcase. Ah. She was a secret chocolate hoarder too. That was why she'd had chocolate on her pretty lips earlier—she'd been trying to ease her anxiety with sugar before attempting to ask Norwood out.

He opened the bag and unwrapped a Bon-Bon, popping it into his mouth.

Kate slipped her phone back into the holster and grabbed the bag away from him with a mild glare.

"Sorry." He held up his hands. "I should know better than to mess with a girl's chocolate."

"I need it for energy." She put the bag back in the briefcase, right next to the rubber bands. "So where did you find the newspaper clipping?"

Tyler gestured to a filing cabinet. Kate pulled open a drawer, sighing with dismay at the sight of the old newspapers and magazine articles crumpled into file folders.

"These aren't even archival quality." She plucked a folder carefully from the drawer. "The acid from the folders is causing all this yellowing."

Yeah, she knew what she was talking about. Tyler's resolve strengthened. His recent lack of sex was enough to explain his preoccupation with Kate's scent and her bra.

But he didn't need her to scratch his itch—he needed to get her on board with the library work. Not only could she help him get the job done much faster than he could ever do on his own, she'd do it to a ridiculously high standard that would exceed even Warren Stone's expectations.

He shoved away from the desk and walked to the overstuffed bookshelves.

"These aren't even in alphabetical order," he remarked casually, studying the book spines.

"I know." Kate approached to look at the adjoining shelf. "It's a travesty, really. Sugar Rush has such a long and rich history that it deserves to be respected and well organized."

"Exactly what I was about to say." *More or less.*

"Before my job interview with Luke, I read up on the history of the company," Kate continued, pulling a book off the shelf. "I thought it was so fascinating that your ancestor...wasn't it Edward Stone? Edward is my father's name, too. Anyway, my favorite part of the story is that Edward Stone came to California during the Gold Rush to seek his fortune, but he never found any gold while mining. But he'd learned how to make chocolate from his father, who had once apprenticed at a chocolate factory in Denmark.

"So Edward made some milk chocolate nonpareils and shared

them with his fellow miners. They were such a hit that he began selling them at general stores. He made enough money to open the first Stone Confectioners' store in San Francisco, and the Gold Rush miners were his biggest customer base.

"He never forgot that either, which is why so many of the later Stone Confectioners' chocolates have been based on Gold Rush themes—Chocolate Nuggets, the Gold Rush bars, 49er Truffles. Luke told me that was also his inspiration for changing the name of the company to Sugar Rush—he wanted to modernize the brand, but also pay homage to its history in the Gold Rush."

She stopped, giving him a somewhat abashed look. "Sorry for going on about it. I just think it's so neat that these men who came to California looking for gold ended up finding chocolate, which is the gold standard of sweets, as far as I'm concerned. And I love working for a company that has such a colorful…and delicious…history. Though of course you already know all about it."

He didn't, actually. An unexpected shame shot through him. He'd heard about the company history his whole life, and a lot of it had stuck in his mind out of sheer repetition, but he hadn't known, or he'd forgotten, details like the ones Kate had just told him. He hadn't even remembered he'd had an ancestor who'd learned chocolate-making in Denmark.

"I'll be quiet now," Kate promised, shuffling a few books on the shelf. "This is a library, after all."

"You don't have to be quiet." Tyler almost wished she'd keep talking—not only did he like the sound of her voice with its faint, throaty quality, this history thing was sort of interesting.

"From what I understand, Fred knew everything about Sugar Rush and its heritage," Kate continued. "But clearly this company has needed a collections management specialist."

"How do you know so much about library collections?" Tyler asked.

"I have a degree in library and information sciences."

Bingo.

She was a perfect, ripe apple that had fallen right into his lap. And though he had a stab of guilt over the thought of playing her —because she really was a nice girl—the reality was that he had a job to do, and he couldn't do it without her.

"Even with your degree, Luke never asked you to work down here?" he asked.

"He hired me as his executive assistant, not the corporate librarian." Kate slipped another book back into place. "Besides, it was Fred's job for forty-five years. From what I heard, he didn't want anyone encroaching on his domain. Luke showed Fred a great deal of respect by allowing him to run the library as he saw fit. But I don't think he realized it might actually have damaged the collection."

She ran a hand over the book spines, her touch graceful and reverent. She had pretty hands—tapered fingers, delicate wrists, short, unpolished nails. An image of her hand sliding lightly across his bare chest flashed in Tyler's mind with unexpected force. His body reacted with a surge of lust.

He stepped away, turning to study a stack of old maps. It'd been...what, almost two months since he'd gotten laid? And then it had been with Savannah, who'd gotten into the unfortunate habit of asking him for money after one of their routine fucks.

Just a little for a mani/pedi? I ran out of my allowance this week, and I really need a new bikini for the party on Saturday.

Like a tool, he'd handed over the cash every time. He had an even harder time saying no to a half-naked damsel in distress, especially one who'd just milked his cock dry.

After the shit hit the fan—or more accurately, the speedboat hit the channel marker—and Savannah had blamed him for everything, he'd put a swift end to those transactions. He wanted a woman in his bed again, but not one like her.

Kate Darling was nothing like Savannah. She stood on tiptoe to reach a book on a higher shelf, the movement lifting her skirt slightly to display her legs. How could *any* guy not notice those incredible legs?

She glanced over and caught him staring. Their gazes met. Heat charged the air suddenly. A flush rose to her cheeks.

Tyler set down a map and approached her. "He's a damn fool."

Her slender throat worked with a swallow. "Who?"

"Norwood. Or he's thick as a plank for not realizing you want to go out with him."

Kate tucked a stray lock of thick, brown hair behind her ear. "Well, we all have our strengths. The dating game is not one of mine."

"Too bad." She had a pretty mouth too—bow-shaped, with a full lower lip and a little notch in her upper lip. He suddenly wanted to put his tongue there and taste her. "I happen to be a pro at the dating game."

"I'll bet you are, Mr. Expert on Victorian Girls' Schools."

Tyler leaned one hand on the bookshelf. Behind her heavy-framed glasses, Kate had light brown eyes, the same color as her hair, and fringed with thick, sooty lashes. Her nose was small and pert, dusted with freckles like cinnamon, and she had the pale skin of a woman who spent most, if not all, of her time indoors. Not to mention she smelled like heaven.

Aside from her glasses and ancient-secretary clothes, Kate was an attractive young woman with a nice, curvy body and a kissable mouth. If she fixed up her exterior package and worked on her flirting skills, a dude like Miles Norwood would find it hard not to notice her.

Hell. *Tyler* was finding it hard not to notice her, even in her current guise. And he was accustomed to women who knew how to show off their assets.

"I need you, Kate Darling," he said.

"Excuse me?"

"You know I'm useless here." He waved a hand at the books, not taking his gaze from hers. "I could work here for a month and not get anything done. Even if I tried, I'd screw it up. And I'd probably damage a lot of the stuff, too. I'd hate to see Sugar Rush's history lost forever just because of bad cataloging or whatever. It's such a shame that our heritage has come to this."

He waved his hand again and expelled a faint sigh for good measure.

"Your brother told me he's put out a call for applications for a new corporate librarian," Kate said. "As soon as one is hired, I'm sure he or she will put everything to rights."

"But in the meantime, I'm the one stuck here." Tyler hesitated for a second, questioning the wisdom of actually touching a mouse like her, but he took the chance and brushed his fingers across her wrist. He'd have preferred touching her bare arm, but her wrist was the only exposed patch of skin from her neck to below her knees. "And if I don't get something done, I'm screwed."

"I'm sure losing access to your trust fund won't *screw* you," Kate replied, her voice a bit dry though she didn't move away or take her eyes from his.

How did she know about his trust fund? He wouldn't have expected Luke to divulge stupid family business to his secretary. And he didn't like that Kate knew how dependent he was on his trust fund.

The button of her shirt was still unfastened between her breasts. He flicked it shut with a twist of his fingers. Kate drew in a sharp breath.

He slid the back of his hand against her breast. Her nipple hardened visibly from the light contact, sending a jolt of heat through him. She was far more responsive than he'd have expected. He wondered about the shape of her breasts, the color of her nipples, the taste of her fine-grained skin…

Kate curled her hand around his wrist. "What…what are you doing?"

"Sorry." His heart was hammering, a totally disproportionate reaction considering he'd barely touched her.

He stepped back and tried to regain the upper hand. "So... Norwood, huh?"

"What about him?"

"Your clothes aside, there's something else you can do to get his attention."

Kate eyed him with faint suspicion. "What?"

He reached behind her head to find the pins capturing her dark hair in that doughnut-shaped knot. With a few twists of his fingers, he pulled out the pins and dropped them to the floor.

Oh yeah.

Kate gasped, a breathy little noise that propelled straight to his dick. Her hair flooded around her shoulders in thick, lush waves, spilling the scent of strawberries into the air. Tyler stepped back, his heart crashing against his ribs with a combination of pleasure and outright awe.

With all that wavy hair as a frame, her face looked softer and even more lovely, like a painting. Her lips parted with surprise, and he was seized with the urge to kiss that notch on her upper lip. What did she taste like? Berries, cinnamon, spice—

"Why did you do that?" Irritably, she reached back to try and pull her hair up again.

"Let a guy see your hair down," Tyler advised. "And he'll be at your feet."

"Well, I don't have much choice now, do I?" she replied, giving up the futile effort of fixing her hair.

Tyler curled his fingers into his palm to restrain himself from tucking a lock of her hair behind her ear, then running his hand through the glossy strands. He'd love to see all that brown silk spilling over his pillow.

The library, dammit.

"Kate." He lowered his head so they were almost eye-level. "You're crazy efficient. Smart. Organized. Educated. How about you give me a hand down here? With your help, we could get the job done in no time and I could be out of everyone's hair in a couple of weeks. Please?" he added as an afterthought.

Her expression was inscrutable, but her eyes lit with wary interest. She was intrigued by the offer—the chaos of the books and papers was both a challenge and a nirvana to an organizer like her.

"I don't think that would be a good idea." Her voice was still breathless, her expression a combination of growing need and caution.

He leaned in closer. The sugar scent of her filled his head, tripping through his blood. Christ. He'd criticized her clothes, but he still couldn't stop thinking about how her body had felt against his. And in that brown suit with her white shirt, glossy hair, and cinnamon freckles, she was like a yummy little pastry he wanted to gobble right up.

Against his better judgment, he lifted a hand to the side of her face, rubbing his thumb over her smooth-as-silk cheek.

"I meant it, Darling," he murmured, his pulse still beating unusually fast. "I need you."

"I think you...you need a lot of girls." Her gaze drifted to his mouth.

"Not like you." He stroked his thumb back and forth on her cheek. The way she was *softening* under his touch infused his blood with heat. His head flooded with images of her lying on his bed, all warm, willing, and eager...

"I'm...I can't do this alone." He swallowed, his voice coming out husky.

"I'm sure you can find someone else to help you," Kate whispered.

"Not like you."

He slipped his hand to the side of her neck, feeling her pulse throbbing against his palm. Jesus, he wanted to strip her suit off, to see that heavy-duty slip hugging her curves all snug and tight, and then he wanted to peel it off her and find her bare skin, her generous cleavage, her hard nipples...He shifted, trying not to wince as his dick pushed insistently against his jeans.

She darted her tongue out to lick her lips. He stared at her mouth, the urge to taste her seizing him. He slid one arm around her waist, flattening his palm against her lower back and pulling her closer.

Kate caught her breath, a little gasping noise. He tensed, expecting her to resist, but instead she curled her hands into the front of his T-shirt. He tightened his hand against the side of her neck. Heat flared through him, swift and hard like the revving of an engine.

He wouldn't kiss her. He wanted to...Christ, he *ached* to kiss her, but he'd channel every ounce of his self-control into *not* kissing her.

As accustomed as he was to women going all pliable under his attention, he'd always been transparent with them. All cards on the table. Dates, sex, friendship, fun. They always knew what he wanted, and it was always what they wanted too.

But Kate...he was trying to get her to do what *he* wanted. And she was making his head spin with the effort of controlling himself. He should stop this right here, but the scent and feel of her weakened whatever resolve he possessed.

"You should first...um, learn about access points." Kate spread her fingers out over his chest. "And authority control."

"Hmm." He turned them both so her back was up against the wall. "Sounds good."

She shot him a shy look from beneath her lashes. Her cheeks were pink. Damn, he wanted her more with every passing second. He'd never had a woman like her before—an organizational efficiency expert with a razor-sharp mind and incredibly awkward social abilities whose ugly clothes concealed a lush, heavenly body. She was a thousand contradictions. He suddenly wanted to know all of them.

He grabbed her skirt and tugged it up far enough to edge his knee between her thighs. As he'd expected, her eyes grew wide with shock.

"Tyler…"

"You smell incredible…" He lowered his head to the side of her neck, inhaling her delicious scent. "One whiff of you, and I'm hard as a rock."

A noise emerged from her throat, a husky whimper that jerked his erection into full stiffness. He groaned, rubbing his jaw against her soft cheek. Before he could think, his fingers were working the buttons of her shirt. Her breasts heaved under her heavy slip.

He considered himself an expert on women's lingerie, but despite his best efforts he found no way of unhooking her slip from the front. As much as he wanted to touch her naked skin, he didn't have the patience to get her clothes off.

Instead he covered her full breasts with his hands, squeezing and caressing their plump fullness. Goddamned perfect fit. Nipples like berries poking against her bodice. He was ready to come just from touching her.

"Oh my God, that feels so good," Kate whispered, her breath brushing against his neck. "But we really shouldn't…"

She moved her hands tentatively downward and slipped them under his shirt. When her cool fingers touched his hot skin, he jerked in reaction. She murmured with pleasure as she traced his abs, trailing her fingertips along the waistband of his jeans and then up to his pecs. Fuck if her light, timid exploration wasn't the most incredible thing he'd felt in ages.

He pushed his knee upward between her legs, tugging her skirt all the way up to her hips. She tensed for an instant. Then she groaned and settled against him, her luscious legs cradling his thigh. Tyler tightened his fingers on her hips. Her heat burned clear through his jeans and however many layers of underclothes she wore.

"Damn, you're hot." He grazed his hand up her stocking-clad thigh. "Come on, Darling. Let me feel you move."

She curled her fingers into his chest. His heartbeat thundered in his ears. She lifted her head, her eyes dazed and her breath puffing sweetly against his lips. He flexed his hands on her hips, aching to feel her writhing and shuddering against his thigh.

"Tyler," she whispered.

"Kate," he whispered back, trailing his lips across her cheek and down to her neck.

She jerked away. He lifted his head.

Like a windshield wiper washing off condensation, the heat disappeared from her expression.

"Nice try," she said dryly.

He stared at her in shock. She smirked, shoving his hands from her hips and slipping away from him. He dragged a hot breath into his lungs, willing his dick to settle down.

"Uh...what..." he stammered.

"I said, nice try." She pulled her skirt down and fastened her jacket quickly. Though her skin was still flushed pink, a derisive glint replaced the arousal in her eyes. "Trying to seduce me into doing your job."

Shit.

He dragged a hand through his hair.

"I wasn't trying to—" he began futilely.

"Yeah right." Kate made a scoffing noise and strode to the desk to pack up her briefcase. "I know about guys like you, Tyler. I grew up around plenty of men who thought they could get what they wanted with a smile and a wink. I realized early on how silly it is to fall for such nonsense. Instead I learned the value of good, hard work. Clearly it's your turn to learn that lesson. However, because both I and the rest of Sugar Rush need the library to operate effectively, I'll throw you a bone."

She pulled her cell phone out of the holster and typed. "Check your email. There's an online library sciences curriculum you can start with. I would be happy to answer questions, but the job itself is yours."

She slipped her phone back into the holster and lifted her head. Their gazes met. A current of heat sizzled between them. He could still feel the shape of her breasts, like they'd been imprinted on his hands.

"Come on, Tyler." Kate snapped her briefcase shut and narrowed her eyes at him. "Let me see you *work*."

With that, she swept out the door, her skirt a straight line around her legs, her hair swishing back and forth like a curtain. The scent of her lingered like the aftermath of sex.

Tyler leaned his shoulder against the bookshelf and shook his head. A sudden laugh broke from his chest. He'd deserved that. And now he liked her even more.

"Well played, Miss Darling," he murmured, his gaze on the empty space she'd left behind. "But I'm not finished with you yet."

CHAPTER 5

Oh my God.

She was so turned on. To the point that she was squeezing her thighs together underneath her desk and hoping no one noticed how flushed she still was.

She'd known Tyler could bring the sexy, but she certainly hadn't expected to experience his brand of seduction firsthand. Moreover, she really hadn't expected her body to throb to the point that she'd been ready to squirm against his strong thigh.

She let out her breath slowly. She'd had to muster every ounce of willpower she possessed to push him away and gather her composure with lightning-quick speed. He could obviously rev her engine, but that didn't mean she would let herself be manipulated.

Then again, she could have pushed him away much sooner. Like, when he first started flirting with her. But she'd been so curious, so unbearably eager to find out just how far he would go and if he'd actually kiss her.

She could imagine Miles kissing her politely, but Tyler? She had no idea. She'd never been kissed by a man like him before.

Disappointment twinged through her. Although she hadn't

had any intention of letting him play her, she *had* been intensely hoping he would kiss her. A little kiss. Just the warm press of his lips against hers.

Then maybe she would have opened her mouth to let him in, and the kiss *might* have gotten hot and wet, even a bit messy. Maybe he would have thrust his hands into her hair, tilted her head back, *devoured* her mouth with his while she writhed shamelessly against his thigh and her arousal burned hotter and hotter...

Kate groaned inwardly. She'd never been uncomfortable in her body, but it had always been just sort of...there. Nothing to write home about. Not a magnet for attraction. She liked touching herself, and her sexual experiences had been okay, but she'd never reveled in her body or loved being inside her own skin.

Her *mind*, on the other hand—that was the source of her confidence and strength. So much so that she didn't often give her body much thought, aside from taking care of it with healthy food, daily walks, and scrupulous hygiene.

But what would it have felt like to surrender to lust, to have let Tyler pull her skirt up and press his hand between her legs...

With a frustrated sigh, she forced her mind back to the reality of the situation.

Help him with the library, indeed. He meant *"you do the work so I don't have to."*

Her arousal dampened at the reminder that he hadn't actually wanted *her* as much as her abilities. Not that she minded being wanted for her skills—after all, they were the reason she was so good at her job—but with all of Tyler's smooth talk about her "killer body" and legs, it would have been a little bit nice if he'd also been attracted to her physically.

Maybe she was shallow to be wanted for her body rather than her mind or personality. But her past relationships hadn't exactly been zinging with sexual chemistry, so Kate did want to know what a hot, purely physical encounter would feel like. Especially if it involved a man like Tyler with his granite arms and intoxicating deep voice, and—

Stop it.

She couldn't let Tyler and his sexiness distract her from her goal of finally asking newly single Miles out on a date. In fact, she needed to come up with a *plan* so her next attempt wasn't such a disaster.

Maybe if she learned more about Miles's ex-girlfriend, she could get some ideas about what he was looking for. She took her phone out of the holster and typed *Melanie McGuffin* into the search engine.

The other woman's social media sites popped up, and by all accounts, Melanie was freaking perfect. Short blond hair, big-toothed smile, slender, toned body. A UCLA graduate, she owned an exclusive clothing boutique in downtown Indigo Bay and hung out with shiny, lovely people who posted pictures of themselves with arms linked and ear-to-ear smiles. *How am I supposed to compete with that?*

Kate sighed. Miles was in a few of the photos, though he didn't look as happy as the rest of the crowd. In a couple, he stood a distance apart, as if he weren't quite comfortable with their evident joviality.

Maybe that was the reason they'd broken up. Maybe Melanie's friends were too fun-loving for Miles. He was serious and thoughtful, after all. He would have neither the time nor the patience for loud groups of people who apparently couldn't stop laughing. Miles was far more suited to quiet evenings at the theater or perhaps discussing Thomas Hardy at a book club.

Melanie might be perfect, but she hadn't been perfect for Miles. And *that* was where Kate would come in.

"Kate, do you have a copy of the meeting agenda?" Luke called from inside his office.

"Right here, sir." She hurried to his desk, extending a copy from her binder. "Also, did you have a chance to review my memo about the need for a new computer and cataloguing data-base in the library?"

"Yeah, you're right." He leafed through the report. "When we hire a new librarian, he or she will need to have some structure in place. Go ahead and order whatever you think is best. I'll sign off on it."

"Are you sure? I'd be happy to show you the different features of each system so you can make an educated decision."

"Kate." Luke gave her a smile. "I trust you. Order anything you want. Maybe even Tyler can do something with it."

Kate's pleasure over his admission of trust dissipated with that parting shot about Tyler. It seemed no one—including her, truth be told—believed Tyler was capable of getting anything done.

Tyler himself didn't seem to think so either. She suspected people didn't often go to him for help with…well, anything. His other brothers all had their own areas of expertise, but from what she could tell, the only thing Tyler had was a reputation for being a womanizer and a reckless rich kid.

But surely there was more to him than that. When it came to *everyone*, there was always more than met the eye.

She sat back down at her desk. Tyler had been right, tough as that was to admit to herself. She really didn't know how to flirt or entice a man. No wonder he thought he could play her with a few hot words and moves.

Except he'd failed. Hah.

She pulled up her web browser again and typed *Tyler Stone*. As she'd expected, dozens of images appeared—some publicity photos of Tyler with his family and more of him out on the town, his arm wrapped around one stunning beauty or another.

In all the photos, whether he was wearing a tuxedo or jeans and a T-shirt, he looked gorgeous—dazzling smile, warm crin-kled eyes, his dark hair glowing under the lights.

Kate wasn't surprised. And why would she be? Tyler had flirted and flattered his way through life, which was probably part of the reason he had no viable work skills. Clearly his talent lay in the dating department, and he couldn't get paid for that unless he was really hard up.

You could take lessons from me.

His words echoed through her head. Too bad there wasn't some sort of "Tyler Stone Dating Curriculum" he could give her in exchange for the information she'd sent him about library studies.

Unless there was.

She started to put her phone away when it buzzed with a text.

T. STONE: I was looking for a book on magic, but it disappeared.

K. DARLING: What you need is a self-help book.

T. STONE: And the geography books are all in the wrong place.

K. DARLING: You have a really bad latitude.

T. STONE: What did one library book say to the other?

K. DARLING: I want to check you out.

T. STONE: Go ahead. I'm right behind you.

CHAPTER 6

*H*e caught the smile on her face the instant before she had a chance to suppress it. She slipped her phone back into the holster and leveled him with her "executive assistant" look.

"May I help you, Mr. Stone?" she asked crisply.

"I come in peace." He held up his hands in a gesture of truce. "And to apologize. But I understand if you want to kick me to the curb after the way I treated you earlier."

"I seem to recall that the player became the played." She arched an eyebrow. "If you can suppress your embarrassment over getting bested by a girl, I'll be glad to listen to your apology."

He almost grinned. Normally he wouldn't particularly like being "bested by a girl," but things seemed to be very different with Kate.

"I'm sorry," he said. "I didn't mean to...well, okay, I did mean to play you, but I shouldn't have. I'm a little desperate here."

"By my estimation, you're a *lot* desperate."

"Well, yeah, but that's not why I...I mean..." Tyler sighed and ran a hand over his face. "Look, I'm sorry, okay? Really. I'm out of my depth. In the library at least. The hot stuff is right in my

wheelhouse. It's been a while since I've had any action, but I'm...
okay, I'll shut up now."

"Here's some advice." Kate crossed her arms. "You didn't have
to go to such lengths. You could have just *asked* me for help."

Guilt stabbed him. Though he'd initially thought she had
secrets under her starchy exterior, she was obviously a nice,
hardworking young woman. And even though she'd one-upped
his attempt to play her, he still felt bad about his behavior.

Not to mention, Luke would kill him if he found out his little
brother had been messing with his assistant.

He sank into the chair beside her desk. He needed her help
more than ever. If he failed at this stupid job, he'd be unable to
make his payments on time, which meant Dan Corrigan would
press charges, which meant the whole fuck-up would get blasted
all over the place.

"Look." He had only one route left, and that was flat-out
honesty. "I know I was an ass, but I really do need your help. You
know way more about this stuff than I ever will, and I have to get
the job done so this *threat* isn't hanging over my family and Sugar
Rush anymore. So what will it take? How can I earn your help?"

Kate studied him for so long that he thought she'd never
respond. Of course she wouldn't. She knew what a player he
could be. Why would she ever agree to help him?

She pushed up from her seat, glancing at the closed door of
Luke's office.

"Come with me." She lowered her voice. "I don't want anyone
to overhear."

Since he was in no position to disobey her orders—not that
that was a bad thing—Tyler followed her down the corridor to a
storage closet. Kate flicked the lights on and locked the door
behind them.

"Cloak and dagger," he remarked. "I like it."

She stood by the door with her arms still crossed and her
expression determined. Their gazes met. Energy lit in the air

between them, something sharp and crackling. Tyler waited, sensing his fortune was about to change…but not without a price.

"I'll make a deal with you," Kate said.

"Okay."

"I'll help you with the library if you give me dating advice."

"Uh…what?"

"Advice," Kate repeated. "You see, I've had a crush on Miles since he started working at Sugar Rush, but he had a girlfriend. Now that they've broken up, I finally have a chance. I really don't want to get it wrong this time."

An unexpected feeling softened Tyler's chest. "What does that have to do with me?"

"I know you're a dating expert," she continued. "And *you* know I have a terrible lack of game. I've never been good at male-female relationships outside of work. Also I've never had… well, I don't really get it. I've never learned all the intricacies of flirting and dating. So maybe you could help me out, give me some pointers and advice on how I can make Miles *want* to go out with me."

Tyler shook his head, not sure he understood this right. "You want me to help you land Miles Norwood? And in exchange, you'll help me organize the library?"

"Yes." Kate looked pleased that he'd grasped the concept so fast.

"What exactly do you want me to do?"

"Give me some pointers on how men like women to approach them." She took her phone from the holster again and scrolled. "Critique my conversational style. Tell me what men expect on dates, what they like to do, how they like women to look and behave. I know there are certain qualities men enjoy in women, and I'm sure I have some of them, but I need advice on how to actually bring them to the surface."

She was the strangest creature he'd ever met. Not to mention she kept throwing him curve balls that he had no idea how to catch. He scratched his neck.

"Here." Kate showed him the screen of her phone, which displayed an attractive, smiling blond woman with a great rack.

"Melanie McGuffin," she explained. "Miles's ex-girlfriend. I need to be more like her."

Tyler frowned. "You don't need to be *more like* anyone."

"I mean, sexier, shinier, more appealing to men. You know."

He did know, but he didn't want to tell her that. For the first time, he realized that he kind of liked Kate's lack of effort with her appearance. It made her different from pretty much every other woman he'd known.

"I've seen all the pictures of you out on the town with tons of women," Kate added. "And you were the one who brought it up when you said I could take lessons from you."

He tried to get his head around this idea. Boat payments aside, if he didn't get the job done, he was facing the next ten years buried under a pile of mildewed books.

Unless he agreed to her ridiculous offer. Which apparently he'd inspired in the first place. *Jackass.*

"What do you think?" Kate looked at him with such hopeful expectation that something twisted in his gut. "Will you do it?"

What the hell was he supposed to say? He'd never finish his job at the library without Kate's help. But he'd never helped a woman get another guy. He was usually the one they wanted.

On the other hand, stuffy Norwood was perfect for efficient Kate—and she wanted him—so what did Tyler have to lose by agreeing to the deal?

Nothing.

His brain flashed with a memory of Kate falling against him, his arms closing around her, the sugary smell of her filling his head.

Nothing. He had *nothing* to lose and everything to gain if

agreeing to this deal meant he could make his payments and be freed from the damned library.

He took a breath and forced out the word, "Okay."

Kate blinked, like she hadn't expected that response. "What?"

"I said *okay*," Tyler said, his voice unexpectedly sharp. "I'll help you get Miles to notice you. Apparently I've now turned into a fifth grade girl. But not a *single* other person knows about this or I'll get laughed out of town for being a freaking Dr. Doolittle or whatever."

"Henry Higgins," Kate corrected. "He was a phonetics professor in *My Fair Lady*. Eliza Doolittle was the Cockney flower seller whom he transforms into a lady."

"Whatever." He started for the door, his shoulders tight with tension.

"Why is this so upsetting to you?"

"I'm not *upset*." He glowered at her. "I just don't know what you expect me to do. Tell you all the things I think are wrong with you?"

"There's nothing *wrong* with me," she said. "I've just spent most of my life as a back-up singer rather than the starring act where relationships are concerned. Think of me as a project, like Henry did with Eliza. You're the professor, and I'm the student. Mutually beneficial."

Just what he wanted. So why was it sticking in his craw?

"But don't expect me to bring you your slippers," Kate added.

"What are you talking about?"

She smiled. "Haven't you ever seen *My Fair Lady*?"

"No." But the title rang a bell. Tyler dug into the smutty part of his memory, which was substantial. "I've seen a porn flick called *My Bare Lady*. Higgins turns Eliza into an adult film star. It's a classic. I can't remember if there are slippers. There's definitely spanking."

Kate's lips twisted with derision, drawing his attention to her mouth. That notch in her upper lip was so fucking tempting, like a raindrop on a windowpane he wanted to lick.

Heat shot through his veins. The air thickened. She cleared her throat and slipped her phone back into the holster. She wasn't wearing her suit jacket, and her hard nipples were visible even under that heavy-duty bra.

He wanted to see her tits naked. He wanted to see *her* naked. She'd fit against him so perfectly he could only imagine what they'd be like together without the barrier of clothes. He wanted her perfect legs wrapped around his hips, her caramel scent filling his head, her breath hot on his neck.

Yeah, like that would happen. Not when she wanted brainy Norwood.

He moved past her to unlock the door. He almost felt the light press of her body against his, her breasts brushing his arm.

Christ. He needed to get laid. Maybe if he told himself that enough times, he'd find another willing girl and finally get thoughts of Kate out of his head.

He *had* to stop thinking about her. Sexually, at least. Because he'd just agreed to help her attract another man.

CHAPTER 7

*S*uccess! Well, not yet, but with Tyler's help she'd soon have a new wardrobe, a new hairstyle, and a new strategy to ask Miles out on a date. She was definitely on the right path to improving her social life.

About time, too. For the past two years, Kate had been so focused on Luke and Sugar Rush that the rest of her life plan had fallen by the wayside. Though at twenty-four she'd had little experience before applying for the job, Luke had been so impressed by her interview that he'd hired her before she'd gotten to the door.

Since then, she'd spent every day, 24/7, proving she was exactly what the CEO believed—a powerfully organized, resourceful, detail-oriented self-starter who maintained her unquestionable integrity and discretion. And now that her professional reputation was well established, she could finally pay more attention to her personal life.

Pleased with how the week had gone, Kate headed home to her tidy little bungalow on the edge of Indigo Bay. She changed into yoga pants and a T-shirt, then called her father for their usual Friday evening chat.

"Hi, Dad."

"Hey, sweetie. How's life by the ocean?"

"It's a shore thing."

He chuckled. The warm deep sound reminded her of home. Her weekly calls with her father were a welcome constant in her life, even if they did leave her feeling lonely. Her father's remarriage three years ago had been one of the reasons she'd taken the job at Sugar Rush—she liked her stepmother and was thankful for her father's happiness, but Barb had taken over the household that had previously been Kate's domain.

Seeing that as a sign that she needed to start her own life, Kate had applied at Sugar Rush, clear across the country from the small North Carolina town where her father and Barb still lived. While she'd never regret the move or the job opportunity, she couldn't prevent the pang of sorrow every time she heard her father's voice.

"I miss you," she said. "How are the guys? And Barb?"

"All good." He rambled on about the men on his crew, most of whom had been working for him for years. "Have you had a chance to look at the March Madness odds yet?"

"Yes, and I'd suggest you bet on the lower seeds on the first day." Kate pulled up a spreadsheet on her computer. "I handicapped the road and neutral site records for all the teams. When the brackets are announced, I'll send you a list of which ones have most balance and depth, but favor the teams with the best defense."

She gave him the stats on his favorite teams before the conversation turned to his expectations for baseball's spring training.

"Hold on, Barb is yelling at me." Her father's voice grew faint as he called, "What? Okay, okay. I'll ask." He got back on the line. "Barb wants to know if you're dating anyone."

Kate grimaced. It was a question Barb asked frequently, and not one Kate ever enjoyed answering.

"She doesn't want you to be lonely," her father added.

"I'm not, Dad."

"So, *are* you dating anyone?"

"Um, yeah." Kate crossed her fingers and ignored a stab of guilt. "Sure. I'm...I'm seeing a guy. His name is Tyler."

Wait. *What?*

"What does this Tyler guy do?" her father asked warily.

"Uh, he's...he's doing some data analytics consulting at Sugar Rush."

"Oh." Relief lightened his voice. "Barb wants to know how long you've been dating him."

"Just...a little while."

"She said to post a picture on Instagram."

"I'm not on social media."

"She said to email me...I mean, *her* one."

"I love you, Dad." Kate couldn't prevent a smile. "Talk to you next week."

She ended the call and stared at her living room, which she'd tried to make homey with striped furniture and store-bought prints and photographs.

Still, not even her house, her job success, and her devotion to Sugar Rush could conceal the fact that she'd been homesick since moving to Indigo Bay. Her career had always been on the right track, but now she was ready for the rest of her life to fall into place. All she needed was a solid relationship with an accomplished, dignified man who would fit neatly into the empty space in her life.

But wasn't Tyler Stone a sneaky one, lurking in her subconscious like that? *Looming* with his cocky grin and player moves. Making her wonder what it would have felt like if he'd kissed her.

She shook her head and grabbed her iPod, sticking the ear buds in her ears as she headed out the door. Wondering was one thing. But it was useless to keep thinking about something that would never happen.

❧

Kate walked up and down Ocean Avenue, casting glances at the high-end boutiques with their beveled glass windows and displays of elegant mini-dresses and designer shoes. She hadn't intended to come to the pricey shopping district during her daily power-walk, but she was here now, and she didn't appear to be leaving.

Tyler's words continued to stream like music in her ears. Raw, impolite music, but music nonetheless.

Killer body. Let me feel you move. Fuck, you're hot.

Even though he'd been trying to manipulate her, she couldn't help wondering what it would feel like to dress and look like a woman who heard those kind of phrases all the time.

She stopped in front of a boutique and straightened her shoulders. She probably couldn't afford a belt buckle at a store like this, but it was certainly a good place to find out what was fashionable nowadays.

Kate took a deep breath, adjusted her fanny pack, and opened the door. She stepped into the hushed, dimly lit interior. Classical music wafted from hidden speakers, and expensive clothing glowed from the racks and walls.

She paused by a display, brushing her hand over the smooth silk blouses. She'd read about the importance of wearing clothes that made you feel powerful and confident, but she'd never known how to find those clothes. So she'd always stuck with basic suits that didn't draw much attention.

She riffled through the clothes, enjoying the tactile pleasure of the woven linen skirts and delicate silk shells. Then she moved to a shelf of folded sweaters and picked up a gorgeous short-sleeved sweater with a V-neck and ribbed hem.

"Excuse me." A tall woman with short blond hair approached, her gaze sweeping coolly over Kate's yoga pants and T-shirt. "May I help you?"

Kate's heart lurched. Melanie McGuffin, even more beautiful in person than she was on social media, stood in front of her. Wearing slim crepe trousers and some sort of flowy tunic, she was like a mannequin come to life.

Kate tightened her grip on the sweater she was holding, belatedly wishing she'd had the foresight to wear something more suitable for high-end clothes shopping

"I'm sorry, but you're crushing that." Melanie smiled thinly and eased the sweater from Kate's hands. "If you'd like to try it on...?" Her voice trailed off dubiously.

"Uh, sure," Kate agreed.

"It's baby cashmere," Melanie said. "A very rare, delicate fiber obtained from the underfleece of Mongolian baby goats."

"Okay."

Melanie's gaze flicked to her breasts. "Actually, I think you'll need a larger size. I don't want this one to stretch." She took another sweater from the rack and headed to the back of the store. "Follow me, please."

Kate followed, feeling like a troll trailing after a princess. Aside from having worked up a sweat on her walk to Ocean Avenue, she had her hair trapped in a frizzy ponytail, ear buds dangling around her neck, and she probably smelled.

Yeah. She definitely should have planned this out beforehand. If anyone ever again laughed at her desire to prepare for things, she'd give them the what for.

"Here you go." Melanie flicked aside a heavy curtain and gestured Kate into the dressing room. "Let me know if you need anything else."

"Thanks."

Kate tried not to look at herself in the mirror—not wanting to feel any worse—as she hurriedly tugged off her T-shirt and pulled the sweater on. She ran her hands over her hair and faced the mirror.

Her eyes widened. Aside from feeling like a cloud, the cashmere hugged her curves in all the right places. The pearl color made her skin look warm and creamy, and even seemed to bring out highlights in her brown hair.

Pleased, Kate smiled at her reflection. This was what all the experts meant when they said clothes should make a woman feel *good*. She could only imagine how she'd feel wearing the sweater after she'd showered and shaved her underarms.

"Everything all right in there?" Melanie sang from the other side of the curtain.

"Fine, thanks."

Kate took the sweater off and folded it carefully before pulling her T-shirt back on. She likely couldn't afford the sweater, but it wouldn't hurt to ask how much it cost.

She started to push back the curtain, then stopped.

"Did you see her?" Melanie's low voice, laced with derision, hissed into the dressing room as she apparently spoke to another salesgirl. "Who shops looking like that? This isn't the lonely virgins' club. She's going to ruin that sweater, I just know it. I should charge her just for trying it on."

Well.

Kate battled a twinge of hurt—because Melanie wasn't worth a full-fledged stab of hurt—as well as the urge to stalk out there and throw a fit. The other woman had a point that Kate didn't look exactly presentable, though that didn't excuse her bitchiness. Probably that was why Miles had given her the boot. Good for him.

Leaving the sweater on the bench, she flicked back the curtain and walked out to the front counter.

Melanie turned, her lips stretching into a smile. "So. How did the sweater work out for you?"

"It didn't, I'm afraid," Kate replied coolly, hitching her ear buds back over her ears. "Too bad because I'm shopping under-cover. You see, I'm looking for a good, *respectful* boutique to recommend to my boss's fiancée for her bridesmaids' gowns. Perhaps you've heard of my boss? Luke Stone, CEO of Sugar Rush. I suppose his fiancée and all her friends will be shopping at your competitors' now. Have a nice day."

She wiggled her fingers and strode out the door, her head high and her heart racing like a greyhound. She rarely, if ever, invoked Luke's name to her advantage, but if ever a situation had called for name-dropping, that was it. Kate suspected Luke wouldn't mind, either. In fact, he would probably applaud.

She hurried home, letting the brisk walk carry away the unpleasantness. When she got home, she further eased her prickly feelings with a hot shower.

But Melanie's "lonely virgin" comment stuck in her mind like a piece of industrial-strength Velcro. Kate wasn't a virgin, though it had been over two years since she'd had sex and she'd never been sure she was even any good at it. So maybe that made her a kind of born-again virgin.

But she wasn't lonely...well, maybe she was a little *solitary.* Okay, a lot solitary. Most twenty-six-year-old women didn't stay at home on weekends reviewing corporate social responsibility reports. But she loved her job and knew she was indispensable. And she was certainly trying to rectify the lack in her social life.

Her encounter with Tyler made her want to rectify the lack in her sex life too.

She closed her laptop, packed it in a bag, and headed out again, her mind working like an engine. She usually stayed home on Friday nights, but she was still smarting over Melanie's remark and fidgety over the thwarted encounter with Tyler—not to mention that she hadn't exactly wanted to *thwart* it in the first place. Maybe being out around people would give her some clarity.

She walked a few blocks to downtown Indigo Bay, heading

toward her favorite restaurant off Ocean Avenue. The Treetop Café was a casual little Mediterranean place where the dress code favored shorts and T-shirts. As she entered, the hostess greeted her with a warm smile.

"Hello, Kate." She took a menu from the hostess station. "We weren't expecting you tonight. Table for one, as usual?"

"Table for one," Kate echoed, following her to the outside terrace. "As usual."

CHAPTER 8

*T*yler squinted at his laptop screen, trying to block out the noise of loud voices and a televised basketball game that permeated his apartment.

"She wasn't anything like Savannah, but she was bangable." In the kitchen, his friend Ben piled roast beef onto a sub roll. "I got her number. Haven't called yet."

"Don't bother." John sat forward on the sofa, focused on the big-screen TV. "Shitty party anyway. You didn't miss much, Ty."

"Says the guy who struck out." Ben grinned before sinking his teeth into his oversized sandwich.

John flipped him off and nudged Tyler in the side. "I'm putting Kansas in my bracket this year. Look up their point differential."

Tyler shook his head. "I'm busy here, man."

John swore and dug his phone out of his pocket, flopping back on the sofa to search. Tyler glanced at the clock on his laptop screen.

He was accustomed to spending his weekends more or less the same way—parties, girls, sports, beer, boating, hanging out with his buddies. Sometimes they'd go bar-hopping in San Francisco or take a road trip to LA. He'd had the same group of friends since college—when they'd also spent their weekends the same way—and he'd always liked their lack of planning.

This was, however, the first time he'd ever spent a Friday night looking at a library sciences curriculum, which turned out to be more complicated than he'd expected. It was more than just alphabetizing and putting books on the shelves—there were things like metadata, classification, and bibliographic databases.

He could try to fake it—stick the books on the shelves, stuff the documents into file folders, and tell his father he was finished, but he'd never been able to fool his father before. No reason why he'd be able to now.

The intercom to his apartment buzzed. He put the laptop aside and shoved up from the sofa to let in the pizza delivery guy. After paying, he left the pizza in the kitchen.

"Didja get a double supreme?" John asked.

"Ben ordered it, not me." Tyler dug around the countertop for his car keys. "I'm taking off for a while."

Restless, he headed down to the parking garage and got into his car. For whatever reason, he was in no mood to hang out with his friends tonight. He pulled out of the garage, thinking he'd stop by and see if Polly needed any help with her bakery.

He drove into Indigo Bay, the expensive town of cobblestone streets and vine-covered cottages nestled south of San Francisco on a rocky stretch of the coastline. The wealthy computer-money crowds of Silicon Valley came to Indigo Bay for both the charming atmosphere and the culture—wine-tasting, fine dining, art galleries, theater, shopping, and plenty of society events. The main street of Ocean Avenue was lined with coffee houses, boutiques, exclusive shops, and restaurants.

Tyler detoured toward a stone building laced with ivy. Luke's fiancée Polly, who owned the Wild Child Bakery half an hour away in the farming town of Rainsville, had recently rented the building for a new branch of her bakery.

The place apparently needed a complete remodel, which Polly was doing with her sister Hannah's help—despite the fact that Luke could have paid professionals to do it in less than a week. Polly was very into being *DIY* about everything.

Work lights glowed around the bakery's interior. Drop cloths covered the floor, and a few round tables were scattered by a wooden counter.

Hannah Lockhart, Evan's girl, sat at one table with a laptop. Polly stood on a ladder, her curly hair hidden by a bandana and her jeans and T-shirt streaked with paint.

"Hey, Tyler." Polly waved a paintbrush at him. "Come to help paint?"

He picked up a clean brush and dunked it into a bucket. "When's opening day?"

"We're aiming for early June." Polly set her brush down and climbed off the ladder. "If we get all the business permits in by then."

Tyler brushed paint over the wall, his tension easing as it always seemed to when he was in Wild Child. Like Evan, he'd gotten into the habit of making the half-hour drive to Rainsville for Wild Child's Declairs, a cross between an éclair and a doughnut that had sparked the bakery's success. Indigo Bay was already buzzing about the opening of Wild Child's new branch.

"How's your job?" Hannah leaned back and looked at Tyler. "Evan said you're working at the Sugar Rush library now."

"It sucks." Tyler focused on making the paint even. "It's not work so much as a punishment for the speedboat incident."

Part of him had to give his father and brothers credit. It was a perfect punishment. They'd known he would hate being strait-jacketed into a job he neither wanted nor knew how to do.

Even getting to the same place at the same time every day messed with his mind. It was the reason he'd had such trouble in school. Though he'd aced all the standardized testing, he could never concentrate well enough to do what they wanted him to do.

"Dinner call." Evan entered the bakery, carrying a paper bag and a tray of drinks. "Hey, Ty. What're you doing here?"

"Helping paint." Tyler dunked the brush into the bucket.

"You want some of my sandwich?" Evan retrieved a wrapped sub out of the bag.

Tyler shook his head. Evan distributed sandwiches and drinks to Hannah and Polly before sitting next to Hannah at the table. She reached out and brushed a lock of hair away from his forehead.

Cute. Tyler hadn't been sure Hannah, a woman who had spent the past decade traveling around the world, would be able to settle in Indigo Bay, but she and Evan fit together like two pieces of a puzzle. Evan had regained most of his strength from his heart surgery last year, and he and Hannah were talking about taking a week-long trip to Venezuela next month, where their other brother Adam was setting up the cocoa bean sustainability project.

Tyler continued painting the wall. He'd never had an interest in working at Sugar Rush, and his father had always been okay with that. Warren Stone hadn't expected any of his children to work for the family business unless they'd wanted to.

Though Tyler had done a few summer stints on the factory floor and gift shop when he was a teenager, he hadn't wanted to work his way up into the corporate ranks. He knew he wouldn't be any good at it, not like Luke and Evan.

The problem was, he'd never figured out what he would be good at, aside from spending his trust fund money and having fun. He knew how to fix old cars, but that was just a hobby—as his father frequently reminded him.

The wooden gate leading to the kitchen swung open.

"He's here!" Polly's friend Mia—a blond beauty who favored tight sweaters and short plaid skirts that gave her a sexy schoolgirl vibe—flew into the room, her long hair flying around her shoulders.

Tyler let his gaze skim over her curvy tits and long legs. He'd have made a move on her ages ago, if she hadn't been Polly's friend. Much as he loved women, there were lines he wouldn't cross. Polly would kick his ass from here to Alcatraz if she thought he was hitting on one of her friends only for sex, which was exactly what he'd be doing with Mia.

Or anyone, for that matter. But because of Polly and Hannah, Mia was off-limits. Too bad because he'd bet she was spectacular in the sack. She was kind of skinny, though. Not much of her to grab.

Unlike Kate, who had a damned perfect figure with the right amount of curves and exactly the right sized breasts, not to mention that he could still feel her legs cradling his thigh like she'd been made for him...

"How do I look?" Mia extended her arms and twirled around.

Since she'd asked, Tyler assessed her pert little ass and long legs encased in sheer white tights decorated with little flowers. Mia's skinniness aside, *that* was how a woman with incredible legs should show them off. Not like Kate in her support hose or whatever.

"You look smoking hot," he told Mia.

She came to a halt and narrowed her eyes, though a flush of pleasure colored her cheeks. "I was asking Polly."

"You look smoking hot," Polly assured her. "Gavin won't be able to resist you."

Tyler and Evan exchanged glances that said, *"Yeah, he will."*

Gavin Knight, owner of Knight Security, which handled all of Sugar Rush's corporate security and the Stones' personal security, had been a family friend for years. He was also a machine when it came to security-related crap and apparently some sort of Zen master of self-control and stoicism.

"He's resisted me for ages now." Mia sighed, her lips pursing in a pout. "He's a freaking statue. If I flashed him my naked boobs, he'd tell me I was a security threat."

"Well, you do have a couple of bombs," Hannah remarked, eyeing the other woman's chest.

"Right?" Mia shook her head. "You'd think a security expert would want to get his hands on them. I'll go let him in the back." She turned and hurried through the kitchen.

"She'd totally let him in the front, too," Hannah remarked.

Tyler and Evan both laughed. Polly shot her sister a mild glare, though her mouth twitched.

"Actually, I admire her persistence," Hannah continued. "What's it been, over a year? And she hasn't given up?"

"It's a quest now," Polly said. "He's the one man who hasn't paid attention to her, so now it's become her personal Mordor. He's the one true ring."

The door swung open again and Mia reappeared, followed by Gavin, a tall, square-jawed man wearing his standard uniform of black trousers and a black shirt with the Knight Security logo. He greeted the others before giving Tyler a nod. "Tyler."

Tyler resisted the urge to respond with *"Sir."* Though Gavin had been Luke and Evan's friend since they were kids, he'd had always had an authoritarian thing going on, not unlike Warren Stone.

So Tyler had always seen Gavin as another older brother, but even more rigid than Luke because of his former military career. And now that Gavin owned a security company and was in charge of keeping people safe, he disapproved even more of Tyler's recklessness.

"I'll take a look at the wiring and see what we can do," Gavin told Polly, setting a toolbox on one of the tables. "I emailed you suggestions for access management and surveillance systems."

"Gavin, this is a bakery, not Tiffany's," Polly reminded him. "We don't need to go over the top."

"It's a scalable system given the size of your space." He opened his sleek laptop. "Indigo Bay isn't immune to crime. I promised Luke I'd give you the best I have."

"I'm sure you always give a girl the best you have," Mia remarked, twirling a strand of long hair around her finger.

Gavin didn't look up from his computer screen. Mia slanted Polly an exasperated frown.

Tyler suppressed a smile. Despite Mia's lack of success with Gavin, the girl knew how to flirt. Any other guy would have been panting at her feet. Kate could take lessons from Mia on how to land Miles Norwood, though for some reason Tyler didn't like the idea of Kate thrusting out her cleavage and batting her eyelashes.

Plus she'd probably do it so badly that Norwood would ask her if she had a backache or something in her eye.

"Polly, you know Luke's assistant?" he asked. "Does she come around here a lot?"

"About once a week," Polly replied. "I adore Kate. She's so efficient. She's helping us keep track of the vendors and permits, and even offered to help with the upgrading of our point of sales system." A frown creased her forehead. "Luke keeps trying to get her to take a vacation, though. He said it's been way too long since she's taken time off."

Evan chuckled. "Coming from Luke, that's saying something."

"It's the truth," Hannah said. "I asked her if she wanted to come to Codswallop with us this weekend, but she said she's working."

All weekend? Tyler had issues with *not* working, but it sounded like Kate took things too far in the other direction.

"What's Codswallop?" he asked.

"A hippie music festival about an hour south," Polly explained. "I took Luke when we were first dating, and tomorrow we're going with Hannah and Evan."

Tyler couldn't imagine either one of his brothers, especially starched-shirt Luke, getting down at a hippie music festival.

Then again, Polly had had an effect on the CEO that no one could have predicted. Tyler had never thought his eldest brother capable of change, but now Luke was doing things like taking off work early and maybe even playing bongo drums and wearing tie-dye T-shirts. He seemed happier, too—not happier about Tyler's behavior, but in general.

Tyler set his brush down. After telling the others he had plans that night, he headed back outside. Restlessness still simmered through him.

He walked along the side-streets of Ocean Avenue toward the beach. He passed a little brick restaurant with a tiny, gated terrace on the side, the heat lamps and strings of colorful lanterns providing a nice glow. He glanced absently at the patrons sitting down for dinner.

He stopped. Kate Darling sat at a table near the fence, studying the paper menu spread out on the table that was set for two.

Tyler's gut tightened. Had she already asked Norwood out? Was this about to be their first date? Was she waiting for him? If she was, then why did the thought stick in Tyler like a thorn?

He shook his head. He was being stupid. So she'd asked Norwood out again. Good for mousy little Kate. A data analyst was the guy for her.

Tyler should just walk away and leave them to their little candlelit dinner.

Instead, he walked right toward her.

CHAPTER 9

*F*inding a perverse satisfaction in getting to Kate's table before Norwood was anywhere in sight, Tyler stopped just outside the terrace fence. "Hey, Darling."

She looked up, her eyebrows lifting. "Tyler. What are you doing here?"

"Just heading down to the beach and saw you." He tilted his head to the empty seat across from her. "Waiting for your dream man?"

"What...oh, you mean Miles?" She shook her head. "No. I'm here alone."

He frowned. "You're eating dinner alone?"

"Yes. This is one of my favorite restaurants." She gestured to a laptop bag near her feet. "I often come here to work and have dinner."

He disliked the idea of her eating dinner alone, but at least she wasn't already having dinner with Norwood.

"Can I join you?" he asked.

She blinked. "You want to join me for dinner?"

"Sure. Unless you want to back out of our agreement."

"I never back out of a decision once it's been made." She indicated the empty chair across from her. "Have a seat."

Tyler entered the restaurant through the front door and told the hostess he was joining a friend on the terrace. "The girl sitting by herself," he added.

"Oh, of course!" The hostess's eyes slid over him as she picked up another menu. "How nice for Kate to have a companion."

Jeez. How often did she eat here alone?

After he was seated across from her, he ordered a beer and opened the menu.

"So what do you recommend?" he asked.

"Either the sand dabs or the baba ganoush. Both excellent."

Tyler ordered baba ganoush along with stuffed peppers and falafel. Kate ordered the sand dabs and a side of dolmas for them to share.

"Also one of my favorites," she explained. "The owner of this place is from Lebanon, and everything is so authentic."

"Sounds like it beats pizza, which is what I was about to have for dinner."

She tilted her head and studied him. "Don't you have big Friday night plans? From what I hear, you're quite the party boy."

Discomfort rustled in his chest. He didn't love the idea that she knew about his bad reputation.

"No, I was just hanging out at home." It was more or less the truth. "What about you? No late-night plans?"

She shook her head. He realized for the first time that she looked different than she had at work—her hair was loose, pulled back with a headband, and she wore a blue T-shirt. Even though the baggy material didn't reveal much, the full curves of her breasts were evident, and God knew Tyler remembered with crystal-clear precision how they'd felt in his hands.

Heat pooled in his groin. He forced himself to focus on the image on her shirt, which was of a cartoon bird lying on its back beneath the words THIS PARROT HAS CEASED TO BE.

His mouth twitched. "You a Monty Python fan?"

"A..." She followed his gaze down. "Oh, sure. I've seen all the episodes, but the dead parrot skit never gets old." She looked up at him. "I'm surprised you got the reference."

"I work with a guy who's an expert on British comedies. He got me hooked on Benny Hill, though given the number of bikini-clad girls on that show, it wasn't a hard sell."

Kate's smile brightened her face and made her even prettier. He wanted to see her smile more often. Except he also liked her serious, schoolmarm look, and the way she pulled her eyebrows together when she was thinking hard about something. Not to mention the cute blush that colored her cheeks when she was embarrassed.

"You said you work with a guy," she remarked. "I was under the impression you didn't have a job."

"It's not a job, just tinkering with old cars at a garage. Charlie has a TV in the office, and he plays old British comedies nonstop."

"So do you have a favorite Python sketch?"

As they launched into a discussion of classic sketches, from "Hell's Grannies" to "Nudge," Tyler's guilt and restlessness eased. Unlike some women, Kate didn't hold a grudge. And even though she'd turned the tables on him in the library, he'd sure as hell known what he'd felt.

She'd been hot. And ready. And she could easily have stopped the encounter long before she'd straddled his thigh. He'd have backed off the second she'd pushed him away. But she'd let him tug her skirt up. She'd slid her hands under his T-shirt and traced his abs with a light, fluttering touch that had ignited a fire in his veins.

Christ. He was starting to get hard from the memory alone. He reached for his beer, grateful for the distraction of the food arriving. He took a bite of baba ganoush and almost groaned as the flavors of smoky eggplant and cumin filled his mouth.

"Right?" Kate smiled at his reaction and plucked a dolma from the plate. "Try this."

He ate the dolma out of her fingers, agreed that it was perfection stuffed in a grape leaf, and dug into the rest of his food.

"I talked to Luke about ordering a new computer and database for the library," Kate said. "He green-lighted everything, so it'll be delivered on Monday morning."

"Thanks." Not that he had any idea what he'd do with new equipment. "I really am sorry for what I did. I'm not usually such a dickhead."

"You mean you're just sometimes a dickhead?"

He acknowledged that remark with a wry grin. "I have a redeeming quality or two. And I know I ragged on you about your clothes, but really…if a guy can't see past that, then maybe he's not worth your time."

Kate sighed. "No, you were right. A woman should always put her best foot forward. But it's not just my clothes. Relationships aren't my thing."

"You've never been in relationship?"

"Of course I've been in a relationship." She gave a little sniff of disgust. "I've been in several. Three, to be exact. But they all failed, and I'm still not sure what happened. So clearly I've been getting it wrong. I just need to figure out why."

Tyler leaned back in his chair and crossed his arms. "What if the men were the ones getting it wrong?"

"Then I missed the memo." She finished off the last dolma. "What about you? Growing up with five brothers, you must have some interesting stories."

"Yeah." He shrugged. "I was lucky. Good family. Had everything I wanted. Never did right by my family, though."

She eyed him perceptively. "I heard you were the rebellious one."

"I was a troublemaker, if that's what you mean. My brothers

were all decent, and Hailey's always been a good girl. She got a lot of attention, being the only daughter."

"Evan too, I imagine, with his heart condition." Kate nodded, as if that made perfect sense. "And your brothers are all so successful."

The last thing he wanted to do was talk about his successful brothers.

"So what do you do outside of the office?" he asked.

"Not much. I work a lot."

"What do you do with your friends?"

Kate bit her lip. "I don't have many friends in Indigo Bay."

Well, shit. That shouldn't surprise him, given what he knew about her 24/7 loyalty to Luke and Sugar Rush. Still, it pissed him off that a young woman like her didn't seem to have much of a life outside of work. She should be out having fun, not stuck behind a desk all the time.

"What about Polly and Hannah?" he asked. "They said you turned down an offer to go to a music festival with them."

"I didn't want to intrude."

"When you're invited somewhere, it's not intruding."

"I know, but they're still making up for all the years they were apart," Kate explained. "So I feel like they should just have the time together as sisters."

Tyler shook his head. "Well, they both like you. You should hang out with them sometime."

"Maybe I will." She picked up the bill the waitress had left on the table, holding up a hand when he started to protest. "I'll take care of this. We wouldn't want to mess up your track record of getting one-upped by Kate Darling."

She winked at him and reached for her bag. A grin tugged at his mouth. He was starting to like getting one-upped by Kate Darling. But still he took a couple of twenties out of his wallet and put them on the bill tray.

"Hey, man." The familiar voice boomed through the air. He turned to see Ben and John ambling toward him.

"Why'd you take off?" Ben asked as they came to a stop beside the fence. "We're going over to that new bar on Green Street. Come on."

"No, thanks." Tyler gestured to Kate, who was still standing beside the table. "This is Kate, Luke's secre...er, executive assistant."

"Oh." Ben blinked. "Sorry, thought you were the waitress."

"Kate, this is Ben and John."

"Hi." She gave them a little wave. "Nice meeting you."

"You too," John said.

Kate indicated to Tyler that she was going inside. After she'd left, Ben punched him on the shoulder.

"Come on, man. The Tipsy Angel is supposed to be a great new place."

Tyler shook his head. "No, I'm done for the night."

"You going out with her?" Ben nodded in the direction Kate had gone. "Interesting choice, especially after Savannah. Looks like you've lowered your fuck buddy standards."

A red mist of anger descended over Tyler's eyes. He got to his feet so fast his chair almost tipped over. He grabbed the front of Ben's shirt and yanked other guy closer. Silence fell over the terrace, the other patrons glancing their way.

"You don't fucking talk about Kate or any other woman like that," Tyler snapped. "Do that again, and I'll kick your ass. Got it?"

"Chill out, man." Ben held up his hands. "Just saying she's not exactly like your other bombshells, right? Fuck buddy or not."

"Shut up." John knocked Ben hard on the back of the head.

"Is there a problem, gentlemen?" The hostess rushed toward them, her expression worried.

"No problem." Tyler released Ben with a shove. "Sorry for the trouble."

John grabbed Ben's arm, dragging him away. Tyler smothered his anger and stalked into the restaurant. He stopped.

Kate stood by the door leading to the terrace. One look at her expression told Tyler she'd overheard what his dickhead friend had just said.

CHAPTER 10

*R*eally?

Kate shook her head in disbelief. Did she have some sort of "Kick Me" sign on her back tonight?

"Shit." Tyler groaned and dragged his hands over his face. "I'm sorry. He's an asshole. Guess it takes one to know one, huh?"

Kate smiled faintly at his attempt at humor. "You're not an asshole, Tyler. You're a little...misguided, and you need to get your shit together, but I know your family. Your parents didn't raise you or any of your brothers to be bad people."

He blinked, as if that thought had never occurred to him. "Still. I'm sorry he insulted you."

Kate slipped her wallet back into her bag and started for the door. It was a good thing she had high self-esteem because taking two hits in one night was a little much, even for a woman who had reasonably strong armor.

But at least this time she'd had someone on her side. Though she really couldn't have cared less what a jerk like Ben thought of her, it was nice to have Tyler leap to her defense and take some of the sting out of the insult. Aside from her father and the quarry guys—and they didn't really count—a man had never defended her.

"You do have interesting friends." She pushed open the front door. "Interesting choice of women too, by the sound of it."

"What does that mean?" He caught up with her on the sidewalk.

"Fuck buddies?" The phrase had an odd effect on her, like it was sparking and popping in her brain. "You don't have the decency to call them girlfriends?"

"I have girlfriends," Tyler replied defensively. "But sometimes a girl and I have an understanding that we're not together, just having fun. Friends with benefits. I don't call them that, though. Not fuck buddies either. I just refer to them as friends. No one else's business if we're sleeping together."

She threw him a derisive frown. "Seems like your *bros* figured it out, though. The girls don't get the idea that you're romancing them?"

"No, because I'm not. I treat them right and all, but there's no long-term promise. It's just sex."

"What about the *friends* part?"

"We're friends, too." He shoved his hands into his pockets as they started toward Ocean Avenue. Discomfort flashed across his face. "It's not a bad thing. The girl and I are both looking for a good time, no matter what we call each other."

"Well, it's the same thing, isn't it?" Kate asked. "Friends with benefits, fuck buddies, sex buddies. Is that what Savannah was? Wasn't she also the speedboat girl?"

"Yeah." He grimaced. "There was an out-of-control party on a yacht anchored in the bay. Savannah Corrigan took the keys to her father's boat and asked me to get her stuff because she wasn't supposed to be at the party in the first place. And, like an idiot, I did."

"How did you crash?"

"I was going too fast because I wanted to get back before we were found out." His mouth twisted. "Didn't exactly go as planned."

"And I'm guessing Savannah didn't tell her father the truth."

Tyler shrugged. "Doesn't matter."

"How can it not matter?" Kate experienced a twinge of indignation on his behalf. "She lied."

"I didn't have to take the boat out. But I can never say no to a pretty girl."

"Sounds like it's the same in the bedroom," she remarked. "How long were you with her?"

"Couple of months," Tyler said. "Can we stop talking about her? The memory of Savannah is like a lingering fart smell in my brain."

Kate laughed. He shot her a grin, and some of the tension seemed to ease from his shoulders.

"Hey, look." She stopped, nodding toward a bar on the other side of the street. A brightly lit window sat between a pizza joint and a board game store. The sign above it read Get Your Geek On Arcade. "I haven't been to an arcade in years."

He cocked his head. "You like arcades?"

"Not only do I like arcades, I hold the all-time *Space Invaders* record at the Pizza Pit on Fourth Street in Wabash, North Carolina."

He grinned. "Well, you're in trouble now because you're on a date with a guy who had dreams of becoming a professional gamer when he was a kid."

A date. Had this really turned into an unexpected *date*?

She arched an eyebrow. "Challenge?"

He strode to the door and pulled it open for her. "Challenge."

The interior was dim and loud, the noise of battles and race-cars pinging from the video-game machines set up on the other side of a snack bar. The proprietor told them all the games were set to free play, so they paid the cover fee and headed into the crowd.

Battles of *Pac-Man, Frogger,* and *Sonic the Hedgehog* filled the next hour. Kate was pleased to discover that Tyler was both surprised and impressed with her gaming skills—after being insulted twice in one night, it was nice to be admired, even if it was for winning an old video game.

"Never would have pegged you as a gamer," he said when they stopped after their third game of *Centipede.*

"I'm not." She retrieved her bag out of the storage locker. "It was just one of the things we did a lot in Wabash."

Tyler held the front door open for her as they exited to the street.

"I think there's more to you than meets the eye, Kate Darling," he remarked.

"Isn't there more to everyone than meets the eye?"

"Maybe. Then there's me, where what you see is what you get."

Kate didn't believe that. She suspected he had more depth than anyone had bothered to discover. But oh, how she did like what she saw. She'd been aware of him all evening, not only his potent masculine presence, but the easy, self-assured way he moved in his own body and the world at large.

"So North Carolina, huh?" he asked. "You grew up there?"

"Yes, my father is the foreman of a granite quarry. My mother died when I was quite young, and my father didn't remarry until a couple of years ago. So for most of my life it was just me and him. Plus a dozen quarry guys who hung around on weekends and evenings. Sometimes it was like having a bunch of overprotective uncles. Other times, like during tax season, it was like having a bunch of needy nephews."

"Why's that?"

"I helped them with their tax prep," Kate explained. "Personal budgets, business stuff. My father is the most loyal and hardworking man you'd ever meet, but he's terribly disorganized. I had to be the one to plan and keep track of things, and when the other guys discovered I was good at it, they also asked me for help. When I was old enough to get a work permit, I became a part-time secretary at the quarry."

"Sounds like you've been an assistant in one form or another for a while now."

"I guess." An old sorrow rose inside her. "When I was twelve, my father came close to bankruptcy. We almost lost our house. He couldn't afford to hire an accountant or advisor, so we had to figure it out together. I learned at a young age that staying organized is critical for both personal and financial security."

He frowned, looking as if he were about to say something else. Instead he kept walking.

"Hey, you want to go somewhere else?" he asked. "Get a drink?"

"No, thanks," She gestured to her T-shirt. "I'm not dressed for going anywhere nice. But if your car is nearby, I'll take a ride home. We can look over the library sciences curriculum, if you're not doing anything else."

He mumbled something under his breath before pausing beside an old blue sports car parked at the curb. Kate stared.

"This is your car?"

"Yeah." He pulled the keys from his pocket.

"It's a Trans Am."

He smiled. "1979. I'm impressed."

"One of my father's friends was really into Pontiacs." Kate touched the fender, experiencing a rush of homesickness. "I figured you'd drive something a lot newer."

"Yeah, well…" His gaze slanted away from her. "Evan gave this to me as a birthday present a few years ago. I've always been into old cars."

He opened the passenger side door for her. After climbing in, Kate admired the leather interior, the high-back bucket seats, and the dash insert. Her father would be impressed with Tyler's appreciation for classic vehicles. Even though he thought Tyler was a data analyst.

Which reminded her...she checked her phone for messages, responding to a few inquiries from Sugar Rush VPs and other assistants.

"Are you ever off the clock?" Tyler asked.

"Not really." She slipped her phone back into her bag and directed him to her house. "I get a lot done on weekends because there aren't any other distractions."

"When was the last time you took a vacation?"

"I'm going to visit my father in the fall."

From the slight twist of his mouth, she could tell that didn't exactly qualify as a "vacation." Well, where else was she supposed to go? A resort in the Bahamas? Hotel room for one?

Tyler probably took his girlfriends to all sorts of exotic places for vacation. Having fun was his thing.

From the sound of it, being a fuck buddy was also Tyler's thing. And *that* gave Kate a heavy, quivery feeling inside. It was perfectly fine to have a visceral reaction to his potent sexuality. She was a normal, healthy woman after all.

She was also no fool. She understood why the youngest Stone brother was so attractive to women. With his rakish good looks and easygoing, teasing attitude, he exuded the promise of good times and great sex.

And she wasn't such a wallflower that she was immune to the appeal of such promises—but she *was* intelligent and self-aware enough to know she would never fall for them.

She wanted a quiet, hard-working man who wasn't afraid of commitment, not a party boy who didn't take anything seriously. Not a man who had no intention of finding a soul mate or even a partner in one of his fuck buddies. Or "friends with benefits."

Scowling a little, she typed "fuck buddy" into her search engine and perused the results for the rest of the drive.

"Nice place." Tyler pulled into the driveway of her house,

peering through the windshield at the neat little front garden with the "Welcome Spring" plaque and porch swing.

"Thanks." She pushed open the door. "I bought it about a year after I moved here. Come on, I'll make some coffee and we can review the website."

Knowing his lack of enthusiasm for library sciences, she half expected him to decline, but he turned off the engine and followed her inside. They went into the kitchen, where Kate started a pot of coffee brewing. She set her laptop on the counter and booted it up.

"So did you have a chance to look at the curriculum?" she asked. "Do you have any questions about it?"

"About a hundred million questions, but I'm not getting a degree in library sciences." Tyler hitched himself up onto the counter. "I just need to finish the damned job. Hell, I need to *start* it."

"I know. That means you need to understand what the job entails." Kate brought the website up onscreen. "The first steps are the basic cataloguing, maybe to a second-level taxonomy, and the installation of a management system. You should also understand the structure of MARC records and the access points of bibliographic records."

"Mmm. Dirty talk."

Dirty talk. She tried not to imagine what Tyler's brand of dirty talk would sound like.

Come on, honey, open your legs nice and wide so I can slide into your hot little pussy and fuck you so hard you'll feel it for days.

God. So much for trying *not* to imagine that.

"Pay attention," she said, though she wasn't certain if she was talking to Tyler or herself. "I might quiz you on this later. Access points include things like titles, authors, and subject headings."

When Tyler didn't respond, she glanced at him. His gaze was oddly intent on her face, and a touch of amusement sparkled in his eyes.

"You need to know this so you'll understand authority control," she said.

"Trust me," he murmured. "I understand both authority and control."

Oh lord. She cleared her throat and turned back to the website. "You also need to establish a controlled vocabulary to maintain consistency."

"Is this what you did with your old boyfriends on your first date?" Tyler asked. "Talked about cataloging and vocabulary?"

"No. But since we were in college, we probably studied."

He lifted an eyebrow in mock disbelief. "So you broke up with them because they bored you to death?"

An old, latent pain curled through Kate. "Um, I didn't break up with them. They broke up with me. I'm still not sure why. That's why I need to figure out what I've been doing wrong."

"Well, what did they tell you?" Tyler asked. "What'd they say in the big break-up speech?"

"Just vague things like it wasn't working out. They all found other girls pretty fast after the break-up." She took a breath and confessed the truth. "Honestly, I think they were bored with me."

"They were bor-*ing* if they couldn't even be bothered to take you out." Tyler shook his head. "Sounds like you dodged a bullet with those douchebags. What about high school boyfriends? Prom and stuff?"

"I didn't go to prom." She held up a hand. "But before you get all worried about poor, sorry little Kate, I *was* asked to go. I just didn't because my father was short-handed at the quarry at the time and I needed to help him out."

In case he thought she was a total loser, she added, "And I wasn't an introverted bookworm with buck teeth and glasses… well, okay, I had to wear glasses, but in high-school I was treasurer of the student council and president of the forensics league. And in college, I was editor of the features section of the university newspaper and coordinator of a scholar's program. In other words, I have always been an active, engaged member of the community."

She'd also been a quiet member of the community, but that was the way she'd both liked and wanted it. She didn't have to draw attention to herself in order to excel at what she did.

"And in all that time, you never found a guy who could rock your world?" Tyler asked.

Kate's flush deepened. "I wasn't looking for a guy who could *rock my world*. Just a man who shares my interests and is a good partner."

He scoffed. "You lie like a rug."

"I am not lying."

"Then why're you doing all this for Norwood?" Tyler narrowed his gaze. "You're not physically attracted to him?"

"Of course I'm attracted to him. But not just because of the way he looks. He's incredibly smart, methodical, and dedicated to his work. Luke brought him in to provide an outside perspective about how Sugar Rush is implementing marketing strategies for all the different product lines, not to mention measuring effectiveness and analytical—"

"Yeah, yeah." Tyler shoved off the counter, a sudden edge to his voice. "He's a genius. I get it. I'm sure he'll turn you on wildly with his knowledge about algorithms, but how do you know he's not a cold fish in the sack?"

"If his *mind* and our conversations turn me on, I'm sure we'd get along with the other things just fine," Kate retorted, stung by his insinuations about both her and Miles's lack of chemistry. "It's the law of attraction. Like attracts like."

"What about that other saying—opposites attract?"

Kate's heart jumped—because no two people were more opposite than she and Tyler, and her body was certainly attracted to his. But that didn't mean a man like him could ever be her soul mate.

"You might have a different set of criteria," she said. "But I want to be with a man who challenges me intellectually. A great conversation is as satisfying as great sex."

Tyler made another scoffing noise. Kate frowned.

"I guess you wouldn't know that since you probably don't say more than two words to all your fuck buddies," she remarked. "Oh, excuse me. I mean *friends with benefits*."

She rolled her eyes to let him know what she thought of that particular euphemism, but he only grinned at her—one of his devastatingly sexy grins that made his eyes crinkle at the corners and had no doubt caused many a woman to want to slither right out of their panties.

Sudden warmth bloomed in Kate's chest, and she focused on the library website. She was too smart, too self-aware, to be affected by Tyler Stone's charm. Certainly he didn't make her want to slither right out of her panties.

Except that he sort of did.

"Trust me," he said. "I like a great conversation. Being with a woman who really gets me, and vice versa. There's nothing like it in the world. But you can have great sex with someone and not say a word...except for some good dirty talk."

Kate tried not to squirm. If Tyler's dirty talk was anything like what she'd imagined, he'd set her off with the power of his voice alone.

"But how do you know if you have chemistry with a woman if you don't have an intelligent conversation with her beforehand?" she asked.

"A kiss tells me everything I need to know."

She turned to face him. He was leaning back against the counter, his arms loosely crossed over his muscular chest, his body relaxed and casual—as if they were discussing their lunch plans rather than sexual attraction.

"A kiss," she repeated dubiously.

He nodded, his gaze slipping to her mouth. Her lips tingled, as if his look were a touch.

"A kiss tells you *everything* you need to know?" she asked. "Sexually?"

"Sure. The kiss is the prelude, the appetizer, the introduction. First base. If a girl is a lousy kisser, chances are she's not going to be any good in the sack."

"Wait a second." Her heart was starting to speed up, and she swore it was a few degrees warmer in here. "You're telling me you first kiss a girl and then decide if you want to sleep with her?"

"No. I'm nondiscriminatory. If I'm attracted to a woman and she's attracted to me, I'll kiss her and sleep with her regardless of what I think of her kissing technique."

"Even if, as you claim, you know she'll be lousy in bed?"

"Sure." He shrugged. "I'm a pretty good teacher when it comes to showing a girl how to get her groove on. Being a lousy lay isn't an unfixable condition."

"So what makes a girl a good kisser? Good enough that you know the earth will shake if you have sex with her?"

"First, she has to know how to give and take," Tyler said. "She has to be responsive, relaxed, and to understand that kissing is like a language in and of itself. You don't have to talk when you're kissing—you should follow the man's lead and let him take control. Unless you want to take control, in which case you need to get aggressive, grip his hair, and use your teeth. Show him how much you want it."

Kate's breath grew shallow. Why had he just gone from *she* to *you*?

"And...and that gives you insight into a woman's sexual performance?"

"Totally. If we're getting hot while kissing on the sofa, if her body is tensing with lust and her nipples are hard, if she opens her mouth and I can taste her heat and desire, if she's greedy, passionate, and wants more...then I know she'll be wild and electric in bed."

Wild and electric.

Though the rational part of Kate's brain told her not to take this conversation any further, the reckless part blurted out, "And what makes a woman good in bed? From your perspective, of course. I assume she has to do more than just show up."

He was silent for a minute, but he didn't take his gaze from her face. A taut kind of energy passed between them.

"Why do you want to know, Darling?"

Kate's throat went dry, her heart now hammering with more than just nervousness. "Um…curiosity."

He leaned closer to her, so close that she could smell the warm, pepperminty scent of him and see the darker ring of brown surrounding his irises. She was caught between him and the counter. The air around them charged with sparks and tension.

"You're good in bed if you're uninhibited." His voice lowered a notch. "If you like being naked and don't get all self-conscious about me kissing you anywhere I want. If you touch me as much as I touch you, if you're not afraid to get messy and raw. If you show me what you like and don't like and you pay attention to what turns me on as much as I'm paying attention to you. If you're vocal—I want to hear you moaning, gasping, begging for more. Fuck, I want to hear you *scream.*

"I want your pussy clenching around my cock. I want to go deep, over and over, and I want you to spread your legs and open yourself up for me. I want us to sweat and groan, to fuck in multiple positions for hours on end. And I want you to come like a goddamned rocket, hard enough that I feel it right to my bones. I want you to take everything I give you and give it all right back. Endlessly."

Kate could only stare at him, her blood hot with arousal, her mind dizzy with images of her and Tyler entwined naked on the sheets, doing all those things and more. Loving every second of their hot, sweaty rawness.

"Well." She darted her tongue out to lick her dry lips. "That was very educational."

And then some.

"What about you?" Tyler watched the movement of her tongue. "What does a guy have to do to satisfy Kate Darling in bed?"

She wished she knew.

"I...I think this conversation has come to an end." She tore her gaze from his and turned to take two mugs out of the cupboard. Her hands trembled as she poured two cups of coffee and pushed one toward him.

She felt Tyler watching her, his gaze tangible, tension still threading through his body and lining the corded muscles of his forearms. Then he wrapped his fingers, warm and possessive, around her wrist.

Her knees weakened. She was certain he could feel her pulse racing. He tugged her gently but insistently toward him.

"If you want me to help you get another guy..." he brought one hand up to touch her cheek, "...I'm going to need a kissing baseline."

She burned beneath his scrutiny. "I...I don't need help with kissing." *And wasn't that the lie of the century?*

"How do you know?" He rubbed his thumb gently beneath her cheekbone, the light touch igniting sparks in her blood. "Maybe those dickwads broke up with you because you're a lousy kisser."

An ache nudged at her heart. Could he tell that she'd actually wondered that herself? Further, she hadn't discounted the possibility that a lackluster performance in bed might have been the reason her boyfriends had hit the road. She'd never had the courage to ask them about her sexual abilities, and they'd either been too polite or too dull themselves to mention it, so Kate had never had any real, honest feedback.

And if she *was* bad in bed—she certainly couldn't recall having done any of the things Tyler had just described in graphic detail

—then her boyfriends hadn't been like him at all in wanting to teach her how to improve.

"I...I'm not a lousy kisser," she stammered. He had a beautiful mouth—a well-shaped lower lip in perfect proportion to the upper.

"I'll be the judge of that."

He took off her glasses and set them on the counter. He slid his hand around to the back of her neck. Heat swept down her spine. And then he lowered his head and kissed her.

Her mind went blank, which was the Kate Darling equivalent of her mind exploding.

All thought fell away, overwhelmed by the cataclysmic burst of pleasure. She drew in a breath the instant before Tyler settled his mouth more firmly against hers. His kiss was warm, firm, and gentle, his tongue sliding over the seam of her lips but not urging her mouth open.

Kate sank into him, allowing her body to press against his, her breasts pillowing against his chest. A tremble rocked through her. He slipped his hands down to her hips, holding her in place as he moved his lips over hers.

She fumbled for something to grab, finding his hair-roughened forearms. She curled her fingers around them, the muscles flexing and tensing beneath her palms. Little fires ignited in her blood, pouring heat right into her core.

God. It usually took her a bit of time to get aroused, but within seconds of their lips touching, she was feeling all melty and lush inside. Exactly the way she'd felt when they were in the library— except then, she'd been poised on the brink, anticipating something that never came. And now, here it was.

Experimentally, she parted her lips. He slipped his tongue into her mouth. Heat bolted through her. Her nipples tightened, and she wiggled a little to rub them against Tyler's chest. She tightened her grip on him, stunned by the electricity crackling through her veins, the striking sense of having found something that had once been lost to her. Or never found at all.

He deepened the kiss, sweeping his tongue across the surface of her teeth as he backed her up against the wall and settled his hands on either side of her head. Dizziness swept through her.

Though trapped between the wall and the muscularity of Tyler's body, she didn't feel claustrophobic or nervous—only sheltered and somehow safe. She let her head fall back, reveling in the sensation of their lips clinging together. He lowered one hand to cup her breast, flicking his thumb over her hardened nipple.

Pleasure filled her veins. She squeezed her thighs together to ease the burgeoning ache.

Tyler's hands tightened on her shoulders. He broke away from her suddenly. Tension coiled through his body.

"Fuck," he bit out, his hands fisting and his expression darkening with regret.

Regret.

Pain filled Kate's chest. Only one thing could assuage the hollow need inside her, the knowledge that all her efficient planning and organization had been smothering the primal desire to be touched.

"Tyler..."

"I'm not trying to play you again."

"I know." She drew in a heavy breath.

"I don't..." He raked a hand through his hair, his shoulders tight. "I don't know what the hell to do with you now, Kate. But I'll tell you one thing."

He turned to face her, his eyes blazing with heat. "You'll be a goddamned firecracker in bed. No question."

A hard shudder rocked through her, centering in her core. She felt as if she were standing in front of something monumental and extraordinary, if she'd only have the courage to step toward it.

"How does it start?" she whispered. "The fuck buddy thing?"

Tyler didn't take his eyes off her. The air thickened.

"Why do you want to know?"

"Curiosity." She swallowed hard. "Do you talk about it first?"

"Sometimes." He paced to the other side of the kitchen. "Mostly it's just understood. We both want it."

"What about medical testing and stuff?"

"We're honest." He took a breath, turning to face her. "If you want to know, I'm clean, but I always use protection."

Yes, she did want to know.

"And does the woman stay the night?" she asked. "Or do you stay the night at her place?"

"Sometimes."

"How do the relationships end?"

"I don't know. They just end."

"But you're on good terms?"

"Yeah." He spread his hands out, faint frustration rising to his eyes. "Look, it's like going to dinner with a friend and splitting the check. We both get a great meal, but neither one of us is indebted to the other."

"Like we just did at the Treetop Café," Kate said. "So it's just sex and friendship."

"Sex and friendship."

"Do you consider us friends?" she asked.

"Sure." Wariness threaded through his voice.

"Good. I do, too." Something clicked inside her, like a key turning in a lock. "So what do you say about us becoming fuck buddies?"

CHAPTER 11

*S*ilence as thick as smoke descended over the kitchen. Kate gripped her hands together, still trying to project an aura of poise despite the fact that her heart was racing madly.

She should have come up with a different way of asking that question—but what other way was there? She hadn't gotten to her position at Sugar Rush by being coy and circumspect—a straightforward approach was always best.

At work, at least. Maybe it was different for this kind of thing.

"Are you fucking kidding me right now?" Tyler finally said.

Oh dear.

She swallowed to ease her dry mouth. "Of course not."

"You *seriously* want to know if you and I can be fuck buddies?"

"I seriously do." She dug into her bag for her phone. "When we were driving back here, I did a quick search on the subject."

Tyler gave a hoarse laugh and thunked his forehead against the wall.

"Just so I understand the details and rules," Kate explained, pulling up the document on the phone. "I really think we qualify. We're friends, but not from the same social group, so there's no chance of things getting messy when it's over. As you said, there's an understanding that emotions and such aren't involved because we're not in a relationship. We have no reason to tell anyone else or get romantic. As long as we use protection, do it when it's convenient for both of us, and keep it straightforward, we meet all the qualifications. So what do you say?"

Tyler lifted his head from the wall, looking as if he'd just been poleaxed. "You're going after Norwood, right? He's the man of your dreams. So why the hell do you want to be fuck buddies with me?"

"For that reason." Kate gave him an earnest look. "You just said that maybe my old boyfriends had broken up with me because I'm a lousy kisser."

He dragged a hand down his face. "You're anything *but* a lousy kisser, Darling. I almost came in my pants just from kissing you."

"I appreciate that, but I'm not all that confident in the sex department either. Based on what I know of you, and of course our previous conversations, you'd be an excellent partner. And it would be nice to go into a relationship feeling as if I at least knew what I was doing. So I was thinking you could give me a few lessons."

He gave another humorless laugh and shook his head with a muttered, "Fuck me."

"That's what I'm asking to do," Kate said patiently. "I've seen the kind of women you date. Clearly you didn't get your womanizer reputation for nothing."

"We're not going to be fuck buddies," he snapped, turning to face her. "If you want to up your sex game, you do it with a guy you're in a relationship with. Not with me."

Kate bristled. "Why not? Because I don't look like a girl who could be a fuck buddy? That's what your friend thought, right?"

"Would you stop putting yourself down?" Tyler's jaw clenched. "When I first saw you, I thought you needed better clothes, but turns out the old lady look is a good thing because you'd distract every man in the office if they could see your body.

And if you weren't Luke's assistant and...*Kate Darling*, I'd have had you naked two hours ago. But you're a nice girl going after a nice guy, even if he does have a stick up his ass, and there is no way I'm giving you lessons about how to fuck him."

"I'm not asking you specifically about Miles," Kate replied tartly. "We don't even know if he'll agree to go out with me, much less sleep with me. But you know I'm romantically interested in another man, so it's not as if we have any secrets or preconceived ideas about what this is about. I'm asking for general knowledge and because...well, frankly, I trust you and I'd rather learn with you than with a guy who makes me nervous."

Only when the words were out of her mouth did Kate realize how true they were. She had always been nervous around men she was romantically interested in, but she wasn't with Tyler. With him, she had the same feeling of satisfied contentment that she had both as the quarry guys' Girl Friday and as Luke's executive assistant—she knew exactly how to help them.

Even though Tyler was a trust fund baby with a nonexistent work ethic, she was at ease with him because he needed her. Yes, he made her all tingly and weak in the knees, but that was just a sign of physical attraction—and yet another reason why she wanted to take things to the next level.

Stony silence fell again. Tension tightened Tyler's jaw. He folded his arms and regarded her with a hard glint in his eyes. "Why do you think you need sex lessons?"

A flush crawled up Kate's neck. She forced her voice to sound calm and measured as she responded with the truth.

"Because in my experience, sex with a man is nice but honestly it's better when I'm...alone."

He didn't move, but the muscles in his biceps twitched. "You mean when you get yourself off?"

"Yes." Her flush burned deeper. "And by all accounts, that's not how it's supposed to be. It should be better with someone else."

Something flared in the depths of his eyes. An arc of electricity sizzled clear across the room, prickling her skin. She shifted. Her heart thudded. Was it getting hot in here?

"I..." She darted her tongue out to lick her lips. "I'm twenty-six. And though I'm exceedingly competent and knowledgeable in a number of areas, sex isn't one of them. So for once, I would like to know what I'm doing. That's all."

He unfolded his arms and crossed the room. Her pulse ratcheted up with every step he took toward her. And when he stopped in front of her, the heady, peppermint scent of him filling her nose, Kate's whole body surged with anticipation.

"That's not *all*," he said. "If we do this, Darling, you'll get more than just the satisfaction of knowing what you're doing. You'll get hot, dirty fucking. You'll get hickeys on your neck, whisker burn between your thighs, and the red imprint of my hand on your ass. You'll get my cock pounding inside you so hard and deep you'll think you can't take it, but then you'll beg for more. You'll get on your hands and knees to take me from behind. You'll come so hard your pussy will squeeze my cock like a vise. You'll get sweaty, raunchy, and totally indecent."

Kate stared at him. His words started a wildfire raging through her blood, setting her alight. She could hardly breathe. Her sex throbbed. Her clothes were too heavy, weighing her down. She squeezed her thighs together and stifled a moan.

"So." He crossed his arms, his gaze burning into her. "Do you still want it?"

God. She wanted it more than ever. She *craved* it, ached for it. She was about to come just thinking about it.

Flexing her fingers on the edge of the counter, she pulled in a ragged breath. "I still want it," she whispered hoarsely.

Tyler was silent. Erotic tension radiated from him, thickening the air between them. Then he gave a short nod, his features hardening with determination.

"Okay," he said.

Kate's heart jolted. That one word promised she was going to have sex with him.

Not just any kind of sex either—the hot, dirty kind he'd described in vividly arousing and graphic detail. Sex with big, hunky Tyler Stone who'd gotten her panties wet with one kiss. It was either going to be spectacular or she was going to wimp out and call the whole thing off.

No. She would not wimp out. She was the one who'd started this, and damned if she wouldn't see it through. "Okay."

They were about to go to a whole new level. She would round out her sexual education, and he would...well, in addition to fulfilling his obligations at the library, he'd get laid. He'd told her it had been a while, so she'd be helping him out.

If she could manage to keep up. From the way she'd seen him eat, not to mention all she'd gleaned from social media, Tyler was a man of big appetites. The bedroom would be no different.

"So when do we start?" she asked before her courage faltered.

Tyler looked at his watch. "Now."

CHAPTER 12

"*N*-now?" Kate stammered.

He approached her with determined intent. "You have somewhere you need to be?"

"No."

"Then now." He stopped in front of her, his dark eyes burning like coals. "No more small talk or getting to know each other. We just get down to it and fuck whenever we want."

A riotous tremble coursed through her. She half expected him to get down to it right here in the kitchen, but he took her hand and led her back to her bedroom, shutting the door behind them.

Nervous excitement flooded her veins. He gripped her shoulders and tugged her closer, his gaze skimming over her and lingering on her breasts, the hard nipples tenting the fabric of her T-shirt. He slid his hands down her arms, then over to cup her breasts, the heat of his palms burning right through her shirt.

"I've been wanting to see you naked since the second you fell into my arms," he murmured, rubbing his thumbs over her nipples. "I'm not waiting any longer."

He grasped the hem of her shirt and tugged it off, tossing it to the floor. His attention snapped to her cleavage, trapped in a white support bra that Kate belatedly wished was something sexier. Before she could dwell on that thought, Tyler reached around to unclasp her bra, releasing the hooks with an expert twist of his fingers. The bra straps slid off her shoulders. Her breasts spilled free, heavy and round.

Goose bumps prickled her skin. She'd never been comfortable with the size of her breasts and had taken pains to conceal them beneath her shapeless clothes. But in private she loved holding and rubbing them, running her fingers around her exquisitely sensitive nipples, which now stuck straight out in clear signal of her arousal.

A flush of self-consciousness rose, but Tyler's appreciative groan told her that he liked the sight of her bare breasts. Or maybe he even loved it, given the way he cupped them again in his big hands and lowered his head to kiss her.

"Fucking perfect," he whispered the instant before his lips touched hers.

Kate melted. His mouth covered hers, his kiss both warm and gentle, as if he were making sure she really was okay with this.

And she was. She stroked her hands over his shoulders to the back of his neck, holding him against her.

Oh bliss...

Exquisite shivers rained through her, building into a wave that made her tremble from the inside out. Tyler's mouth moved against hers with increasing urgency, his tongue sliding out to part the seam of her lips and delve inside.

A gasp caught in Kate's throat as their tongues touched, firing her with heat. His hands moved over her breasts, rubbing and squeezing, his long fingers plucking at her tight nipples and sending shocks right to her core.

"Christ." He lifted his head, his breath hot against her mouth and his eyes smoldering. "You're so fucking responsive. You're wet already, aren't you?"

She drew in a breath and nodded. She'd been aching from the

minute he'd started talking about kissing, and then detoured into *"I want you to spread your legs and open yourself up for me."* She pressed her thighs together, unable to stifle a small moan.

A wicked smile tugged at Tyler's mouth. He pinched one of her nipples and edged his hand down into the waistband of her yoga pants. Before she could grasp a thought, his hand was moving down her panties and into her sex.

"Ah, *fuck*." His groan escaped on a rush of breath and stirred the tendrils of hair at her temple.

Kate choked out a gasp and gripped the front of his T-shirt to maintain her balance. He edged his hand farther between her legs, working one finger into her cleft while circling his thumb around her swollen clit.

"I knew you were a firecracker," he said, sliding his finger up and down. "How often do you touch yourself, Darling?"

She swallowed. "O-often. At least every other night."

"And what do you fantasize about when you get yourself off?"

"All sorts of things," she replied breathlessly. "Sometimes kinky stuff like spanking or getting tied up. Mostly just good hard fucking. Being...um, taken, you know?""

"Hmm." His chest rumbled with the sound. "Your old boyfriends never did that?"

"Not the way it looks in the movies." She arched her lower body toward him when his finger probed inside her. "Tyler, that feels incredible."

He lowered his head to her mouth again, his kiss scorching her. He grasped her hips and turned her toward the bed.

Kate fell backward onto the flowered comforter, her gaze locked onto him as he peeled her pants and underwear off her legs. He took off her socks too, a grin flashing over his face at the sight of her pink painted toenails.

"Pretty." He kissed her big toe.

Kissed. Her. Big. Toe.

Affection and tenderness pushed at the walls of her heart.

Tyler ran his hands over her bare legs, his gaze on her naked body.

With her large breasts and round hips, Kate knew she didn't look like his previous girlfriends—or even his previous fuck buddies—but his lust for her was evident in the erotic tension of his muscles and the unmistakable erection pushing against his fly.

She rose to her elbows, anticipation welling inside her. "I want to see you, too."

Tyler shucked his T-shirt over his head and dropped his hand to his fly. Fascinated, Kate watched as he worked the buttons and shed his jeans, kicking them off along with his socks.

Oh my...

His body was incredible—taut, golden-brown skin stretching over hard muscles that looked as if they had been chiseled from granite. His well-defined pecs sloped down to a washboard stomach lined with ridges that she wanted to trace with the tip of her tongue.

For the moment, she settled on devouring him with her gaze, skimming past his pelvis to his corded thighs before sweeping back up to settle on the unnervingly big cock trapped beneath his boxer briefs.

Her throat went dry, her heart pulsing a fast rhythm. Her sex contracted in response to the sight of his arousal, both with excitement and wariness because she was quite certain she'd never seen so large an erection up close and personal.

She sat up. Tyler approached her, and then *the bulge* was right in front of her. She slowly ran her fingers over the hard heaviness, tracing the length all the way down to where it pulsed against his thigh.

Drumming up a latent courage, she grasped his boxer briefs and tugged them over his hips. His cock sprang free. She stared in awe at the thought of him pushing that thick ridge of flesh into her body.

"Can I touch you?" she whispered.

He gave a hoarse laugh. "God, yes. *Please.*"

She encircled the shaft with her hand, loving the pulsing sensation against her palm. Everything about him was so alive, so charged with energy and power. She licked her lips with the urge to taste him.

He slid one hand into her hair, working the band holding it away from her face. Her hair fell in waves around her shoulders, and he muttered a noise of appreciation before sinking his hands into the dark strands.

The sensation was warm and pleasurable, a welcome addition to the heat building inside her with the force of a volcano on the verge of eruption. She opened her mouth, letting him nudge his cock against her lips. She darted her tongue out to lick the tip, her senses filling with his musky scent and taste.

With a moan, she squirmed to the edge of the bed and settled her hands on his hips, holding him still as she opened her mouth wider and sucked him in.

"Oh, shit." He groaned, driving his hands deeper into her hair. "Christ, Darling, the second I saw you, I wanted those pretty lips wrapped around my dick...yeah, use your tongue...ah, fuck, that's good..."

He pushed his hips forward, and she instinctively slackened her throat muscles so he could thrust gently. His fingers tightened against her scalp, stilling her movements as he slipped out of her mouth. She ran her tongue over her lips, the lingering taste of him still a heady aphrodisiac.

Her whole body flushed with arousal and anticipation. He crawled onto the bed, his eyes brimming with lust. He straddled her waist and grabbed her wrists, pinning them on either side of her head. Sexual intent radiated from him like the burn of the sun.

He bent his head to kiss her again, his mouth a welcome, hot pressure against hers. Her curves yielded to the hard planes of his chest, fitting into him like two hands clasping. The kiss length-ened, deepened. She stroked his smooth back, tracing the muscles with her fingertips. She was softening, melting, opening for him.

Tyler eased back and reached for his jeans, fumbling to grab a condom from his wallet. Kate watched him, her breathing fast. Never before had she felt like this, as if all her nerve endings were on fire, as if only he could assuage the ache growing and expanding inside her.

He rolled the condom over his shaft, then made a place for himself between her thighs.

He looked up, his gaze meeting hers with an electric jolt. "Spread them nice and wide, Darling."

Kate bit her lip, battling back anxiety as she spread her legs. Not only had it been a while since she'd had sex at all, she'd certainly never been with a man who was nearly as big and potent as Tyler.

He tucked his hands beneath her thighs, pushing them upward. He grasped his shaft and rubbed the tip of his cock slowly over her folds, as if he were giving her a chance to get used to both the size and feel of him.

She squirmed, her need arcing higher and higher. She couldn't believe this was *her*, all spread out and open while this insanely hot man stroked her so intimately. She'd have wondered how in the world this had even happened, if her hips hadn't started rotating almost of their own volition, a wordless plea for more.

Tyler muttered something low in his throat, his chest heaving and his eyes glazing over as he watched her working herself on him. She moaned, running her hands over her breasts and belly. She couldn't wait any longer.

"Tyler." Her voice was strained, desperate. She fisted her hands in the sheets and lifted her head to look at him. "Hurry."

His jaw clenched. He pushed her legs wider apart, easing into her slowly...slowly...Kate's thighs trembled with strain, her body working to accommodate him.

He filled and stretched her by exquisitely slow degrees. Incredible sensations flooded her. She tightened her grip on the sheets, clenching instinctively to prevent the penetration even as much as she wanted it. Tyler paused, sweat breaking out on his forehead as he rubbed her clit with his thumb.

"I'll go slow," he said, his voice husky with urgency. "But don't tense up."

The stimulation was enough to send her into a frenzy of aching need. She released the sheet and touched her breasts, pinching her hard nipples.

"Do it," she whispered. "Fuck me."

With a groan, he sank into her another inch. She arched upward.

"Jesus, you feel good," he hissed, shifting into her even farther. "So fucking hot and tight...wider, honey...oh, fuck..."

He thrust once more, and then he was fully seated inside her, filling her so completely that his blood pulsed in time with hers. Kate dragged a hot breath into her lungs, not sure she could take much more of this even though it was far from over.

It was, in fact, only beginning. He pulled back and pushed forward, jostling her body against the bed. And then she was falling, sinking into the push-and-pull cadence of their bodies, the deep thrust of his cock in and out of her. His grunts filled the hot air above her. His fingers dug into the tender skin of her thighs, her breasts, her hips. Her legs began to ache from being spread so wide apart, even as she reveled in the constant slick thrust of his shaft.

Her mind fogged with pleasure. Only when she felt the pressure of his fingers on her clit again did her body begin the ascent toward release.

"Tyler." She gasped, raking her hand down his chest. "It's happening."

"Yeah." His jaw clenched. "Tighten your pussy around my dick, sweetheart. That's it...you're going to come so nice and hard...I want to feel it all the way to my bones."

Kate moaned, lifting her legs in a blatant display of exposure that she'd never thought herself capable of. Tension coiled through her, tighter and tighter, before breaking with a delicious explosion of bliss. She cried out, quivering and shaking as her body contracted around Tyler's shaft and his fingers continued to draw the sensations from her.

She opened her eyes, her blood still throbbing as she watched him. Tension corded every one of his muscles. His pace slowed. He thrust inside her once, twice, then sank deep with a shout, his body arching above her.

Beautiful, Kate thought in a daze. He was a beautiful specimen of masculinity.

He groaned and rolled off her, his chest heaving. He discarded the condom and threw an arm over his eyes. Sweat trickled down his temple.

"That was incredible, Darling. You don't need sex lessons."

Pleasure swept through her. She turned onto her side to face him, tucking her hands under her head.

"I definitely need experience," she said. "I just haven't done very much. I think this was only the third time, if that, that I've given a man a blowjob. My first boyfriend didn't like it...well, he didn't like the way I did it, I guess. I've never done it to completion, though."

"Rule number one." Tyler lifted his arm to look at her, his expression shuttered. "Don't bring up other guys before, during, or after you and I fuck."

Kate winced. "Sorry."

"Rule number two..." He lifted his arm, indicating that she should tuck herself against his side. "We always cuddle."

CHAPTER 13

*K*ate couldn't sleep. Arousal continued to course through her veins, intensified by the warm strength of Tyler's body beside her. He rolled to his side, his chest rising and falling with the rhythm of his breath. She ran her fingers over his back, loving the way his muscles moved beneath his taut, tanned skin.

She eased out of bed, pulling on a cotton robe before going to the kitchen. She filled a glass with water and turned on her laptop.

As it warmed up, she checked her phone. Five texts from Sugar Rush employees popped up, including one from Luke asking if she could bring the information for the next all-company email to the Wild Child Bakery in Rainsville on Saturday.

A pang of guilt shot through her. Though none of the issues were time sensitive, she had a reputation for responding to messages within five minutes—not five hours. She quickly replied to all of them, promising Luke she'd drop the paperwork off at the bakery before ten.

She looked at her laptop, the multiple folders organized on

the desktop. She'd had plans to work last night, but wow…hadn't those plans gone totally awry?

And she couldn't exactly muster up any interest in working right now, not with her blood still pulsing and her sex damp and quivering. She was half tempted to go back to bed and wake Tyler up for…

"You getting my quiz ready?" His deep voice rolled through the darkened kitchen.

Kate turned away from the computer. Her nerves lit up at the sight of him leaning against the doorjamb in nothing but his boxer briefs. The dim light carved shadows over his chest, delineating all his muscles and washboard abdomen with that trail of hair pointing the way straight to bliss.

For a minute, she couldn't believe she'd had sex with him, this big, hunky male with his messy dark hair and chiseled body. No wonder he was such a popular fuck buddy. Women everywhere would…

…and *that* thought could stop right there.

"Maybe." Kate rested her hips on the counter and eyed him pointedly. "What does the acronym MARC stand for?"

"Making A Really pretty girl Come." He rubbed the scruff on his jaw. "A girl named Kate."

She stifled a giggle. "And what is the purpose of authority control?"

"Consistency." He started walking…no, *stalking* toward her like a predator seeking its prey.

"What else?" Kate's breathing grew shallow with every step that brought him closer.

"Organization." He stopped in front of her. The air warmed with his body heat. "Cooperative cataloging. Access control."

"You did do some homework."

"My teacher told me to." His eyes darkened as his gaze slid to the V neckline of her loosely belted robe. "But now she has to obey my orders."

Kate's knees weakened. She reached behind her to grasp the counter and keep her balance. Tyler hooked his finger into the belt of her robe and slowly pulled it off. The robe separated, revealing her flushed, naked body. Her nipples were still hard, her skin marked from his whisker burn and the pressure of his grip.

Kate shivered, automatically moving to close the robe. Tyler grabbed her arms and stepped closer, locking his lower body to hers and pushing her back against the counter. He was already half hard, his erection pushing against her belly. Fresh arousal flared through her.

"My orders," he murmured, grinding his hips slowly against her, "are for you to do exactly what I tell you to do. Because I have *authority control.*"

He took hold of her waist and lifted her onto the counter, sliding his hands between her thighs to spread them wider. Kate drew in a breath, her fingers tightening on the counter. Through the thin barrier of his boxer briefs, his cock throbbed against the folds of her sex, the hard ridge stimulating her still-tender clit.

With a groan, she edged forward to wiggle against him. The robe fell off her shoulders and pooled around her waist, leaving her almost naked. Tyler gave a muffled laugh and slipped his hand beneath her chin. He lifted her face, his eyes brewing with lust as he lowered his mouth to hers.

Arousal burst in Kate like an exploding star. He kissed her like she was the only thing that existed for him at that moment. Like he wanted to devour her, absorb her, fill himself up with only her. His hands flexed on her waist, curved around to grip her bottom and pull her more securely toward him. Caged in his arms, she was drowning in a sweet, hot pool of sensation.

Unlocking her fingers from the counter's edge, she placed them on his arms, gripping his strong biceps. She loved the ripple of his muscles under her palms. She loved being secure in the knowledge that she could touch him to her heart's content.

She parted her lips under his, shivering with delight as his tongue swept into her mouth. He tasted like decadent, exotic things—peppermint fudge, amaretto cookies, sugar-laced marzipan.

He slid one hand over her thigh, pushing her robe aside and edging his fingers between her legs. Kate twitched, heat rising to her chest when he flicked his thumb against her clit. She reached between their bodies, grazing her hand across his washboard abs before cupping his erection in her palm.

"Do you have another condom?" she whispered, rubbing her cheek over his jaw.

"No. But that won't stop me." A glint appeared in his eyes. He moved his hands to her breasts, caressing them with a leisurely ease that soon had her panting for more.

"Tyler, I can't wait much longer."

"Yeah, you can, greedy girl." He pressed his lips to the side of her neck and circled her nipples with his thumbs. "You will. Because I said so."

Oh my God, this was so fucking hot. A sheen of sweat dampened her body. She looked down, mesmerized by the sight of Tyler's big hands rubbing her breasts, his cock straining against his boxer briefs. She tightened her grip on him, gratified when he grunted with restrained pleasure.

She started to slide her hand into his waistband, aching to touch the warm heat of his shaft, but he grabbed her wrist to stop her.

"Not yet," he said.

Kate pulled in a breath. "Then what?"

His mouth curved with a smile. He took her hands and placed them beneath her thighs, pressing them apart.

"Open up, Darling," he murmured.

Kate's heart lurched. A flush scorched her cheeks. Tyler paused, as if waiting for her to get accustomed to the idea—in which case, he would be waiting for a very long time.

Reminding herself this kind of experience was exactly what she'd wanted, what she'd asked him for, Kate gripped her thighs and spread her legs wider. Her robe slithered farther off her body, clinging only to her arms.

"Ah, fuck." Tyler stepped back to look at her and groaned, an appreciative rumble that eased her trepidation. A little.

Her breath came in shallow pants. Cooler air brushed against her sex, spread for his hot gaze and whatever else he planned to do with her. She'd never felt so exposed, so utterly open.

Erotic tension strained his muscles, and a wet circle dampened the front of his briefs. He was as close to the edge as she was. Before she even realized what he was about to do, he knelt in front of her.

"Tyler..."

"Don't move. Keep yourself spread open nice and wide for me."

She trembled with shocked anticipation as he pressed his hands to her inner thighs. Then he leaned forward, stroking his tongue smoothly over her cleft. Kate yelped, bucking toward him and nearly toppling off the counter.

Tyler held her steady, his warm laugh brushing against her folds. "Hold still, Darling. I won't let you fall."

Kate dug her fingers into her sweaty thighs. She stared down at his dark head moving between her legs.

"Tyler, that feels amazing."

He made a muffled noise and delved deeper, licking her folds up one side and down the other. Exquisite shudders ran through her in a never-ending stream, setting her blood on fire.

Never in a million years had she imagined herself ever doing something like this—sitting naked and spread-eagled on her kitchen counter while her boss's youngest brother licked her pussy like an ice-cream cone.

But oh lord, it was the most incredible thing *ever*. Blissful sensations tingled through her body. The teasing strokes of

Tyler's lips and tongue contrasted with his hard grip and the brush of his thick hair against her inner thighs.

"Christ, you taste good," he muttered. "Sweet like honey. Open just a little wider now..."

He edged his finger into her, working it back and forth a few times before moving lower to the ring of her anus.

Kate gasped, her fingers slipping away from her thighs. "Tyler, I don't..."

"I won't hurt you." His eyes smoldered, and his cheekbones were flushed with heat. "I promise."

Her heart hammered so loud she could hear it in her head. She spread her legs again, wincing when his finger probed at the tight, forbidden opening. Sparks flew down her spine. He closed his lips around her clit, pushing his finger in farther, farther...

"Tyler!" she shrieked. "Oh my *God*..."

"Come on, Darling. Give it to me."

She gave up the fight. All lingering inhibitions fell away. She thrust her hips toward him and submitted to his erotic ministrations. She'd had no idea her body could feel like this—electric and flaring, like firecrackers were exploding in her veins. She trembled, a stream of moans spilling from her lips as her body climbed toward the peak. Every part of her gripped and clutched him, tightening and releasing at the same time.

"Please," she gasped.

He sucked her clit and slipped his thumb inside her sex, penetrating her in both places at the same time. The triple stimulation sent her flying over the cliff. With a cry, she grabbed hold of his hair. Her body quaked and shook, submerging her in rapturous sensation.

Only when she began coming down the other side did Tyler ease away from her and get to his feet. His chest heaved, and his own body was still tight with unfulfilled tension, but his eyes gleamed with warm pleasure.

"You're amazing," he whispered before covering her mouth with his.

A moan lodged in her throat. The flavor of her own body mixed with *him* made her dizzy with the anticipation of all the other things they could do together. She smoothed her hand down his abdomen and into his boxer briefs. This time, he didn't stop her.

Kate pulled her mouth from his, their breath hot and heavy in the space between them. She eased his thick cock out, pushing his briefs down to his thighs. Just the sight of his shaft resting in her palm quickened her arousal. She closed her fingers around him and stroked.

"Fuck, yeah." Tyler hissed out his approval, resting one hand on the counter behind her and the other on the back of her neck. "Faster...just like that..."

Kate watched with rapt fascination as she slid her hand up and down his shaft, pausing only to rub her thumb over the swollen head. He pushed forward to fuck his cock into her fist. A heady sense of power filled her.

"Do it, Tyler," she urged, curling her other hand against his chest. "Come all over me."

She felt the wave roll and peak through his body the instant before he gave a low groan. He thrust into her fist and shot all over her bare thighs. A fresh wave of pleasure coursed through her.

Tyler swore on a single breath, then gathered her against him. God, but she loved the press of their sweaty, naked bodies, the steel of his arms locking her close, the potent scent of their release filling her nose. She slipped her arms around his waist and rested her forehead on his chest.

"Damn." He pressed his lips against her temple and pulled her robe back over her shoulders. "I'm starting to like library sciences."

"You definitely have a strong command of authority control."

After another kiss, Kate eased away and cleaned herself off with a paper towel before fastening the belt of her robe. Tyler tugged his boxer briefs back over his hips and rubbed his damp chest.

"Are you hungry?" he asked. "I make pretty good pancakes."

Kate laughed. "It's 2:00 a.m."

"So?" He opened the refrigerator. "Is there a law that I can't make pancakes at 2:00 a.m.?"

"Well, no, but..."

"Got any bacon?" He glanced over his shoulder at her, an eyebrow raised in inquiry.

She shrugged and opened a cabinet to take out the flour. A few minutes later, they started making pancakes.

Despite two active rounds of sex, which would probably put most men right to sleep again, Tyler was full of energy. He bounded around the kitchen, humming under his breath, opening all her cabinets, cracking eggs with one hand, and showing off how he could flip the pancakes without using a spatula.

When she found herself sitting at her little kitchen table, having pancakes, hot cocoa, and bacon at 2:00 a.m. with a man who was proving to be far different—and so much better—than she'd initially believed, Kate wondered if asking Tyler to be her fuck buddy had been a good idea after all.

She liked him, of course. A lot. She wouldn't have asked for something so intimate if she didn't. But she was starting to realize she could potentially like him so much more. Maybe even in ways that went beyond straightforward, casual, and "no romance." She could end up liking him far differently than one fuck buddy should like the other.

She pushed her plate away and reached for her mug of hot cocoa. She felt like a different woman than the one she'd been this morning.

Wow. Had it only been this morning when she'd fallen into

Tyler's arms? Now they were having a midnight snack after two rounds of insanely hot sex, the likes of which she'd once thought she would never experience.

She didn't even know how long this thing between them would last. She hadn't thought to put a deadline to their relationship...if one could even call it that.

"So what's on your agenda for the rest of the weekend?" Tyler forked another pancake onto his plate and drenched it with butter and syrup. The smooth muscles of his shoulders gleamed in the light.

For some reason, Kate's chest tightened. Her body still felt the thrust of his cock, the press of his fingers, the heat of his kiss.

"Mostly work." She took a sip of cocoa, forcing her voice to sound casual. "And starting my new self-improvement plan. So far your advice has been spot on. You were definitely right about my clothes. I'll do some shopping, find a few new things to wear to work and for going out in the evening."

A flash of darkness crossed his expression. It seemed to ricochet right back and lodge in her heart.

Kate rose to take her empty plate to the sink, excusing herself to go to the bathroom. She closed the door and regarded herself in the mirror, pressing her hands to her hot cheeks. Her robe gaped open at the neck to reveal her cleavage, and her skin was still reddened from Tyler's touch. Her hair was a tousled mess around her flushed face, and her eyes were heavy-lidded and dark with sexual satiation.

God. She even looked like a different woman.

Maybe she was.

After using the toilet, she splashed water on her face and started back to the kitchen.

Tyler stood in the living room, dressed in the jeans and T-shirt he'd been wearing earlier that evening.

Kate stopped. Her heart began a slow descent to her stomach. "Are you leaving?"

"Yeah, it's getting late." He gestured to the clock, his tone casual despite the tension lacing his shoulders. "Or early, as the case may be. Figure I should take off, leave you to get some sleep. I put the dishes and stuff in the dishwasher."

"Okay." Kate didn't know what to do. Was there an etiquette for this sort of goodbye? "Well, I had a really nice time."

"Me too. Thanks for a great night." He dug his keys out of his pocket and headed for the foyer.

Something shriveled inside Kate as she watched him open the front door. Then he stopped and turned. Their eyes met, a sharp, hot energy crackling in the air.

He let go of the doorknob and strode back, stopping right in front of her. When they were this close, a force seemed to encircle them, wrapping them in a world where nothing else existed.

"You're right, Darling." Tyler looked at her as if he could see right to the center of her soul, his eyes glittering like pieces of topaz. "You want to land old Norwood, you need to wear sexier clothes, stuff that shows you have an incredible body and phenomenal tits, suits that fit better and show off your perfect legs.

"And your hair...keep it down so a guy can imagine running his fingers through it, seeing it spread over a pillow. You don't need makeup...one look at your lips and any man in the world would want to kiss you, but I've been with enough women to know they think makeup is important. So figure out how to enhance what you already have—incredible eyes, kissable lips, skin so perfect it's like cream."

Aside from her heart racing like a bullet train, Kate couldn't move.

Tyler brushed his fingers across her cheek. Her spine tingled.

"Also stop looking down so much," he continued. "It makes you seem uncertain. When you talk to Norwood, look him in the eye. Smile at him...your real smile, which will make him weak in the knees. You need to find out what he likes to do—theater or concerts or whatever—and ask him to something specific. Don't do that crap about *you wouldn't want to go out with me, would you?* either. Men like confident women. Be direct. *Miles, the San Francisco string orchestra has a performance of Concerto in Whatever this weekend. Would you like to go with me?* If he's into you, he'll say yes. Or if he's busy, he'll suggest an alternative idea. Either way, you'll know."

Kate gripped her hands together. Her head spun with disbelief that after such an extraordinary night, she would ever be able to look at another man, much less try and attract one.

And yet...that had been the whole point.

"Got it?" Tyler asked.

She swallowed and managed to whisper, "Got it."

He gave a short nod and stepped away from her. His expression was shuttered, but his eyes still glowed with that inner fire and energy that was such an intrinsic part of him.

"For the record," he said, "you're the most incredible first date I've ever had. And honestly? You don't need to do anything differently when you go out with another guy. Just be Kate Darling. If that's not everything a man could dream of, then he doesn't deserve you."

He walked out, closing the door behind him. It was a long time before Kate was able to move.

CHAPTER 14

$\mathcal{T}$yler drove home without knowing how he got there. He sat in his car, unable to get Kate out of his head. Everything about her. The warmth of her naked body, the sound of her gasping little moans, the way she'd traced the lines of his chest with her forefinger. The perfect fit of his hands into the curve of her waist, the smoothness of her ass and fucking gorgeous breasts.

And all the other stuff he'd learned in so short a time—the fact that she knew all the lyrics to "The Lumberjack Song," her encyclopedic knowledge of library stuff, her pretty painted toenails.

It was kind of cute how her wardrobe was so boring, but she took the time to polish her nails. Not to mention all the things he'd seen in her bathroom—expensive lotions, powders, bath salts, loofahs. Underneath it all, Kate Darling was the most sensual woman he'd ever met.

He wanted more of her. For *him*, not because he was "improving" her for another man. Just the thought of her asking Norwood to the symphony or whatever made him clench his fists with anger.

What the hell was wrong with him? He'd never gotten territorial about a girlfrie...fuck bud...*friend with benefits* before.

Jealousy wasn't his thing. He was loyal to the girls he was with, and he'd been in love a couple of times, but he never worried that they'd be interested in another man. Not because he was an arrogant ass—though he guessed to a degree, he was—but because he treated women right and told it like it was. There were never any secrets, misunderstandings, confusion.

Hell, he rarely even fought with them. He just gave them what they wanted, made sure they were happy, and life was always good.

Why should it be any different with Kate? She'd been honest from the start. She'd asked him for dating advice, then she'd taken it to the next level with the fuck buddy thing—all because she was working up the courage to ask another guy out on a date and start a real adult relationship.

Good for her.

Too bad for him that he was letting a hot fuck and 2:00 a.m. pancakes mess with his head.

He finally got out of the car and let himself into his apartment. As usual, the place was a disaster—the kitchen counters piled with dirty dishes, empty pizza boxes, and beer cans, the living room strewn with chips bags, unwashed T-shirts, and old socks.

Since he wasn't tired, he changed into track pants and went out for a two-mile run, hoping the exercise would get rid of his tension. But all it made him want to do was run back to Kate's neat little house.

He wanted to crawl into her bed, which was too small for both of them, and fall asleep with her tucked right against his side. Then he wanted to wake up when the sun rose and eat leftover pancakes while she quizzed him about cataloging.

And wasn't he just losing his shit?

After a shower and more grumbling, he drove inland for half

an hour, turning off the interstate near the farming community of Rainsville.

He guided his car down a dirt road and parked at the side of a three-bay garage. One car sat in an open bay, junkyard cars cluttered the adjoining field, and a black lab lounged at the front door of the office. As Tyler approached, the dog got to his feet and ambled over to greet him.

"Hey, Bandit." Tyler scratched the dog behind the ears and produced a treat that he'd taken out of the stash in his glove compartment. The dog wiggled happily and trotted back to his spot.

Tyler entered the office, where Charlie, the grizzled old army vet who owned the garage, was seated behind a grimy, paper-strewn desk. The smells of oil and engine fluid filled the room. An episode of *Fawlty Towers* played on the old TV in the corner.

"Got anything for me to do?" Tyler sank into the metal folding chair in front of the desk.

"Nah." Charlie peered at a grease-stained invoice. "You get the taillights in yet?"

Tyler shook his head. "No delivery date either."

At least he'd already paid for the parts he needed for the old Mustang he'd been restoring for the past few years. He'd used the money his mother had willed to him after her death—each child getting an equal share—though his brothers had put their portions back into the Rebecca Stone Foundation.

Old shame curled through him. It was stupid to be twenty-seven and relying on his family's money, but he didn't know what the hell else to do. He couldn't even figure out how to organize a library by himself, so it wasn't like he'd ever be able to tell his father he wanted to work his way up in the company.

Bandit wandered through the open door and settled at his feet. He absently stroked his hand over the dog's head. Charlie heaved a sigh and tossed the invoice onto a pile of papers.

Tyler eyed the messy desk—invoices, crumpled receipts, sales catalogs. Kate would get all up in arms if she saw what a disaster the garage paperwork was. He pictured her standing there with her hands on her hips, lecturing Charlie about a projected balance sheet and business ratios. The image made his insides get all soft and tender.

He took a haphazard pile of receipts from the desk and leafed through them. "You ever think about getting some sort of filing system? Or a computer?"

Charlie made a scoffing noise. "Too old to learn how to use a computer. And with insurance rates going through the roof, plus all that competition over in Rainsville, it's a small wonder I'm not turning a profit. Lost the car show sponsor and exhibit space, too."

"You serious?"

Charlie nodded. "Not worth it, they said. Didn't get enough ROI last year."

"So what's going to happen to the show?"

"It's not going to happen. Not this year anyway."

Tyler frowned at his friend's defeated tone. Charlie had been organizing a classic car show in the small town of Fordwell for the past five years—and though it had never been a huge draw like some shows, classic car enthusiasts from surrounding neighborhoods usually turned out for it. There was a judged competition, exhibitions, food trucks, sometimes a local band.

"I was going to enter the Mustang," he said.

"I know." Charlie shrugged. "Check out the one in LA for next year."

Next year. He'd probably still be working at the library.

Tyler tossed the paperwork back on the desk. He'd started hanging out at Charlie's Garage after completing a technical course in auto repair four years ago. Back then, he'd thought he might even work for Charlie one day, but his friend had never made enough to be able to afford employees. Sometimes Charlie's army buddies hung around and did a few repairs, but the turnover wasn't enough to keep many customers coming back.

Tyler rented out the space for his Mustang, which at least made him feel like he was partially contributing to Charlie's income. A veteran who'd done three tours in Iraq, Charlie's transition to civilian life had been less painful than those of his comrades-in-arms, many of whom were still struggling to get the government assistance they needed.

At least Tyler had been of some help there, convincing his father and Aunt Julia to channel some of the money from the Rebecca Stone Foundation into local veterans' programs. He'd wanted to somehow help men like Charlie and also Gavin Knight, who'd served at least half a dozen tours as a Marine.

He still hadn't been actually *doing* anything, just using Sugar Rush money again, but maybe it had made a difference. He hoped so, anyway.

He shoved to his feet and went out to the garage. A tarp covered his Mustang, and he tugged it off to examine the vehicle. He and Charlie had rebuilt the engine and frame, replaced the floorboards and upholstery, and painted it the original silvery blue. Some detail work was still needed, and he'd been waiting forever for the original taillights, but the car was almost finished.

He draped the tarp back over the car. He could ask his father or Luke if Sugar Rush would sponsor the car show, but that wouldn't be different from every single other time he'd relied on his family's money to get something done.

He headed back to his Trans Am. Kate was the reason he was suddenly so antsy. She was only a year younger than him, but she had a high-powered job, a house, and probably a dozen investment and retirement accounts. She even had a plan for her love life. He had a trust fund and...stuff that was paid for with his trust fund.

On his way back to Indigo Bay, he detoured to Rainsville,

where the Wild Child Bakery sat at the lower level of an old building that had recently been restored to its former glory.

Tyler went inside, appreciating the warm, homey atmosphere with numerous plants, colorful prints on the walls, and rustic wooden tables. People sat drinking coffee, reading books and newspapers, playing board games. Hannah, Polly, and their friend Ramona bustled around behind the counter, their voices rising cheerfully over the clatter of plates.

After greeting them and buying a doughnut and coffee, he sat at a table by the window. Not until he'd started coming here regularly had he appreciated all that Polly had created—Wild Child was a gathering place for so many people, a home away from home. They came for concerts, poetry readings, writing workshops.

Tyler would have envied Polly's seemingly effortless abilities if he hadn't known she'd made Wild Child such a success through hard work, creativity, and learning from Luke's business expertise.

"Hey, man."

Speak of the devil.

Luke pulled out the chair opposite Tyler's and sat down with a cup of coffee. "What're you doing here?"

"Just hanging out," Tyler said. "You?"

"Waiting for Polly's shift to end. We're going to the Codswallop music festival for the rest of the weekend."

Tyler sat back in his chair. His brother was wearing cargo shorts and a T-shirt, and dark stubble lined his jaw. Far cry from CEO Luke Stone with his tailored suits and ties.

"Yeah, she told me," Tyler said. "What'd you do there?"

"Aside from get a contact high?" Luke grinned. "Listen to bands, eat, dance, sit around a campfire, nap in a hammock. Watch Polly hula-hoop."

"You stay in a hotel?"

"A tent."

Tyler raised his brows. "Seriously?"

Luke gestured to where Polly was restocking a tray of Declairs. "Whatever she wants, man."

"Dude, you are fucking whipped."

"Like cream. Never been happier."

Tyler picked at his doughnut. An uncomfortable feeling rustled inside him. He'd always figured he was whipped, too—by women in general—but he wasn't all that happy about it. Made him feel like an ass, actually.

But Luke had just one woman he'd do anything for. One woman he couldn't say no to. One woman he wanted to keep happy. One woman who made him happy in return.

Maybe that was the difference between being jerked around and being…in love.

He shook that thought off.

"So where is this festival?" he asked.

"Field down near San Miguel, off Highway 5."

"Yeah?" An idea sparked in Tyler's mind. "How big is the field?"

"Few acres, I guess. Belongs to a farmer who's been renting it out to the festival for years."

"Does he rent it out to anyone or just Codswallop?"

"No idea." Luke shrugged. "Why, you need it for something?"

"Maybe. Does Polly have the farmer's contact info?"

"If she doesn't, she can get it for you." Luke studied him for a moment. "What've you got in mind?"

Tyler took a bite of doughnut to avoid having to respond. He didn't want to tell Luke about looking for a venue for a classic car show. None of his brothers had ever disparaged his interest in cars, and Evan had always supported it, but it wasn't an actual job.

The bakery door opened, letting in a rush of cool air. Kate walked in with her briefcase, her stride brisk and purposeful.

Tyler's heart crashed against his ribcage. She wore one of her straight black skirts and a white blouse, but his body reacted to her as if she'd been standing in front of him wearing lacy red lingerie.

No, that wasn't true. It had nothing to do with what she was wearing. He just reacted to *her*.

"Oh, good, you haven't left yet." She spotted Luke and hurried over to the table, her steps slowing when she saw Tyler sitting there.

He frowned. He didn't like being the *second* one she noticed.

"Morning, Kate." Luke stood to take a file folder from her. "Ty, you can thank Kate for ordering the new equipment for the library."

"I already did."

Kate darted him a quick glance, a flush rising to her cheeks. She set her briefcase on a nearby table. "Nice to see you again, Tyler. Luke, I brought you the projected growth charts from the chewing gum sectors as well."

"Great, thanks." Luke leafed through the report. "We need to include data about the accelerated growth of the European and Asian markets. And I want reports from the presidents of the global divisions for the overall financial plan, with North America remaining the main reportable segment."

"And a customer base of retail markets, wholesale distributers, vendors, drugstores, and concessionaries." Kate took a yellow legal pad from her briefcase and wrote some notes. "With a marketing emphasis on brand recognition and superior product quality. Did you want me to include an update on the Cocoa Bean Team?"

"If Evan has finished the new mission statement on Sugar Rush's corporate responsibility, yes."

Kate nodded and continued writing, glancing up and meeting Tyler's gaze with a sudden start—as if she'd felt him watching her. Her serious, concentrated expression disappeared for half an instant into a slight smile before she turned back to Luke, who was saying something about "joint ventures" and "strategic objectives." She continued writing, obviously understanding everything he was saying.

Irritation gripped Tyler.

"Good, thank you." Luke nodded after finishing another list of things for her to do. "Can you have the draft on my desk by midweek?"

"Of course, sir."

"And the SEC and Section 16 filings?"

Tyler shoved to his feet, knocking against the table hard enough that his coffee splashed over the edge of the cup. Both Luke and Kate glanced at him.

"It's the weekend, *sir*," Tyler snapped at his brother. "Do you pay Kate extra to be your assistant on the weekends, or is she just not allowed to have a life of her own?"

Kate gasped, her wide-eyed gaze flying from him to Luke in shock. Luke looked at him in bafflement.

"Sir, I'm sorry," Kate said quickly. "It's really not a problem for me to—"

"You don't have to call him *sir*," Tyler interrupted, his hands flexing and unflexing.

"She knows that." Luke quickly recovered from the surprise of the outburst, his expression hardening. "And her job is not your business."

The fuck it's not, Tyler wanted to snap. *She's* my business. *Kate is my business.*

"Look, um…" Kate stepped closer to Tyler, the back of her hand brushing against his. "I'm happy to work on weekends occasionally, and Luke knows that."

"You work more than *occasionally* on weekends," Tyler retorted. "Do you ever say no to him?"

Her eyes flashed. "Luke would never ask me to do something if it were inconvenient for me."

"Yeah?" A thousand emotions simmered through him—jealousy, anger, frustration, need. "But you would never tell him if it were inconvenient, would you? You just do whatever the hell he wants whenever the hell he wants it."

"Watch it, man." Eyes narrowed, Luke stepped between him and Kate, putting his hand on Tyler's chest and pushing him backward. "You're crossing a line."

Tyler's breath burned in his lungs. He'd already crossed the line. He was so far on the other side that he couldn't even *see* the fucking line anymore.

A hush fell over the bakery. Behind Luke, Kate clutched her notebook, her face pale.

Tyler shoved Luke's hand off his chest and stalked out the door. Resentment clawed at him. He couldn't compete with his brothers, especially Luke. He'd known that when he was a kid— they were all older, smarter, goddamned *better*. Why would he ever think he could compete with the CEO over his super-assistant?

"Tyler."

Kate's voice stopped him in his tracks. He turned, his jaw tightening as he watched her hurry toward him, her black shoes clacking on the pavement and her briefcase clutched in her hand.

She came to a halt in front of him, her gaze searching his face, her breath fast.

"Well," she finally said. "That was quite a show."

The tension in his shoulders eased a little. He rubbed the back of his neck.

"I...it just pisses me off that he wants you at his beck and call all the fucking time. Why should you be?"

Her forehead creased. "Well, I told him when he first hired me that I was available twenty-four seven. And I was. I didn't know anyone or have any friends when I first moved here, and I had no real EA experience...so it made sense to devote all my time to learning on the job. I wanted to do the best I could."

"That was two years ago," Tyler reminded her bitterly. "Pretty sure you know how to do your job now. And you don't need to jump every time he calls."

"Actually, I do." She slanted her gaze away from him. "I need to be indispensable."

"Everything okay out here?" Luke walked toward them from the bakery, the lines of his body tense. "Ty, you want to tell me what's going on?"

Tyler held up his hands, expelling his breath in a rush. "Nothing, man. Just being an ass."

Luke looked from him to Kate. "Kate?"

"Everything is fine, sir. Tyler and I had a little misunderstanding earlier, but we've worked it out. I assure you this will not affect my job performance."

Tyler couldn't stop a curse from escaping. Kate shot him a warning look.

"If there's a problem between you two, I need to know about it," Luke said.

"No problem." Kate and Tyler both spoke at the same time.

Though Luke didn't appear convinced, he gave a short nod and stepped back. "I'm going. Kate, you call me any time if you need to."

"Yes, sir."

Luke pointed at Tyler—a "watch yourself" gesture—and strode back to the bakery. Kate moved toward Tyler.

"Why did you do that?" she asked.

His hands flexed. What the fuck was he supposed to say? That he didn't want to show her how to attract another man? That now he was jealous of his damned brother, who had all of her time and attention? That she was the first woman he'd ever felt so possessive about and he wanted her to belong only to him?

Yeah, spill his guts and then listen to her little speech about how they were just temporary fuck buddies and he wasn't the one she really wanted. Not for good anyway.

He turned, yanking open the passenger side door of his car.

"Get in," he ordered Kate.

She hesitated, glancing back at the door of Wild Child closing behind Luke. Tyler's blood burned. The second of waiting felt like an hour. Then she climbed into the car, putting her briefcase on the floor.

Tyler slammed the door and got into the driver's seat. He reversed and pulled out of the lot, peeling onto the street with a squeal of the tires.

"Tyler, slow down." Kate put her hand on his thigh. "Can we please talk about this?"

He gripped the steering wheel. He didn't want to talk. Too much shit was tangled up in his chest, making it hard to breathe. He swerved, pulling the car off the road and into the shadow of a deserted barn.

After killing the engine, he looked at Kate. She was watching him, all flushed and beautiful with her hair like silk and her eyes sharp and intelligent. He took her glasses off and set them on the dashboard.

He rested his hand against the side of her face. The feeling of her breath on his wrist, right where his pulse beat rapidly, eased some of his anger. Then she turned her head and pressed a kiss against the center of his palm.

A hard shudder rocked through him. Before he could grab her, haul her toward him, Kate was unbuckling her seatbelt and closing the distance between them.

Their mouths collided in a hot, hungry kiss that jolted him with lust. His head filled with her taste, her scent, the feel of her lush body against his.

He grabbed her hips, yanking her heavy skirt up to her hips. His heart hammered. He gripped her stockings and yanked, ripping them at the thigh. Kate gasped, her eyes widening in shock. He pushed the seat back and hauled her onto his lap so she was straddling his thighs.

"What if someone..." Kate's words trailed into a moan as he

pulled the torn nylon away and put his hand between her thighs. Her panties were already damp. His dick stiffened.

"Fuck," he muttered. "I knew you'd be ready."

"I've been ready since you walked out last night." Kate put her hands on either side of his jaw and lowered her head to kiss him. "I feel like you flipped a switch inside me. Turned on a light."

She'd done the same to him. A blazing hot, white light glowed in the center of his chest with the force of a hundred suns. He pushed her underwear to the side and drew his finger over her heat, the little button of her clit.

Kate shuddered. "Wait."

She drew away from him to unbutton her shirt. Her fingers trembled. Tyler's breath stopped when she tossed the shirt onto the other seat and worked the clasp of her bra. Her breasts popped out, her nipples so pink and tempting he lowered his head to close his lips around one and suck.

"Tyler…" She gasped, driving one hand into his hair and putting the other on his groin. "I need you."

He fumbled to yank open his jeans and push them down his thighs. He was already hard enough to ache. Kate licked her lips and grasped his cock, working her hand up and down in a perfect rhythm.

"Do you have a condom?" she whispered.

"Glove compartment."

She leaned over to find the condom, releasing him only long enough to unwrap the packet and sheathe his erection. He clutched her waist, lifting her and positioning her right above him.

With a low moan, she sank down onto his cock. Tyler rested his head against the back of the seat, his whole body tensing with pleasure as her tight heat enclosed his shaft. He dug his fingers into her hips and thrust upward once.

"Move." He slipped his hand back to give her ass a little slap.

"God, Tyler…" Kate clutched his shoulders, her breath coming in hot puffs against his face as she lifted her body and brought it down again, enveloping him in bliss. "This is so…"

He half expected her to say something like *so wrong, so dangerous, so illegal.*

"…incredible," she finished, squirming so her ass rubbed against his thighs. "I had no idea it could feel like this."

"I'll show you a thousand other things that feel even better." He palmed one of her breasts, tweaking her nipple. "Work yourself on me. Nice and fast."

Perspiration broke out on her skin. She adjusted her position, tightening her knees around his hips before she started moving up and down in earnest.

Fuck, yeah.

That was what he wanted—her gorgeous tits bouncing, her head thrown back, her whole body writhing like she couldn't get enough. Again and again she enclosed him, driving him to orgasm as fast as she was driving herself. Little moans burst from her throat every time she slammed her body downward.

The windows fogged. The smacking noise of flesh hitting flesh filled the car. Sweat trickled down his temple. His muscles strained with the effort of holding back, but just when he thought he couldn't stop himself, Kate came with a sharp cry, her body rippling and convulsing. He grabbed her hips and thrust upward, shooting inside her with a force that shook the earth.

She gasped, falling against him in a sweet, damp bundle of heat, her breath warm against his neck.

"Wow," she whispered. "We could get arrested for this."

He squeezed her ass. "Totally worth jail time."

She giggled and pressed a kiss on his shoulder. She drew her hand down his chest and let it stop right over his heart.

CHAPTER 15

*K*ate never knew she could feel like this. Like glitter was sparkling through her veins. Like she was inside a shiny, translucent soap bubble, dipping and swaying through a lush tropical forest. Like her heart had infinite possibilities, a universe dusted with stars.

Needless to say, she found it difficult to concentrate on work when she returned to Sugar Rush on Monday morning. Her mind kept drifting to Tyler, replaying the time they'd spent together over the weekend.

Everything about him was imprinted in her memory—the timbre of his deep voice, his sexy smile, the way he looked at her like she was a tasty little candy he wanted to eat right up.

And of course, she couldn't stop thinking of all the ways he'd touched her, kissed her, *licked* her. Her body hummed, as if it were awakening after a long state of dormancy.

But overlying all her warm, gooey feelings was a flashing red *Danger* sign, reminding her that a fuck buddy friendship was almost the opposite of an honest-to-God relationship. And the latter was what she wanted. She couldn't let her feelings for Tyler run loose and wild, regardless of her current state of starry-eyed bliss.

"...and so an analysis of purchasing trends can lead to a far more efficient global distribution system." Miles Norwood turned off his laser pointer and faced the executives seated around the boardroom table.

Kate straightened, forcing her expression into one of polite interest. This was the first time in the past two years that she hadn't paid strict attention to what was said at a board meeting. That would never do.

"Sugar Rush can continue to use data to track cocoa-farming production in Africa and South America," Miles continued, "in conjunction with Evan Stone's Cocoa Bean Team."

The executives stirred, murmuring to each other as they leafed through the packet of cocoa bean crop data Kate had compiled. After answering questions about his presentation, Miles gathered his notes and resumed his seat at the table.

"Next item is the report on edible candy pencils." Warren Stone nodded toward the sales director, who indicated for them all to turn to the correct page in the sales report.

Kate gazed surreptitiously at Miles. He wore a tan suit and tie with not a strand of his golden hair out of place. Not like Tyler with his messy dark hair and torn jeans that hugged his incredibly muscular legs.

She tightened her grip on her pen and wrote a few notes, trying to focus on what the sales director was saying. By the time the meeting ended, she hoped she'd assimilated at least half of what the executives had discussed.

She collected her things and made her way to the door, finding herself right beside Miles. Usually his presence caused her heart to flutter, but this time only her nose twitched at the potent smell of his cologne. Had he always smelled like the perfume section of a department store?

"Nice work," she said politely. "Sounds like your analysis will also help the company gather revenue data much faster."

"I expect so." He paused, adjusting the knot of his tie. "By the way, I enjoyed the smoothie from the Gumdrop Bistro. Thanks for the recommendation."

"Sure."

All she had to do was ask if he wanted to join her for another smoothie later today. Or right now. *I was just on my way over there for a Blueberry Blast. Care to join me?*

The question formed easily in her mind, but the words lodged in her throat. Miles gave her a nod of farewell before heading to the tech department offices.

Kate turned in the opposite direction. She should wait to ask him out until she'd had a chance to get new clothes, anyway. Put her best foot forward and all that.

She joined Luke in his office—noting that he appeared rather sunburned after his weekend at the music festival—to review several action items and his afternoon schedule.

"Will there be anything else, sir?" she asked, rising to her feet.

"Yes."

Here it comes. She braced herself for an interrogation about Tyler.

Luke leafed through some papers. "Have you ever attended a conference for administrative professionals?"

"A conference? No."

"There's one in Florida next month." He extended a brochure and a set of forms. "Registration is still open. Sugar Rush will pay for your tickets, hotel, and a per diem. Considering how quickly you became indispensable not only to me but to all the executives at Sugar Rush, it would be a great way for you to network."

"Network for what?"

"Your future," Luke said. "You're the best EA this company has ever seen. But at some point, we should sit down and talk about your career goals."

"This is my goal, sir. Being your assistant. I'm able to use all my skills, and frankly I love the job."

"I'm glad to know that. But I don't need to point out that you're quite young. You shouldn't expect to be my assistant for your entire future career."

Kate had no idea what else she should expect. She'd been looking for basic secretary work after graduating from college, and she'd applied for the Sugar Rush EA position almost on a whim. The coastal California location had been highly appealing, not to mention she'd always loved Sugar Rush chocolates, and the job description had been tailor-made to her strengths.

But she'd also been surprised by the call for an interview, then downright shocked when Luke had offered her the job on the spot. Since that day, she'd never considered doing anything else.

Where did an executive assistant to the CEO go from here? Wasn't this already the top of the line?

"Thank you. I'd love to attend the conference." She hesitated. "But I feel the need to apologize for what happened on Saturday at Wild Child. It was a mistake, not to mention highly inappropriate."

Luke nodded, though his expression was somber. "Kate, your personal life is none of my business. And what Tyler said made sense. I hadn't realized I've been taking it for granted that you're available on weekends. Not at all fair of me, especially since I've made it a point to keep my own weekends to myself. So from now on, please consider weekends your time off."

Kate's hand tightened on the brochure. If he'd told her this a week ago, she'd have wondered what she would possibly do with all that spare time. But now, immediately, an image of Tyler appeared in her mind.

What if she could spend it all with *him*? She would be giddy with happiness. Not to mention drenched in sexual satisfaction.

She cleared her throat. "Thank you, sir. But I'm happy to be available whenever you need me."

"I appreciate that." Luke continued regarding her. "But I've learned that a personal life is as important as work. And since I value you as both my assistant and friend…well, I'd advise you to be careful."

"Yes, sir."

Kate returned to her desk, her feelings jumbled up. Much as she appreciated Luke sending her to the conference, she didn't like the sense that he was warning her away from his brother.

Then again, he had reason to. Tyler hadn't exactly been a model citizen of late.

She sat at her desk and reviewed the conference brochure. Stiletto heels clicked sharply up the stairs, like nails poking through her concentration.

Kate's guard shot into place. She knew *those heels* like she knew how to create a budget spreadsheet.

She straightened, schooling her expression into one of cool impassivity. Julia Bennett, the younger sister of the late Rebecca Stone, approached Luke's office, her regal walk seeming to command the air molecules to bow at her passing.

Over the past twelve years, Julia had reigned as both the Stone family matriarch and one of the most revered stylists and fashionistas in the state. Kate had witnessed *The Julia Effect* firsthand countless times, which resulted in a combination of awe, fear, and occasional heroine-worship among the other employees.

None of which meant Kate would let Julia get the better of her.

She stepped in front of Luke's door, crossing her arms and straightening her shoulders. After discovering that visits with his aunt often left Luke with a headache, Kate had taken it upon herself to protect him from the woman's overbearing presence.

Or at least, she tried.

Julia stopped in front of her, hands on hips. In her mid-forties, she had an effortless beauty—sleek, blond hair falling to her shoulders in an elegant pageboy and curving *just so* at the ends, some sort of tweed designer suit that fit her gorgeous, toned figure to perfection, and of course those four-inch heels that announced her arrival like a contemporary herald.

"Good morning," Kate said in her usual cool, polite voice. "Mr. Stone's morning schedule is full."

Julia skimmed her gaze over Kate's suit, which she'd scored from a Target clearance rack. Clearly Julia could tell, if the slight flaring of her nostrils was any indication of her distaste.

"As much as I can appreciate your loyalty to my nephew," she replied, her own voice besting Kate's coolness by a good thirty degrees below freezing, "I'm weary of this little game. Please step aside."

"No one sees Mr. Stone without an appointment. But as a favor to you, I'll let him know you're here."

Kate knew from experience not to step away from the door because Julia would barge right into the office. She pulled her cell phone from the holster and brought up Luke's number. "Mr. Stone, your aunt is here asking to see you."

A gusty sigh came through the phone. "All right, let her in."

Kate had expected that, too, because unless he was in the middle of a meeting, Luke always deigned to see his aunt. It rankled Kate a bit since she would have liked to actually block Julia from entering, for no other reason than the satisfaction of proving she had power.

But she would never undermine Luke's authority, least of all in front of his aunt, so she opened the door and stepped aside.

Julia swept past her in a rush of cool, expensively perfumed air. Luke looked up from his computer.

"Your little poodle guard dog is getting wearisome." Julia came to a halt in front of his desk.

"What do you want, Julia?" Luke asked.

Kate slipped out, closing the door behind her. As she returned to her desk, it occurred to her that despite their rancor, she *could* technically ask Julia, the Walking Fashion Magazine, for a teensy bit of advice about her wardrobe. At the very least, Julia could tell her if she was an "autumn" or a "spring" or whatever those terms meant.

Yeah, right.

Even if Kate opened herself up to ridicule by asking for advice from The Great One, she'd never be able to afford Julia's services. While she suspected Julia had more class than to make a bitchy "lonely virgin" comment about her, Kate wasn't sure she wanted to take the risk.

Then again, she'd taken a huge risk with Tyler...and that was paying off in ways she'd never imagined.

"Tell Polly I have her new dress in," Julia called to Luke as she came out of his office. "She needs to stop by and have it fitted properly."

The *Polly* remark gave Kate a sudden burst of courage. In the past, Julia had helped Polly with the right dresses and whatnot. And Polly was so nice...if she got along with Julia, maybe there was hope.

"Excuse me," Kate said quickly.

Julia stopped midstride, her perfectly arched eyebrow lifting.

"Look, I know we're not the best of friends," Kate said in a rush. "But I also know you're an amazing stylist, and I'd like to improve my wardrobe. Unfortunately, I don't know anything about fashion. And I can't afford too much either, but I was thinking maybe you could give me some tips."

She waited. Her heart raced.

Julia's blue gaze slid up and down her figure as if she were looking at her through a microscope. Then, astonishingly, her red lips parted in a genuine smile.

"Why, Kate," she said. "I thought you'd never ask."

*a*fter setting up an appointment to visit Julia's studio later in the week, Kate took a quick lunch break and then triple-checked the afternoon schedule to make certain she wouldn't be dropping any balls by spending an hour at the library.

Her simmering excitement increased tenfold at the thought of seeing Tyler again. Of course, she had to keep the situation professional since they were at work, but just being in the same room with him would be like Christmas Eve and her birthday wrapped into one package.

The *Danger* sign flashed. Kate ignored it. She *had* to go to the library. The electronics company had set up the new computer this morning, and she needed to install the collections management system. She also had to show Tyler how to use it, thereby fulfilling her part of the bargain.

Suppressing the reminder that they had a "deal," she picked up her briefcase of office supplies and took the elevator to the lower level. As soon as the elevator doors opened, the beat of "Funkytown" thumped through the basement.

What in the…?

She paused at the half-open library door. A media player and speaker sat on a table, blasting the music. On the mezzanine, Tyler, dressed in jeans and a white T-shirt, was holding a stack of books and...dancing.

Kate covered her mouth to prevent a laugh from escaping, even as her gaze locked on to him. He shifted and rocked, his hips jerking from side to side, his pelvis thrusting with a vigor that would have put Elvis to shame.

Even with an armful of books, Tyler moved with a rhythmic, masculine grace, in tune with the catchy beat and perfectly at home in his body.

Envy and need curled through Kate. In one weekend, he'd given her a whole new experience with her own body. What would it be like to feel music flowing through her, compelling her to move the way Tyler was, with his hip thrusts and arm pops or whatever they were called? No wonder he didn't like sitting at a desk—the man was a celestial object, in constant kinetic motion.

She couldn't take her eyes off him. Ribbons of heat unfurled in her veins, warming her from the inside out. She wasn't surprised he could dance like this, given her firsthand knowledge of what else he could do with his body.

She grasped the doorjamb and pressed her thighs together, shocked by the burgeoning throb between her legs even though she could have watched him forever, captivated.

Only when Tyler spun around and came to a halt, his gaze crashing with hers, did Kate realize the music had faded to a stop. And he'd caught her staring at him with her mouth agape and sweat dotting her upper lip.

"Excuse me." She cleared her throat, pushing away from the doorjamb. "I apologize for interrupting *Dance Fever*, but I need to get some work done."

"By all means." He leaned his elbows on the railing, his eyes fixing on her like twin laser beams.

Kate yanked her attention from him and strode to the desk, hitting the off button on the media player when "Shake Your Groove Thing" started to play. She couldn't let their fuck buddy friendship interfere with her professionalism. She just had to keep the two things compartmentalized, like she did in her filing system.

She turned on the bright, shiny new computer and sat down. Her heart was beating unnaturally fast.

Tyler's footsteps sounded on the stairs. She felt him approaching, the air around him charged with energy, his presence flooding her spine with heat.

"So what's shakin', Darling?" he asked.

"Your ass, apparently," she remarked dryly. "'Funkytown'?"

"Nothing beats the disco music of the seventies."

"I wouldn't know. I don't dance."

God, she sounded like an eighty-year-old. A persnickety eighty-year-old at that.

"You don't dance," Tyler repeated. "At *all*?"

"I have better things to do."

"Like research library database systems." He did an eye-roll with his voice. "Fantastic."

"You know, we can call off the deal." She slanted him a glance.

"No, we're good." He winked at her.

Yes, we're good. Too good. Crazy good.

"I talked to Luke earlier this morning." Kate held up her hand when irritation tightened his jaw. "It's okay. He apologized and said he wanted me to start really taking weekends off, like he does. Your speech had an impact."

Tyler looked faintly surprised, as if he wasn't accustomed to having an impact on his older brother. "That's great."

Kate didn't bother telling him she didn't know what she'd do on weekends—at least not after their friends-with-benefits relationship was over. Just the thought made her heart hurt.

"You're here to do some cataloguing or whatever?" Tyler asked.

"I'm here to install the new database and get it up and running." She logged into the computer. "It's an incredible system with customizable metadata structures and tools for comprehensive collections management."

A deep rumbling noise erupted in his chest, sending a flame of heat through her lower body. He'd made that exact same sound when he'd been buried deep inside her with his mouth pressed to her neck and his fingers digging into her hips.

"I love it when you talk like that," he murmured.

"I am ignoring you because we are at work." She brought up the database software and started the installation process.

"Your coldness doesn't change the fact that you look really good, Darling."

Kate shot him a scowl, pressing her lips together to prevent a smile. He was—of course—*leaning* against the desk with his legs crossed at the ankle and his arms folded across his broad chest. The overhead light glinted off his corded forearms, dusted with gold-tipped hair.

Oh, he looked good, too. *Edible* good.

"How was the rest of your weekend?" he asked.

Spent in a post-lust haze reliving every second of having sex with you and getting aroused all over again.

"Fine," she replied. "Yours?"

"Fine." His eyes twinkled, as if he knew quite well that was a major understatement. "Can I come over tonight?"

"We shouldn't discuss personal stuff at work."

"I need to go over the..." he leaned closer to her, his breath brushing her hair as he murmured in a husky voice, "...*controlled vocabulary*."

A giggle escaped her throat. She forced her attention back to her task.

"You might want to pay attention," she said, though she wasn't quite sure if she was talking to Tyler or herself. "You need this to finish your job."

"You're my ticket to freedom, Darling," he replied. "There's no agreement that I have to actually learn anything. However, since you're my teacher, I'll pay attention."

"Didn't you pay attention in school?" She glanced at him. "What did you study in college?"

"Business. But I dropped out."

"You dropped out of college?"

"Junior year." Tyler scratched his chin and shrugged. "Didn't go over well with the old man, as you can imagine."

"Why did you drop out?"

"I didn't like it. Hated sitting in class, doing homework, all that stuff. I went to a tech college for a while to learn auto repair. I liked that a lot more because I was actually doing something."

"Well, believe it or not, library work is *actually doing something*." Kate picked up a book from a nearby shelf and opened it to the copyright page. "This is where you find the information to input into the bibliographic index. The index is composed of bibliographic records, or metadata, that include information like title, author, ISBN, and keywords. Those are the data elements that users need to retrieve a resource."

"Just hearing you talk like that gets me hot."

"Bring me an armload of books, Stone." She turned back to the computer. "If I'm going to be the brains, you get to be the brawn."

"As long as I can dance, I'll be anything you want me to be."

Kate shot him a repressive look. He responded with a wink before shoving away from the desk and heading to the stacks. He returned with a pile of books, then turned the volume up on the media player and strutted his way back to the photographs.

Kate thought for sure the music and Tyler would be a distraction, but she found herself getting the system set up with rapid efficiency. As soon as she finished inputting the books into the database, he appeared to whisk them away and bring her a new stack. He never seemed to stop moving, whether he was dancing, playing air guitar, roaming the mezzanine, or shelving books.

They worked in compatible silence—disco music in the background—for a while before Tyler called, "Hey, Darling, you got any chocolate in your briefcase?"

Kate reached for the bag of Whipped Creams tucked beside her paperclips. She pushed away from the desk and went up the stairs to the mezzanine.

"Don't get chocolate on the books." She handed him the bag. "Don't you get tired of all the Sugar Rush candy?"

He shrugged, popping a Whipped Cream into his mouth. "Not really. I don't work here, so I don't get any freebies and I don't keep a stash of Sugar Rush candy at home. I like the Fruit Puffles, though. You got any of those?"

Kate shook her head. "I prefer the more traditional stuff. When I was a kid, there was this candy store called Grenville's in downtown Wabash. They had all sorts of retro candy, like candy drops, gumballs, jawbreakers. They made everything by hand, and they'd always tell you the history of whatever candy you just bought.

"They didn't have much chocolate, but they always carried Stone Confectioners' Gold Rush bars. And every Friday night on his way home from the quarry, my father would stop at Grenville's and get two Gold Rush bars for me, one with nuts and one without. I savored them all weekend."

She stopped, embarrassed that she was being a Chatty Katie again. Tyler was merely looking at her with that sharp brown gaze of his, as if waiting for her to explain why she was telling him all that. At least he didn't look bored, only slightly baffled.

"I like history," she explained lamely. "And chocolate. Even though I usually make decisions methodically, I think I applied for the Sugar Rush job because of my emotional connection to Grenville's. In fact, I was really disappointed to discover that

Sugar Rush no longer makes Gold Rush bars...um, I'll just get back to the computer."

She returned to the desk, her cheeks warm. Tyler couldn't have made his disdain for the library—and by proxy, Sugar Rush history—more clear. He certainly wouldn't want to hear about her "emotional connection" to Gold Rush bars.

"Hey, speaking of old Sugar Rush candy." He approached with a tattered, leather-bound book. "I found this earlier today when I was sorting out the ledgers. Looks like a bunch of recipes."

"Really?" Kate turned. "Do they have dates?"

"Some of them. I was reading in one of the books that Edward Stone's wife created a lot of the formulas for chocolate and candy when he opened another store in San Francisco. Some of the recipes include some weird stuff."

He flipped to another page and read, "'Common chocolate is frequently mixed with ground peas and maize or potato flour, to which an amount of brown sugar or treacle is added, with mutton suet causing it to adhere together.'"

"Er...yum?" Kate threw him a grin. "Although that kind of thing would be interesting to add to the historical section on the Sugar Rush website."

Tyler put the open book on the desk. They studied the scrawled, loopy writing, which included recipes for chocolate cream, chocolate drops, chocolate milk, and chocolate powder.

"It would be fun to try some of these," Kate said.

"If you could get the ratios right." He gestured to a recipe for Chocolate Drops. "Most of them don't even say if you should use a cup or a teaspoon of something."

"Still, it's all a part of Sugar Rush history." She flipped to the front of the book. "Come on, I'll show you how to input this into the system and create a bibliographic record."

She half expected Tyler to make some flippant comment and dance away again, but instead he pulled up a chair and sat beside her. After creating a record for the book, he retrieved a few more to log in to the system. They'd gotten through a dozen books before Kate realized she'd been at the library for much longer than her planned hour.

"I need to get back to my desk." She retrieved her phone from the holster and checked her messages. "You can keep working on these, and just text me if you have any questions."

"I have a question." Tyler brushed his hand against her thigh. "When do I get to make you come again?"

Oh my God.

Though she was tempted to say, *"Right now, please,"* Kate focused on packing up her briefcase. Warmth bloomed in her chest, her nerves already sparking with anticipation of another sexy night with him.

He moved behind her, his fingers tickling the back of her neck.

"You smell so good." He nuzzled his nose into the curve of her shoulder, one hand sliding up into her hair. "Like birthday cake and butterscotch. And fresh coconuts from a tropical island."

Kate smiled, her blood warming from his touch. "Your father and Luke are going to ask you about this system. How are the resources organized?"

"Alphabetical order. Dewey Decimal system. Let's fuck."

Heat crashed into her blood at his raw command. Kate swallowed hard and pushed her elbow backward to nudge him away from her. Much as the idea excited her, they were *at work.*

"You said you wanted lessons." He slid his hand down to fondle her breast beneath her suit jacket. "Lesson number five or whatever. Be spontaneous."

"Spontaneous shouldn't also mean *unprofessional.*"

"Fuck professionalism." He squeezed her breast. "Let's be dirty librarians and get between the covers."

Kate stifled a laugh, even as her arousal mounted. Before she could work up the resolve to pull away, Tyler was tugging her out of the chair and turning her to face him. Her blood went into full boil at the sight of the mischievous glint in his eyes.

The urge to touch him bloomed inside her with sudden force, like a lid exploding off a pressure cooker. With a moan of surrender, she leaned forward and met him halfway in a hot, open-mouthed kiss.

Tyler muttered something in his throat and locked his granite-like arms around her, compressing their bodies together. He pushed her back up against the wall and put his hands on either side of her head.

Dizziness swept through her. She curled her hands into the front of his T-shirt, her nerves already on fire and her core throbbing.

He deepened the kiss, sweeping his tongue across the surface of her teeth. He glided one hand into her jacket to cup her breast, flicking his thumb over her hardened nipple.

Pleasure washed through her. She squeezed her thighs together to ease the burgeoning ache. He moved his hand to the side, tracing the strap of her cell phone holster. His chuckle brushed against her lips.

"Never thought a cell phone holster could be sexy, but on you, it is."

He moved his hand to her thigh and fisted his grip into the fabric of her skirt. Kate's heart crashed against her chest when he slowly pulled the hem up over her legs. His fingers grazed her nylon-clad thigh.

She trembled. Even through the thick stocking, she could feel the callouses on his fingers, the warmth of his big palm. He moved his hand up higher, higher...all the way up to the crease of her hip and over her belly...

He lifted his head his breath hot against her lips as he rested his forehead against hers. His fingers dug into the waistband of her nylons, but didn't make much progress on their downward quest.

"It's like Fort Knox," he muttered. "You know, it would be a lot easier to get my hand in here if you were wearing a thong."

"I tried a thong once and felt like I had permanent wedgie." She bit her lip on a moan when he moved his hand up to fondle her breast again. "I don't find sexy underwear very comfortable."

"You haven't found the right sexy underwear then. You could just get naked and wear nothing but your cell phone holster. That would be something to see." He trailed his lips from her mouth to her ear, then sucked her earlobe.

Kate gasped, a bolt of heat shooting right to her core. He could probably make her come without even touching her between the legs.

He settled his lips over hers again, his fingers gently pinching her nipple. She was lightheaded with sensation, the heat of his body and his breath, the possessive caress of his—

Tyler pulled away from her so fast that Kate almost lost her balance.

What the—?

She grabbed his arm to steady herself the instant before he pushed her back into the shadows of the alcove. A second later, a male voice rang into the library.

"Working hard, Tyler?"

Kate's heart plummeted to her toes. That deep voice, like a wave rolling across a marble floor, was unmistakable.

Warren Stone, family patriarch and president of Sugar Rush, had come to check on his son.

CHAPTER 17

*S*hit.

In the time that he'd heard the footsteps coming down the tiled corridor and managed to save Kate from acute embarrassment, Tyler hadn't had time to steel himself for his father's arrival.

He sank into the desk chair, partly to hide the evidence of his raging hard-on and partly because his knees were so weak from kissing and touching Kate that he couldn't stand upright much longer.

"Hey, Dad." At least his voice was somewhat steady. "Working hard, yes indeed."

Warren stopped in front of the desk. Even now, Tyler felt the effect of his father's intimidating presence. Tall and broad-shouldered with a thatch of metal-gray hair and strong features, Warren Stone looked as if he should be issuing decrees on *Game of Thrones*.

Only his perfectly tailored Armani suit, the silk tie patterned with jellybeans and the breast pocket bearing a crisply folded, matching handkerchief, belied the fact that Warren was the modern day king of a candy company.

Tyler stood to put himself on a somewhat level playing field. At least his erection had withered. "What are you doing here?"

"Came to see how things are going," Warren replied.

Of course. Frustration prickled Tyler's spine. His father would never believe he'd just get the job done without periodic check-ins. Even more than hating his father's mistrust, Tyler hated the fact that there was a good reason for it. He'd never done anything to earn his father's trust or respect. Not like all his other brothers had.

Warren crossed the room, his dark gaze scanning the piles of books that showed scant evidence of having been organized. "What's your plan for getting started?"

"Uh, I'm trying to get the bookshelves alphabetized," Tyler said. "And figuring out what all is even in here. Seems to me someone should have supervised old Fred years ago."

"Yes, that was clearly an oversight. But there was no denying Fred's devotion to Sugar Rush." Warren picked up a book and flipped through the pages. "Have you discovered anything interesting yet?"

Christ. Now he was supposed to give a report?

"About what?" he asked irritably.

Warren set the book down. "Work."

"I discovered that it sucks."

His father frowned. "Better than wasting your time hanging around an old garage, isn't it? As least you're getting paid here."

"Mr. Stone!" Kate's voice suddenly sailed through the room like a fresh breeze.

She came out of the alcove, looking sharp and crisply put-together as always, with no indication that Tyler had just had his hand down her shirt and his tongue in her mouth.

She crossed the room, straightening her glasses with one hand and extending the other to Warren. "Pleasure to see you, sir. I was just looking for archival photographs for the revamp of the website."

"Excellent." Appearing faintly bemused by her presence, Warren shook her hand. "Nice to see you as well, Kate."

"I was also explaining the new fully integrated library system to Tyler. Luke approved it the other day, and all the new equipment was delivered this morning. If you'll step over here, please?"

She strode to the desk, indicating that Tyler should get out of her way before she tapped a few keys on the computer and brought up the database screen.

"As you see, sir, Tyler can use the system for traditional services like cataloguing, lending, and acquisitions as well as stronger knowledge management capabilities. The program has a manual input screen and a streamlined function that allows you to update MARC records automatically."

She turned, gesturing Tyler to the stacks. "Tyler will get some books, and we can show you how the system works with both digital and print assets, each of which can also be supplemented with searchable file attachments."

Warren gave a slight cough. "As interesting as that sounds..." he pushed back his cuff to look his gold wristwatch, "...I need to get back to my office. I appreciate you helping Tyler get started, Miss Darling."

"My pleasure, sir." She beamed at him. "It would have been near impossible for him to get anything useful done without the proper equipment. I'm glad that Luke had the foresight to recognize that overhauling the Sugar Rush library requires a certain degree of expertise and knowledge. Tyler seems to be doing very well, considering he doesn't have a background in library sciences."

Faint irritation scraped Tyler's insides. Kate was trying to help, but this was starting to sound like a parent-teacher conference. He'd never liked those.

His father glanced at him, one eyebrow lifting. "As Tyler knows, no one expects him to do the scientific work. Just to organize things enough so that when we hire a new librarian, he or she will have an easier time getting started."

He gave them both a swift nod and headed to the door. After he'd gone, Tyler picked up a book and leafed through it. His chest was tight with a feeling of uselessness—not that that was unusual after an encounter with his father.

As Tyler knows, no one expects him to do...anything.

"Hey." Kate rested her hand on his arm. "You okay?"

He put the book back on the cart. "Yeah. Fine."

"You look upset."

"I'm not." He pulled his arm away from her, unable to explain the other stuff simmering inside him.

It was like the other day with Luke, when he and Kate had been speaking a language Tyler didn't understand. And now he didn't like the evidence that she could also converse with Warren Stone much more easily than he had ever been able to. Nor the fact that she'd had to "rescue" him because he couldn't just talk to his father like a normal person.

"Evan told me that your father is into making model cars and planes," Kate remarked. "Sounds like you have a similar interest with your Trans Am and all."

"Not really."

He doubted Evan had told Kate that their father started making models after their mother died in a car accident. Their sister Hailey had been badly injured in the accident. Warren had spent so much time in the hospital at her bedside that one day Spencer had brought him a model airplane kit to give him something else to focus on.

In the twelve years since Rebecca Stone's death, Warren had built countless models in his office workshop. And while they'd all been grateful that Warren had an outlet for his grief, as far as Tyler could tell, the hobby had ended up only further isolating his father.

Maybe old cars had isolated him, too. Yeah, he had his

buddies and a string of girlfriends, but he'd never felt...*compatible* with anyone. Not until Kate. Who was after another guy.

He rolled his shoulders back, forcing the tension from his neck. Stupid of him to be pissy about her well-intentioned help. At least with her here, he hadn't had to deal with his father alone.

"Hey, thanks for the save," he said. "You're good at this stuff."

"Well, I've seen your father in action in the boardroom." Kate tugged her suit jacket over her hips and turned to the desk. "I know he can be quite formidable, even more so than Luke at times."

She straightened some papers in her briefcase before snapping it closed and whipped her cell phone from the holster to check the screen. Tyler liked her efficient movements. She reminded him of an industrious little bird, like a sparrow building a nest.

"All right, then." Kate slipped her phone back into the holster and picked up her briefcase. "I need to get back to my desk. You can continue to put books into the system, but use the basic entry screen. Call or text me if you have any questions."

"I sure will."

"I'll stop by again before I leave for the day." She strode to the door.

"Kate."

She turned to look at him.

"Tonight," he said. "Six o'clock. Be ready."

A pink flush of pleasure colored her skin, her brown eyes lighting with an anticipation she couldn't conceal. Then she gave him a swift nod and hurried away.

Tyler grinned and turned the media player back on. "Stayin' Alive" burst through the room. He sat back down at the computer and continued retrieving MARC records and inputting resources into the system.

When he got tired of sitting, he took a dance break, then started to separate the materials by type—photographs, maps, documents, ephemera (a word Kate had told him meant "things that originally weren't supposed to last long, like newspapers, tickets, and posters"), and books.

As much as he'd hated being banished here, the more he worked, the faster time passed. Now that he knew what he was doing, it was a hell of a lot better than sitting around feeling useless. He'd celebrate the day he was released, but now he actually believed he could get the job done to his father's satisfaction.

Thanks to Kate.

He riffled through a file folder, absently scanning what looked like more recipes for Sugar Rush chocolate products of the past. With Evan's cocoa bean project and the recent acquisition of Alpine Chocolates, chocolate had been a big thing on the company agenda for the past year.

He sat at the desk to review the haphazard pile of papers. He found three other candy recipes, which he read carefully before texting his brother Spencer. *Where are u?*

SPENCE: Lab.
TYLER: Can u come to library? Need to ask u something.
SPENCE: I'm going to lunch in 10 minutes. Meet you at Gumdrop Bistro.

Tyler slipped the recipes into an acid-free, archival quality envelope and headed out of the building. The afternoon sun hung behind a thin layer of ocean fog, and the salty breeze made him briefly wish that he could be out surfing or boating.

He crossed the manicured gardens, nodding at a few employees he recognized, before reaching the brightly colored Gumdrop Bistro with its gumdrop-shaped tables and cushiony chairs.

Spencer sat at a table by the window, studying a newspaper on his tablet. He glanced up over the tops of his glasses when Tyler sat in the chair across from him.

"I hear you've been showing up for work," Spencer remarked, pushing his tablet away.

"I guess miracles can happen, after all."

"Maybe that means tomorrow you'll actually shave before coming to the office."

Tyler shrugged off the jab. He opened the envelope and pulled out the recipes.

"Actually the library is kind of cool. All that historical stuff. I mean, some of it is dead boring, like the accounting ledgers, but Sugar Rush has an interesting history. Did you know we launched a bunch of rescue and aid efforts after the San Francisco earthquake in 1906? When the company was headquartered in the city, our building was the only one in a three-mile radius that wasn't destroyed by the quake."

Spencer raised his eyebrows—not as if the information was new to him, but as if he were surprised that Tyler found it interesting.

"That's true," he said. "Our great-grandmother took that as a sign that Stone Confectioners had been spared for a reason. That reason being that the company had an obligation to help others in need. That's why social consciousness has been part of the company philosophy for so long."

"Cool." Tyler put the recipes on the table and tapped them with his finger. "I also found these. Old recipes for different chocolate and candy products. Do you know if we make them anymore?"

Spencer leafed through the recipes. "Not that I know of. Why?"

"Do you think you can recreate them?" Tyler asked. "In the lab, I mean. Do you have all those ingredients?"

"Not all of them. Some of these things aren't available or used anymore. Why do you want to know?"

"I thought it would be cool to see if it's even possible to remake chocolate and candy that's historically authentic. As much as it can be, anyway. Kind of a Stone Confectioners revival."

A spark appeared in his brother's eyes, which was exactly what Tyler had been expecting. Spencer loved a challenge—especially one that could be created through science.

"I can try," Spencer finally said. "Might take me a while to figure out the ratios and ingredients, though."

"No prob. I'm not going anywhere. Not for the foreseeable future, anyway."

"Okay." Spencer nodded and put the recipes back in the envelope. "I'll take these and see what I can come up with."

"Wait a sec. No can do." Tyler took the envelope from his brother. "These are delicate original documents that you can't just manhandle. I'll digitize and email them to you."

Faint surprise flashed in Spencer's expression, a reaction that pleased Tyler. He thanked his brother and walked away.

Turned out it was fun to surprise his family by being responsible. And a heck of a lot better than disappointing them at every turn.

Speaking of surprises...

He pulled out his cell and dialed.

"Yes?" a woman responded in a sexy, throaty tone.

"Veronica, it's Tyler Stone."

"Tyler!" Her voice warmed considerably. "How wonderful to hear from you. It's been so long. When are you coming to see me again?"

"Tonight, if you're available."

"Indeed, I am."

CHAPTER 18

"*A*nother café au lait, sweetheart?" Veronica, a gorgeous, curvaceous woman in her mid-forties, stopped by Tyler's chair and rested her hand on his shoulder.

"No, I'm good, thanks."

"All right." She glanced toward the curtained dressing area on the other side of the room. "Shall I see what's keeping Miss Darling?"

"No, she'll come out when she's ready." He injected a "please leave now" tone to his voice. "Thanks."

"Very well. Just ring if you need anything." She indicated the bell on the table and left the room in a waft of expensive perfume, closing the door behind her.

Tyler took another sip of coffee, sank deeper into the plush chair, and waited some more. Most women he knew shopped at the exclusive lingerie boutique *LuLa* for their overpriced bits of silk and lace, and it wasn't the first time he'd sat in the private dressing room waiting for a girl to come out and display her assets in a push-up bra or G-string.

It was, however, the first time he'd ever waited for a woman like Kate. A woman who'd already proven to be the opposite of what he'd initially thought. A woman who, every time he thought he'd figured her out, kept surprising him. A woman who was anything but a cliché.

"Darling," he called.

"Hold on." Behind the curtain, Kate's voice sounded tense. "Can't you just let me pick out a few things I like and be done with it?"

"Nope. You wanted my opinion, and I can't give that to you without seeing what you're wearing."

"I think you just want to ogle me."

"Yes, I do. Among other things."

A muffled laugh emerged. The curtains twitched. "Ready?"

"Considering I've been sitting here for half an hour and I haven't even seen you in a bathrobe, yeah, I'd say I'm ready."

"Okay." She poked her head around the side of the curtain, her hair tousled around her heart-shaped face. "Veronica told me it's called a merry widow."

"I love merry widows."

Kate stepped out from behind the curtain. All the breath escaped Tyler's lungs in one hard *whoosh*. His coffee sloshed over the cup. He managed to set it down on the table, then he just stared at her.

Holy mother of God. He'd known she'd look great in sexy lingerie, but he hadn't expected her to look like...*this*. Like a goddamned sexpot bombshell with the lace bodice skimming over her curved waist and hips, her long legs encased in black fishnets, and her tits pillowed up to display her cleavage, a deep valley of temptation that he wanted to thrust his cock into right then and there.

He groaned, shifting to ease his instantly hard dick. Kate frowned and adjusted the straps of the merry widow.

"What's wrong?" she asked. "Doesn't it look good?"

"Yeah, it looks good. It looks fucking incredible." He dropped his hand to his groin. "You look like Betty Boop."

Kate laughed and walked over to view herself in the mirror. Tyler craned his neck a little to get a glimpse of her ass, which peeked out from beneath a lace ruffle like a perfect, round moon. He wanted to see her ass bouncing against him as he thrust into her from behind.

"I can't say it's the most comfortable thing I've ever worn." Kate slid her hands around to the front and plumped up her breasts. "But it feels pretty sexy."

Tyler tore his gaze from her, wincing as his erection pushed against his jeans. A knock sounded at the door before Veronica, the boutique's owner, came in again. He groaned inwardly.

"How is everything here?" She closed the door. "Oh, that's a perfect fit, my dear. Is it chafing anywhere?"

"I don't think so."

"Move around a little and see if it's uncomfortable. We can always adjust the fit."

Kate walked around the room. Tyler couldn't stop himself from watching her, even though his self-control stretched tighter and tighter with every passing second. Her tits bounced, her hips rocked, her ass swayed, her hair swished back and forth.

He gritted his teeth, wanting to rip that expensive thing from her lush body and plunge his dick between her warm, wet thighs—

"I'll try on the bustier next." Kate disappeared behind the curtain again.

Veronica left with the assurance that she'd be back momentarily. Tyler resisted the urge to lock the door behind her and have his way with Kate right on the dressing room floor.

Veronica happened to be a good friend of his aunt Julia. His bad behavior would get back to Julia in light speed, and God knew he didn't need any extra family aggravation. Not to mention, he never wanted his indecency to hurt Kate.

She paraded out again—this time in a royal blue lace bustier and matching panties. The material was so sheer that the dark circles of her nipples were visible—and hard.

Tyler wiped a trickle of sweat from his temple, resisting the urge to grab his crotch and give his erection a relieving squeeze.

"Oh, lovely!" Veronica sailed back into the room, a pleased smile curving her lipsticked mouth. "I have some matching thigh-highs for this one, too."

Tyler suffered through five more rounds of lingerie modeling before Kate decided on what she wanted to purchase. Veronica ordered the salesgirls to package all the items in pink boxes lined with tissue paper. She waved away Kate's attempts to give her a credit card.

"That's not right." Kate looked at Tyler with dismay. "I told Tyler I wouldn't let him pay for anything."

"He's not, dear," Veronica assured her. "Consider it a favor to his aunt."

Kate paled. "I appreciate that, but the last thing I want is to be indebted to Ms. Bennett."

Veronica considered that, then gave a brief nod. "How about I give them to you wholesale?"

After some conferring, while Tyler stood by the door still trying to get his dick to calm the fuck down, Kate made the purchases, and the salesgirls started toward the door with six beribboned boxes set in a tower.

"I'll take them." He gathered the boxes, shoving the glass door open with his hip as he waited for Kate to precede him.

"I will admit," she said, after they'd gotten back into his car, "that that was more fun than I thought it would be."

Not so much for him. He'd always liked watching girlfriends —not that Kate was technically a girlfriend—model their lingerie for him, but he couldn't remember ever being *this* turned on by it. Like he was ready to take out his cock right now and jerk off like a fifteen-year-old. If he weren't in the middle of bustling down-town Indigo Bay, he might have done just that.

He inhaled a deep breath, smothering his lust to the point where he could drive safely to Kate's house. He was supposed to meet his friends back at his house so they could caravan up to the city for a blues concert, but his current interest in music was less than nothing.

He pulled into the driveway and took all the lingerie boxes out of the trunk while she opened the front door. Tyler set the boxes on the coffee table and straightened, his chest heaving and his heart pounding in total disproportion to his actual physical exertion.

"Thanks." Kate gave him a bright smile, blinking at him like a little owl with those big-framed glasses. "I know you have to get going, but—oh!"

Her gasp of surprise was lost under the pressure of his mouth. Before she could finish, Tyler had crossed the room in three strides and hauled her into his arms. His mouth crashed down on hers without tenderness or finesse. Pure raw lust spilled through his veins. Kate's brief shock gave way to surrender as she twined her arms around his neck and arched her body against his.

Tyler guided her over to the sofa, not taking his mouth from hers. He worked his hand between them to unfasten the buttons of his fly and shove his jeans over his hips. Through his boxer briefs, his erection nudged against Kate's thigh. She drew in a sharp breath, pulling away from him slightly.

"Good lord, Tyler," she breathed. "Was it the lingerie?"

"Damn right." He clenched his teeth to prevent himself from throwing her onto the sofa and shoving between her legs without preamble. "Go put one of them on for me."

"Now?"

"Yes, *now*."

"But why? If you want to—"

"So I can take it off you, woman." He released her and gave her ass a gentle slap. "Go on. The black one."

Kate flashed him a smile, grabbed the boxes, and hurried into her bedroom. When she returned an eternity later, Tyler's heart almost hammered out of his chest.

She was a fucking goddess with her perfect breasts, curvy hips, and those mile-long legs. He thanked every god of every religion that Kate had spent her life wearing clothes that hid her gorgeous body because men would have been crawling after her like slaves if they'd known her secrets.

He clenched and unclenched his fists, not wanting any other man in the universe except him knowing Kate Darling's secrets.

Hell, he didn't want any other man knowing anything about her. He wanted her all to himself...and that thought had to stop right there before he started getting any more possessive of her than he already was.

"You know..." Kate slipped her hand over her thigh, her fingers toying with the flimsy string holding her panties together. "I was getting aroused knowing you were watching me."

Tyler stripped off his jeans and stalked toward her, his lust firing hotter than before. At least in the lingerie shop he'd been restrained by the fact that Veronica could walk in any second. But here...

With a groan, he yanked Kate into his arms again and kissed her until his head spun and she was moaning and squirming against him. He got them both onto the sofa as she tugged off his boxer briefs, and then his dick was throbbing in her warm hand and he almost shot all over her new lace panties.

"Wait." He pulled away from her, his breath heavy. He wasn't going to lose control before doing what he'd fantasized about.

He got to his feet and tugged her to a sitting position, unable to take his eyes off her. With her skin flushed pink, her eyes filled with arousal and her hair spilling around her shoulders, she looked like a woman out of a dream.

He rubbed her breasts, flicking his fingers over her hard nipples. Much as he wanted to suck on them, he had another agenda in mind. He tugged her bra down to expose her tits, pressure tightening his groin at the sight of them—full, creamy, and topped with round, pink nipples.

Kate shivered, her breath catching. He rubbed the crevices beneath her breasts and pushed them together to create a deep valley of cleavage. He inhaled a hard breath, struggling for some modicum of control.

"Tyler?" As if sensing his sudden restraint, she looked up at him. "What's wrong?"

What *was* wrong? Beneath the thick layer of lust, he knew the basic truth—he didn't want to ever do anything to push her away. He'd told her he liked sex raw and dirty, but with her lack of experience, she might think even his brand of *tame* sex was too much.

"I want you to know you can always tell me if you don't want to do something." He lifted one hand to touch her hair. "Or if you want me to stop. Just tell me, and I will."

Kate gave a breathless laugh, wiggling her hips on the sofa cushion. "Tyler, I am deeply appreciative of your concern, but I am begging you *not* to stop. Whatever you want to do, I'm all in. I want to learn, to experience things with you, to do things I've never done before. So please *don't stop.*"

Her plea sank into him, firing his lust hotter. He pushed her breasts together.

"Hold them like this," he ordered, his voice rough with desire. "I'm going to fuck your tits."

Kate's eyes widened. "You're going to what?"

"I'll show you. Hold them."

A visible shudder went through her. She lifted her hands and cupped her breasts, her fingers circling her nipples. He grabbed his shaft and stroked it up and down, then moved closer to her, positioned himself right at the underside of her breasts, and thrust.

"*Oh!*" Kate gasped, her teeth biting down on her lower lip.

Pleasure and heat flooded Tyler in a wave as he sank into the depths of her cushiony flesh. He pulled back and thrust again, his pathway eased by both Kate's perspiration and his own fluids.

"Oh my God, Tyler, that feels so...amazing." Kate tore her gaze from him and looked down at her pillowed breasts. "A little weird and totally dirty, but amazing."

"Hold them tighter." He grunted, plunging forward to sink as far as he could into the soft heaven of her tits.

Kate panted, shifting to the edge of the sofa, her thighs rubbing together. She stared in fascination at the sight of his cock appearing and disappearing between her breasts. He increased the pace, his urgency ratcheting higher with every thrust.

He drove his hands into her hair. He dragged in a hard breath and stilled.

"Lick it," he said hoarsely.

Kate let out a little whimper that told him she was already as close to the edge as he was. She lowered her head and touched her pink tongue to his cock. Heat shot through him. He tightened his fingers on her hair. She swirled her tongue around down his shaft as far as she could before enclosing the head between her lips and sucking.

"That's so sexy," she whispered, pulling back to look up at him. "Can you come like this?"

"Yeah." Hell, he was struggling *not* to come like this. "You want me to?"

She nodded, opening her mouth to lick his cock again. A groan shook his chest. He drew back and plunged forward, fucking her breasts until his blood burned with urgent fire. Kate's gasps and whimpers only fueled his lust, and it wasn't long before pressure gripped his lower body.

With a shout, he thrust as far as he could and came, shooting all over her pretty tits and chest. Kate shuddered and squeezed her breasts around his shaft, milking the last sensations from his body.

Tyler clutched the arm of a nearby chair, collapsing onto the seat with a groan. He watched through half-lidded eyes as Kate rubbed her hands over her breasts, leaving them glossy and damp. She licked her finger and shot him a grin.

"You're a naughty girl, Darling," he murmured.

"Mmm. And a good student, considering the things you're teaching me."

Though Tyler didn't like the reference to his *teaching*, he did agree she was a good student. Hell. The best student. No wonder she'd graduated *summa cum laude*.

"Fast learner, too," he said. "You never let a guy do that before?"

"Rule number one, don't talk about other guys," she reminded him. "But the answer is no. I like it, though. A lot."

"Me too." He let his gaze drift over her breasts and down to her thighs, which she was still pressing together. "Now get yourself off."

Her eyebrows lifted. "You mean..."

"You know what I mean." He jerked his chin to indicate her lingerie. "You're soaking right through your panties, aren't you?"

"Well, I think they're meant to inspire sexy stuff, but not withstand it." Kate moved back on the sofa and spread her legs partway, but then locked them together again. A flush colored her cheeks. "I don't think I can do this."

"You want me to?"

She lifted her head, her breath catching. Tyler shifted across to the sofa and hauled her into his lap, settling her ass on his thighs. Her heat enveloped him, her body sinking against his. He slid his hand up her smooth leg and between her thighs, edging his finger into her pussy just far enough to encourage her to spread her legs wider.

Kate squirmed, her breath brushing against his neck, her body already tensing with need. He circled his thumb over her folds. Shivers rocketed through her as she started the climb to release.

"Come on, honey," he urged. "Work yourself on my finger. Show me how much you want it. You're so fucking perfect... that's it...next time I'll sink my cock into you, let you ride me until you beg me to rub your clit and make you come..."

Kate groaned, thrusting her hips forward to impale herself on his finger. He pushed another finger into her and massaged her clit, unable to take his eyes from her face. She leaned back on his other arm, her long lashes fluttering against her cheeks, her face flushed. She parted her lips on a groan.

"Tyler, I feel it...harder, please...I'm going to come...now!" With a shriek, she bucked against his hand, her body shaking.

Tyler held her, slowing the pace of his fingers when she went limp against him. Lingering shudders coursed through her.

"Pretty." He brushed his lips across hers and tightened his arms around her, not wanting to let her go.

Ever.

$\mathcal{F}$or the first time in his life, Tyler looked forward to going to work. Though he'd never been good at routine, there was something comfortingly predictable about Sugar Rush.

Over the next few days, he arrived at the main office at nine sharp every morning. The receptionist, Nancy, always greeted him with a warm smile and offer of coffee and muffins. He chatted with her and other employees, and more people started coming into the library to ask him for resources. He did his best to help them—sometimes succeeding, sometimes having to admit he had no idea where to look.

Then he'd wait until Kate arrived during her lunch hour, and they'd search until they figured it out. Spencer came in with questions about the old Sugar Rush recipes, assuring Tyler that he was working on the formulas in the lab.

All in all, it was a heck of a lot different than he'd expected. He even liked the process of putting the books and documents in order, seeing it all come together in the database. It was a little like restoring a classic car piece by piece.

After work on Thursday, he headed to Rainsville before his

scheduled after-work date with Kate. He stopped at Wild Child first, where Polly greeted him with a wave.

"Here's the info." She pushed a scrap of paper across the counter. "George Leonard. My friend Tom knows him. Says he's a really nice guy, very laid-back. He rents the field to supplement his income, so he has to charge for it but apparently he's flexible with pricing depending on the event."

"That's great, thanks." Tyler glanced at the name of the farmer who owned the Codswallop festival field. "I'll give him a call this weekend. Hey, you got any Declairs?"

"In my secret stash, yes. Have a seat, and I'll bring you a couple."

Tyler ambled to an empty table. Hannah sat nearby, working on her laptop.

"Hey," he greeted. "Writing a blog post?"

She nodded. "I got a letter from a woman who was widowed when she was forty-five. She moved back to her hometown and went to have lunch at the local diner. Turned out it's now owned by a guy she'd dated in high school. She sat at the counter, and he brought her a grilled cheese sandwich, tomato soup, and a piece of apple pie without her even having to order. That had been her favorite lunch at the diner in high school, and all those years later, he still remembered. Needless to say, they've been happily married for three years now."

Tyler guessed there was a lot more to it than grilled cheese and apple pie, but it was a cute story. Kate would like hearing it. Girls were into that kind of thing.

"She sent me pictures, too, and she said I could post them along with the story." Hannah turned the laptop screen toward Tyler so he could see the photos of a happy, smiling couple.

"Nice," he offered.

"Maybe Hannah will have to write a post about you and Kate." Polly approached with a plate of chocolate-dipped Declairs and a cup of coffee.

Tyler scowled. "What are you talking about?"

"I was there the other day," she reminded him. "When you got all up in Luke's face about Kate. A Stone brother doesn't get *that* possessive about a girl unless he's into her in a seriously big way."

"Kate?" Hannah leaned toward Tyler, her eyes lighting with intrigue. "Really? That's awesome."

"We're just friends."

Polly and Hannah exchanged knowing looks.

"You had steam coming out of your ears," Polly said. "And the way she was looking at you...whew. I almost had to turn the fan on."

Tyler glared at them, annoyed that he hadn't had more self-control but also a little intrigued that Kate had been looking at him with her own feelings on transparent display.

"I would love to write about you and Kate." Hannah rubbed her hands together with a gleeful smile. "Two people who couldn't be more different, and you hook up because—"

"No one," Tyler interrupted, "is writing anything. There's nothing to write about. Kate and I are just friends, okay? We're not a real life love story."

"Okay, okay." Hannah turned back to her computer. "But if anything changes, I need to be the first to know. Because that would be *huge.*"

She and Polly grinned at each other before Polly headed back to the counter. Tyler pulled out his phone, pretending to check messages as he ate the Declairs so he wouldn't have to converse with Hannah.

Truth be told, he kind of liked her blog—though he wouldn't have actually admitted he sometimes read it. The blog had once been about Hannah's travel adventures, but in the past year it had evolved into *Locked Hearts*, featuring stories about true love. The blog had skyrocketed in popularity, and Hannah received hundreds of letters a month from couples wanting to share their stories.

Still, the skeptical part of Tyler knew that not all the stories would really end happily ever after. Most of them were probably happy *for now*...until something bad happened.

His parents had once thought theirs would be a "happily ever after" marriage with seven good kids and a successful candy company. They'd envisioned grandchildren, growing old together, retirement, vacations. Then a split-second had changed everything.

He brought his empty plate and cup to the counter, said goodbye to Polly and Hannah, and headed out to his car. He drove to Charlie's Garage. His friend was working on an old Chevy.

"Hey, man, I have an idea for you." Tyler approached, tossing Bandit a dog treat.

Charlie levered himself up from peering under the hood. "What's that?"

Tyler dug the contact info from his pocket and explained about the Codswallop festival and the farmer who might rent out the field.

"I don't know what he'll charge, but it sounds perfect for the car show," he said. "Plenty of room, good location for people to come from different parts of the state. We could have stages, bands, food booths, a swap meet. What do you think?"

Charlie adjusted his greasy baseball cap on his head and sighed. "I think it's great, kid. But not this year."

Disappointment speared Tyler, sharp and sudden. "Why not?"

"Because we still don't have a sponsor."

Tyler battled his conscience for a second. Much as he'd been struggling with his dependence on Sugar Rush, he'd put his pride aside for Charlie's sake and for the car show.

"So I'll ask Luke," he said. "Sugar Rush can sponsor it."

For a second, it appeared Charlie might waver, but then he shook his head. "Nah. I'm done here. Time for me to retire anyway."

"What do you mean, you're done?" Tyler's disappointment shifted to irritation. "You're throwing in the towel?"

Charlie shrugged, unperturbed by the sharp note in Tyler's voice. "Profits have been down for a while. Can't hold on to my clients. I figure it's time to close up shop."

Tyler didn't know what to say. He'd been coming to Charlie's Garage ever since he'd dropped out of college. In some ways, it was more of a home to him than his own apartment. Which wasn't even really *his* anyway.

"I'll give you a loan," he said without thinking. "You just need to advertise more, put together a decent business plan."

Charlie waved a hand dismissively. "Nah. There's no big loss here, kid. I've got a pension, so I'll be okay. Maybe I'll go work for someone else, if I get bored."

Tyler's hands fisted. Not only did it piss him off that Charlie could talk so casually about shutting down the garage, he was even angrier with himself for not being able to do anything about it. Thanks to his own stupidity, everything he earned working at the library had to go toward the boat payments.

Yeah, he could ask Luke or his father for money to give Charlie a loan, but then what? Even if by some miracle they *didn't* refuse, Tyler would be indebted to them even more, and he'd have put his friend in the same position.

The Sugar Rush Candy Company cast one hell of a long shadow. So did his own screw-ups.

He stalked back to his car, ignoring Charlie's call of, "Come on, kid..."

He drove back to Indigo Bay with the windows open and the radio blaring. If he hadn't been such a dickhead his whole life, maybe he'd actually have enough money to help his friend, even sponsor the car show himself.

Too late for that now.

He let himself into his apartment, groaning at the sight of his friends sprawled around the living room. A video game battle blasted from the Xbox, tablets and phones pinged, and music fired out of the high-level speakers mounted in the corners of the living room.

Why had he thought it was a good idea to give them a key?

"Hey, man," John called.

Tyler grabbed a bottle of water from the fridge and retreated to his bedroom, which wasn't much cleaner with all his clothes and shit strewn everywhere.

"What's going on?" John appeared in the bedroom doorway, his forehead creased.

Tyler shrugged. "You know Charlie, the garage owner? He's shutting down."

"Oh. Well, he's old, right? Ready to retire."

"Yeah, but..." Tyler took a swallow of water, unable to explain why he was all knotted up inside. "I dunno. I guess he's just always been there. Now he won't be."

"Can you buy the place?"

"No. Even if I could afford it, I don't know anything about running a business. Just one of the reasons I've never wanted to work for Sugar Rush."

"What about the car show?"

"Over. No sponsor, no venue. So Charlie figures there's no point."

"You don't need a sponsor to run a show, not really," John said. "I mean, yeah, it helps a lot but you can totally do something smaller and just rent out vendor booths to recoup the cost."

"Doesn't matter. Charlie doesn't want to do it anyway."

"So why don't you?"

Tyler sighed. Once again, he had no idea where he'd even start. Not that he'd admit that to John.

He glanced at the clock, his frustration slipping away suddenly. "Hey, I gotta get ready to go."

"Where're you going?"

Any other time, Tyler would have told his friend he was

seeing a girl. But he was already sharing Kate with all of Sugar Rush, Luke, Polly, his other brothers, and the fucking possibility of Miles Norwood. He wanted her to himself as much as he could get her.

"Just have stuff to do."

"You coming to the party up in San Jose tomorrow night?" John backed out of the room. "Should be a good one."

"I don't know." Tyler went into the bathroom for a quick shower. He changed clothes and grabbed his keys.

"Turn down the music, would you?" he told the guys as he headed out the door. "And clean up your shit. You all need to be gone by the time I get back."

As he navigated the streets to Kate's house, all the gnarled emotions stuck in his chest began to unravel. He parked in the driveway and took a deep breath at the sight of her little house with the tidy flower garden. He approached the door and knocked.

"Come in," Kate called.

Tyler tried the knob and found it unlocked. He went inside.

"Kate?"

"Hi." She peeked out from behind the bedroom door and waved. "Get yourself a drink and have a seat. I'll be right out."

Accustomed to women not being ready on time, Tyler dug around in her fridge for a soda, then settled on the sofa. He leaned his head on the back and closed his eyes.

Aside from Kate rustling in the other room, silence filled his ears. Reminded him of the library. Maybe he was getting used to quiet, or at least appreciating it more. The last of the tension eased from his shoulders.

"Ta da."

He opened his eyes. Kate stood in front of him, wearing a pale blue suit that fit her to perfection. The skirt fell above her knees, showing off her long legs, and the white shirt displayed her breasts in a way that was both attractive and modest at the same time. The jacket molded to her curves rather than falling in a straight unrelieved line like all her other suits.

As if that weren't enough, she had a new haircut that made her hair fall in smooth waves to her shoulders, and her features were artfully enhanced with makeup that emphasized her high cheekbones and pretty eyes.

"Wow," he managed to say.

"Not bad, hmm?" Kate smoothed down her skirt. "I took the plunge and asked your aunt for advice. Did you know she has a whole room full of clothes that designers and shop owners have sent her for *free*? She said I could have some of the suits, but they have to be altered. Three of them fit already though, so I have new stuff to wear to work. This is a Chanel suit. I've never even touched a Chanel suit, and now look at me. I'm wearing one."

Tyler's insides grew weak with tenderness and affection. She was so fucking adorable. He'd never dated a woman who thought it was an actual novelty to wear designer clothes.

"You look amazing, Kate. Where are your glasses?"

"Contacts. I don't wear them often, but Julia told me I need to get frames that fit better. Then she unleashed this Italian guy named Enzo on me, and he did all this stuff to my hair and face. And look, the shoes match the suit perfectly." She extended her foot to show him the blue leather pumps she wore. "This is called a block heel. Julia said I walked like a Minotaur in the stilettos. I figured that was not a compliment."

She glanced up and smiled at him. His heart gave a little jump, like it was tied directly to her smile.

"Want to see another one?" she asked.

"Sure."

"Okay, wait here." She hurried back to the bedroom.

Tyler waited, leafing through the magazines and DVDs on her coffee table. A cell phone buzzed. He reached for his, before remembering he'd left it in the car. He shuffled through the magazines and found Kate's phone lighting up with a call from someone named *Ed*.

Jealousy rustled in his gut. Who the fuck was Ed? A Sugar Rush VP bugging her after work? Didn't he know Kate wasn't on the clock?

Without thinking, Tyler hit the *accept call* button. "Kate Darling's phone."

Silence filled the line before an older man's voice asked, "Uh, is Kate there?"

"Can I tell her who's calling?"

"Her father."

Relief swamped Tyler, fast and strong enough to be surprising. What the hell was wrong with him?

"Sorry," he said, getting to his feet. "I didn't...she's just in the other room."

"Is this Tyler?"

"Uh, yes."

"Oh, good to talk to you. This is Ed Darling. She told me about you."

Tyler didn't know what to say. She'd told her father *what* about him? That he was the Stone family loser? That they were coworkers? That they were *more than that*?

"Nice talking to you too," he finally said, remembering what Kate had told him about needing to help save her father from near-bankruptcy.

He hated the idea of a young Kate having to take responsibility for her father's fuck-ups—even more than he hated the knowledge that he'd never taken responsibility for his own fuck-ups. At least, not until now.

"How long have you been dating her?" Ed asked.

"Not long." Tyler paced to the dining room and back, glancing at the closed bedroom door.

She'd told her father they were *dating*. For a girl like Kate, telling her father something like that was no small thing.

"So you're working with her at Sugar Rush?" Ed asked.

"That's correct."

"Must be an interesting job, data analysis."

Tyler froze. "Data analysis?"

"Isn't that what you do? That's what Kate told me, I think. You're doing some data analysis consulting for Sugar Rush?"

What the fuck?

"Hold on." He forced his voice to remain steady. "I'll get her for you."

"No, that's okay. I'll call her back later, if she's busy. Take care, Tyler."

Before Tyler could respond, Ed ended the call. He set the phone down, his heart hammering. She'd told her father they were "dating," but she'd also told him he was a data analyst?

"Ready?" Kate peeked out from the bedroom.

Tyler couldn't move. Kate drew her brows together, as if she sensed his sudden shift in mood, and came out of the bedroom. She looked different—not just because of the designer tweed suit she wore, but because of what he'd just heard.

"What happened?" she asked. "I heard you talking on the phone. Is everything okay?"

"It was your phone." He tilted his head to the coffee table. "It rang, and I answered it."

Her forehead furrowed. "You answered my phone?"

"I didn't…" He paced away from her, shoving his hands into his pockets. "I didn't recognize the name, and figured it was no big deal."

"So you thought it was okay to answer it?" Irritation scraped her voice. "That's overstepping your boundaries."

"The fuck buddy boundaries, you mean?" Tyler snapped. "Are those the boundaries you're talking about? The ones about not *getting involved* outside of the occasional fuck? Is that why we'd planned to go to dinner tonight and why you wanted to show me your new clothes? Because we're just fucking and having fun?"

Her jaw tightened. "None of that gives you the right to answer my phone. Who called?"

"Your father."

"My father." Trepidation flashed in her brown eyes. "Did he say he'd call back?"

"Yeah. We introduced ourselves." He crossed his arms. "He said you told him we were *dating*. He also asked me how my *data analysis* work was going at Sugar Rush."

Kate stared at him for a second before closing her eyes with a groan. "Tyler…"

"Kate." Anger flooded his veins. "Why did you tell your father I'm a data analyst? I get that Norwood is your dream guy, but don't drag me into lies about your social life. Or lack thereof."

Kate flinched, the arrow hitting its mark. Tyler smothered a rush of guilt. He fought the urge to cross the room and grab her, haul her against him, make her admit that she didn't belong to anyone but him.

"I'm sorry." She spread her hands, her brown eyes shadowed with distress. "My father has just always worried so much about me, especially when I moved out here. And he and my step-mother ask all the time about who I'm dating or what I'm doing with friends…and of course, I never have a good answer. So sometimes I fudge the truth a little, just to stop them from worrying. And last week after what happened in the library…I couldn't stop thinking about you. So when my father asked if I was dating anyone, your name just popped out."

"Along with the lie that I'm a data analyst."

"Well, I—"

"You couldn't stop thinking about Norwood either, apparently."

Guilt flashed across her face. Tyler turned, staring at the family photos that lined the fireplace mantel.

Kate's father was a tall, bearded man with a wide smile—the kind of man who likely wanted nothing but the best for his only daughter. Like Warren Stone wanted nothing but the best for all seven of his children.

Tyler ran a hand through his hair, his shoulders slumping. He couldn't compete with an MIT grad who had his own company. He didn't want to, either. Living with five older brothers had taught him that he was who he was. Yeah, he needed to get his shit together, but he couldn't pretend to be a different person.

Not even if Kate wanted him to be.

If he dug deep enough, he knew exactly why she'd told her father he was a data analyst. What else was there?

Hey, Dad, I'm dating the family fuckup Tyler Stone, who crashed a speedboat and now has to work at the Sugar Rush library to pay off the damage.

"I need to go." He walked to the door. "I have some stuff to do."

"Okay." Bitterness laced her voice. "Let me know when you're up for some *fun* again."

Tyler left without looking back.

CHAPTER 20

*T*yler flopped onto his bed, his blood still simmering with frustration. He rested his hands behind his head and stared at the ceiling.

No question this thing with Kate was a hell of a lot different than his previous fuck buddy relationships. Given the way he'd reacted the second he saw her, he should have known from the start that everything would be different with her.

Maybe he had known. Maybe that was why he'd agreed to this whole *My Fair Lady* deal in the first place. Because everything was different.

She made him want all the things he'd never had—a girl who was a *friend* with more than just "benefits." One whom he could talk to, hang out with, feel good around. A girl whose body he craved like an addiction. A girl who believed he was capable of more than anyone else thought. Even himself.

A knock sounded at the front door. Tyler groaned and went to answer it. If it were his jackass friends again…

Kate stood in the hallway, still dressed in her designer suit with her leather bag over her shoulder. She was also holding an old boom box. His heart did a somersault, wary hope rising in his chest.

"Hi," she said. "Can I come in?"

Tyler stepped aside, pulling the door open wider to let her precede him. Kate set the boom box on the counter and glanced around. Embarrassment rose in him over the mess—beer cans and chip bags scattered over the tables, the counters cluttered with dirty dishes, unwashed T-shirts and socks strewn on the floor.

He braced himself for Kate's disapproval, or even an outright scolding. Instead she plugged the boom box into an outlet and pointed to the sofa.

"Sit down."

Tyler shoved a sweatshirt off the sofa and did as she ordered. His earlier frustration shifted to faint intrigue.

Was she going to lecture him about library sciences? Give him a quiz? In her tweed suit and gray pumps, she sure as hell looked the part of a sharp, put-together teacher. Maybe she'd whip a pointer out of her bag and order him to—

Kate hit the play button on the boom box. "Night Fever" burst from the speakers.

She hesitated, taking a deep breath. Then she put her hands in front of her, like she was gripping ski poles, and started wiggling her hips and knees.

"What are you doing?" he asked.

"Dancing."

"Are you sure?"

"It's called the Bunny Slope. Check this one out." She shifted position and flapped her hands around in what appeared to be a bad imitation of a Jackie Chan martial arts sequence. "I did some research and learned a few groovy disco moves. This is the Hustle."

She launched into a marching beat, swinging her hips back and forth awkwardly.

Tyler laughed. Amusement and wild affection flooded him. "Darling, you're a terrible dancer."

"Don't be so quick to judge. Watch this." She turned and put her hands on her knees, presenting him with her ass—perfectly displayed in the figure-hugging skirt. She arched her back and moved her ass up and down.

"What's that one?" Tyler asked.

"Twerking." She shot him a smile over her shoulder. "Not a disco move, but I thought you'd appreciate it."

"Oh, I do." He could have watched her bouncy version of twerking for hours, even if it did look like she was having a convulsion.

"This is The Robot." She faced him again, tilting her head and putting her arms at ninety-degree angles. She jerked a few steps to the right, then the left. "The Funky Chicken." She flapped her arms like wings and knocked her knees together. "And the famous *Saturday Night Fever* finale."

She thrust her arm into the air, index finger pointing toward the ceiling, and came to a stop just as the song ended. Silence filled the air.

Tyler clapped.

Kate smiled, pushing a swath of hair away from her forehead. Her face was flushed with exertion, her eyes bright.

"So did you like it?" she asked.

"I loved it."

I love you.

The confession flew right from his heart through his head, ricocheting around every part of him.

He got to his feet and approached her. Uncertainty rose to her eyes when he took hold of her hips and pulled her closer.

"Can we please be okay again?" she asked.

He brushed his knuckles across her cheek. His heart felt astonishingly light.

"We're okay, Darling. We were never really *not* okay."

Relief flashed over her expression. She leaned her forehead on his chest. His head filled with her sugary scent. He wrapped his arms around her, locking her body against his.

"I'm so sorry, Tyler."

"Forget it." He tightened his hold on her. "I was pissed at first, but it would take a lot more than that to do us any real damage. I dig you way too much, foxy lady."

She gave a muffled giggle. "You're pretty far out yourself, cool cat."

"You Sexy Thing" started on the boom box. Tyler moved his hands down to Kate's ass, giving it a gentle squeeze.

"This is a slow disco dance." He rocked her from side to side in time to the music. "Full body contact, lots of ass gripping, and the girl rubs herself all over the guy."

"Hmm." She shifted, pressing her breasts against him. "What's it called?"

"The Tyler."

Kate laughed. "No wonder it's my favorite move of all."

CHAPTER 21

"One pepperoni, one everything." Tyler returned to the living room, carrying two pizza boxes.

Kate's stomach rumbled with anticipation. He pushed aside the remote controls on the coffee table before putting the boxes down.

"Do you live on takeout pizza?" she asked.

"Of course not." He threw her a look of mild offense. "There's also frozen pizza, fast food, potato chips, and sub sandwiches."

Kate shook her head and accepted the greasy slice of pizza he offered her. She wasn't surprised by his bachelor pad apartment with its huge TV, foosball table, and massive speakers—not to mention the utter mess—but she liked it because it was his domain. His cave. And he'd let her in.

Tyler flopped beside her on the sofa. He reached for the remote and unpaused the Monty Python marathon they were watching. Kate curled her legs underneath her and bit into the pizza.

Messy apartment aside, she could get used to this. Sitting on the sofa with him, watching TV and eating pizza. Or having him over for a home-cooked dinner and board games before they moved into the bedroom for some raunchy fun.

She imagined spending her new "weekends off" with him, taking trips to Napa or Yosemite, driving his Trans Am along the winding coastal highway. Maybe even bringing him back to Wabash, where her father would drag Tyler over to the quarry and lecture him about the processes of extracting granite. She'd take him to the Pizza Pit and show him the proof of her still-standing highest score on *Space Invaders*.

And then they'd ride a fucking magical purple unicorn over a glittering rainbow and land on clouds made of cotton candy.

Kate set the paper plate down and wiped her fingers on a napkin. Fuck bud...okay, *friends with benefits*. They were not boyfriend and girlfriend. They were not dating. They were temporarily having fun.

Dammit. She still couldn't believe her feelings for him had deepened so much, so fast. They'd only known each other for a week—*a week!*—and she was getting all dreamy about their future...when they didn't even have one. Not together.

"More?" Tyler extended the open box toward her.

Kate shook her head. "I should head home."

"Stay here."

"With you?"

"No, I'll go to a hotel," he replied dryly. "You can stay here by yourself."

She pinched his arm. "I have to be up early for work tomorrow."

"I have an alarm clock." Tyler popped the lid of a soda can and took a long swallow. "We'll get you home in time to get ready, then we can go in to work together."

Well, wasn't that all warm and cozy? A pang speared through Kate's chest. In the past, she'd pictured herself doing that exact kind of thing, but with a devoted businessman who'd ask her to fasten his cufflinks before they sat down for a breakfast of egg whites and toast spread with avocado.

She had never pictured waking up in a chaotic bachelor pad, eating cold pizza, and probably being late for work because a rakishly sexy hunk had seduced her in the shower. Pushing her right up against the tile wall and spreading her legs so he could plunge into her from behind.

A shiver ran down her spine. Truth be told, she desperately wanted the latter version of *morning*. For now.

"Okay." She gave a casual shrug. "As long as I'm up by five."

"You might not get any sleep at all, Miss Darling." He edged closer to her, a gleam appearing in his dark eyes. "Your twerking was damned sexy. I need to see it again, except this time I want you to be naked."

Kate smiled. Tyler lifted an eyebrow.

"I'm not joking," he said.

Her heart bumped against her ribs. "I'm not twerking naked for you."

"We'll see about that." He stood, wrapping his hand around her wrist. "Come on."

Kate's pulse sped up. She got to her feet, allowing him to lead her down the hall to his bedroom—which was no cleaner than the rest of the apartment with an unmade bed and rumpled clothes scattered everywhere.

But it was Tyler's, and *he* was evident everywhere, from the framed prints of superhero movie posters and classic cars to the sci-fi novels on the bookshelf and the state-of-the-art computer.

He tugged her toward him, his eyes warming as he lifted his hands to cup her face. He lowered his mouth to hers, but in the instant before their lips made contact, Kate put her hand up to stop him.

"I'm really not twerking naked."

He lifted his head and stepped away from her. For an instant, Kate thought he was annoyed, but then he grabbed the back collar of his T-shirt and yanked it over his head. Her breath caught. She loved looking at his muscular chest, all those sculpted muscles she couldn't wait to touch again.

His gaze still on her, Tyler unbuttoned his jeans and shoved them down. Kate's whole body reacted to the sight of him almost naked, the impressive bulge of his cock resting alongside his thigh. He shucked off the boxer briefs, tossing them to the side. Then he stretched out on the bed, putting one hand behind his head and wrapping the other around his cock.

Kate bit her lip. Her sex was already starting to pulse. Tyler stroked himself, rubbing his hand up and down his thick shaft. She got downright wet.

"You want to try new stuff, right?" he asked.

She nodded.

"Have you ever ridden a guy before?"

"Probably."

"So this is like that, except backward."

Her stomach clenched. "Oh, no."

"It's called reverse cowgirl," Tyler explained.

"I know what it's *called*," Kate replied a touch irritably. "I just don't want to do it."

"Why not?"

A flush rose to her cheeks. The truth was that she did want to do it—very much—but anxiety rose in her like a tidal wave. A big tidal wave. And not just because Tyler was stretched out on his bed like some sort of naked Greek hero with his muscles all rippled and sloping, his skin bronzed, and his dark hair rakishly tousled.

Oh yeah…and his hard cock sticking straight up like a sundial pointing the way straight to orgasmic heaven.

Kate shifted, rubbing her legs together. Her new designer suit felt heavy, like it was weighing her down. She fidgeted—crossing and uncrossing her arms, fiddling with a lock of her hair.

"Okay." Tyler heaved a sigh and took his hand away from his

erection. "I promised I wouldn't do anything you don't want to do."

He rolled over and reached for his boxer briefs.

"Wait," Kate said quickly. "I guess...I mean, maybe I could *try* it."

Tyler settled back on the bed, his eyebrow lifting as he took hold of his cock again. "Are you making a decision or not, Darling?"

He stroked up his shaft, rubbing his thumb around the tight head. She almost moaned aloud, her gaze locked to the sight of his fist moving up and down. Maybe if she were naked, he'd get distracted enough to the point that he wouldn't care about having sex in that particular position.

"Yes, I'm making a decision," she muttered.

"Atta girl."

She'd told him she never backed out of a decision once she'd made it. She slipped out of her shoes and unzipped her skirt. Tyler's hot eyes followed her every movement as she stepped out of the skirt and started unbuttoning her blouse.

She was glad she'd had the foresight to put on her new lingerie before modeling the designer suits for him. The purple bra and panty set hugged her curves and plumped up her breasts in a way that made her feel powerfully sexy.

She glanced at Tyler, who was staring at her cleavage as she removed her silk blouse. His breath escaped on a hiss.

"Damned if you don't look incredible," he said. "Get over here."

She approached the bed. Her blood thickened at the thought of straddling his hips, positioning herself right over his thick cock and then sliding herself slowly onto him...

"*Here*," Tyler growled, indicating the mattress.

Kate climbed onto the bed and knelt beside him, resting a hand on his chest. She bent to press her lips to his, loving the heavy beat of his heart beneath her palm, the way he captured her lower lip between his teeth and gathered her hair in his fist to hold her in place.

Even lying on his back, *control* radiated from Tyler like an aura. He shifted her position with minute tugs of his hand until she was splayed over his chest with her knee sliding between his legs.

Heat flared between them, igniting her need. He pushed his leg upward between her thighs, and Kate flashbacked to that first encounter in the library when he'd commanded her to *move.*

With a moan, she pressed her sex against his thigh, the rock-hard length delicious against her cleft. She wiggled up and down. Tension coiled through his muscles. He pulled her down for another kiss, sliding his hands down her back and into her panties.

He gripped her ass, positioning her farther up his thigh.

"Turn around," he ordered, his voice rough. "And ride my dick."

"God, Tyler." Kate lifted her head, staring down into his lust-dark eyes. Her hair fell in a curtain on either side of his face. "I'm nervous."

"Why?"

"It's embarrassing. My rear is kind of big, and in that position it'd be right *there*..."

He groaned, sliding one hand farther down to the folds of her sex. Kate gasped, curling her fingers against his chest.

"First, your ass is goddamned fucking perfect," Tyler said, "which is exactly why I want to see it bouncing up and down right *there*. Second, your little pussy is already nice and wet, which means this idea turns you on as much as it does me. Third, you never...I repeat, *never* need to be embarrassed or shy around me, okay? And you need to trust that I'm not going to do anything that makes you uncomfortable. God knows there are a million dirty things I want to do with you, but if you ever want me to stop, you just have to say so. Remember that."

Kate nodded. She'd already done so much more with him than she'd ever done with another man—and *loved* every minute of it. Why would this be any different?

"And in this position, you're in control," Tyler said. "I just get to lie here and enjoy the show."

The thought of being the one in control mitigated some of her anxiety.

"Okay."

He smiled and plucked at her panties. "Then take these off and turn around."

A tremble rocked her. She slithered out of her panties, aware of his gaze raking down her body. He unfastened her bra, groaning at the sight of her bare breasts. He grabbed a condom package from the nightstand and rolled the sheath over his erection.

"The lousy part is I don't get to watch your tits if your back is turned," he said, taking hold of her hips. "Next time I'll put a mirror at the foot of the bed so I can see you from both the front and back. And so you can see yourself."

"Tyler!" Kate's arousal skyrocketed.

He chuckled, putting one of her legs over his hips so she was facing his feet. "Turn around and let me see your gorgeous ass move, Darling."

Kate's teeth sank into her lower lip. She scooted backward and straddled his waist. She felt strangely vulnerable not being able to see his face or read his expressions.

She took a breath and grasped his shaft, positioning herself right over him. Oh lord, he was staring at her bottom. Slowly she lowered her body, feeling the head of his cock penetrate her. Tyler's grip on her hips tightened.

"Ah, fuck, yeah…" He thrust his hips upward.

Kate moaned. Sweat trickled between her breasts as she lowered herself onto him inch by exquisite inch. When he was fully seated inside her, she stopped and took a breath.

"Oh my God, Tyler..."

She leaned forward, bracing her hands on his thighs. He felt impossibly big. She lifted herself up and down experimentally, adjusting to both the position and his sheer size. She swiveled her hips and wiggled a little from side to side.

"Fucking amazing." Tyler stroked his hands over her ass, parting her cheeks. Kate shuddered, pausing for a heart-stopping second when he ran his finger down the cleft of her bottom. Her spine tingled.

"Tyler..."

"Kate." He withdrew his finger and squeezed her cheeks. "After you come, I'm going to rub my dick up and down your ass, over your pussy, and then I'm going to shoot all over your pretty cheeks. I can't wait to see you dripping with my come."

Lord in heaven, he was going to be the death of her. Or the *life* of her.

His raw words sank deep inside her, setting her nerves on fire. Shaking with excitement, she continued riding him, her arousal mounting higher and higher with each thrust. Her thighs trembled with strain, and her body burned.

All lingering embarrassment slipped away, replaced by the drenching heat of pleasure. She braced her hands on his thighs and circled her hips before moving up and down.

A dim part of her realized she *was* sort of twerking naked, given the way her bottom was bouncing, but wow, did it feel good. She felt Tyler's gaze scrape hotly over her back, his hands sliding everywhere he could reach, his body heavy and hard beneath her.

Then he spanked her, a light stinging slap that sparked through her. She gripped the bedcovers beside his legs and leaned forward, rounding her ass out further to indicate she wanted more. He grunted his approval before spanking her again, the little smacks creating a pattern of heat that intensified her arousal to the breaking point.

"Tyler, I'm so...so close."

"Touch yourself, Kate." His voice was hoarse with lust. "Bring yourself off."

Kate slipped her fingers into her cleft. One light press of her fingers, and an orgasm exploded through her, tearing a cry from her throat. She shuddered, clenching around his shaft. The sensations flowed and ebbed.

Tyler cursed, one hand digging into her hip as he slid out of her. Panting, Kate twisted to peer at him over her shoulder. Her heart slammed into her chest at the sight of him—eyes smoldering, sweat glistening on his muscles, and his jaw set with restraint.

He pulled the condom off and, true to his word, rubbed his thick cock between her bottom cheeks. Kate shivered, her fists tightening on the bed sheets. He gave a rough shout, his body tensing beneath hers before warm seed splashed over her ass.

Kate lowered her head and closed her eyes, fighting to catch her breath. Her whole body trembled with lingering aftershocks over having indulged in something both dirty and delicious.

He expelled his breath on a hard sigh and tugged her back toward him. She collapsed at his side, her eyes closed. He brushed his hand against her forehead, pushing her hair away from her face. She opened her eyes to find him watching her, his expression warm with affection.

Her heart tightened, like it was being gently enclosed in his hand.

"Okay?" he asked.

"Oh, yes. I can't wait to try the mirror next time."

He grinned and pressed his lips against her temple. She tucked herself against his side and closed her eyes, letting sleep wash over her.

She woke with a sudden start, disoriented and thirsty. She peered at the clock. 1:00 a.m.

Beside her, Tyler was sound asleep. She rose to one elbow to look at him. She traced his dark eyebrows, touched the spiky lashes resting against his cheekbones, and rubbed her finger over his beautiful mouth.

A warm, smooth feeling, like a shiny red ribbon, wound through her heart. *Not love.* She knew better than to fall in love with Tyler. But she liked him a lot, and in many ways—not all of which were physical—he'd become as close a friend to her as any she'd ever had.

She eased out of bed, pulling Tyler's discarded T-shirt over her head before going to get a drink of water from the fridge. As she drank it, she surveyed the mess.

She rummaged through the cupboards for black plastic garbage bags and went on a cleaning spree. She dumped the trash into the bags, cleaned up the living room, wiped down the granite countertops, hung sweatshirts in the front closet, and swept the floor. She was just putting away half-finished bags of chips and crackers when the front door opened.

Her heart leapt into her throat. Before she could call Tyler's name, male voices rose from the foyer. Three men ambled into the kitchen, two of whom Kate recognized from last Friday night at the Treetop Café. With them were two pretty girls wearing heavy makeup, miniskirts, and tight T-shirts.

They all stopped at the sight of her. One of the guys—Ben, she remembered—set a grocery bag and a twelve-pack of beer on the counter.

"Oh, hey, sorry," he said. "Didn't know Tyler had a girl over."

"I didn't realize he was supposed to check with you first."

Ben blinked, like he didn't understand her caustic tone. The two girls exchanged glances. One of the other guys—John—scratched his head.

"Uh, sorry about this," he said. "I texted Tyler that we were stopping by again, but I guess his phone was off or something."

Or something.

Kate felt one of the girls looking at her. The scrutiny made her acutely conscious of the fact that she wasn't wearing anything under Tyler's T-shirt. Not to mention, their combined fluids and sweat still lingered on her skin. She suppressed the urge to dart back into the bedroom and close the door.

Ben squinted at her. "Aren't you the girl Tyler was having dinner with the other night?"

"Kate," she replied stiffly.

"Yeah." He looked her up and down. "Nice to see you again. Didn't know you and Tyler had hooked up."

"Shut *up*, man." John smacked Ben on the back of the head.

Kate crossed her arms and leveled Ben with a cold look.

"We were just over at the Snowflake Club and thought we'd come here for a little after-party." He headed toward the fridge. "You can join us, if you want."

"What's going on?" Tyler's irritated voice pierced through the air. He stood in the bedroom doorway, wearing only his jeans and a dark frown.

"Tyler!" One of the girls swept over and wrapped her arms around him. "Omigod, I haven't seen you in *so* long. You look amazing."

She kissed his cheek, leaving a red imprint of her lips, and patted his bare chest. Tyler scowled and moved away from her.

"Get the hell out, all of you," he snapped.

"Miscommunication," John said quickly, stepping forward to grab the twelve-pack. "We're going. Sorry about the interruption."

"You don't have to go." Kate started toward the bedroom. "I need to leave anyway."

Tyler grabbed her arm as she tried to pass him in the doorway.

"You're not going anywhere," he said. "They're leaving. *Now*," he added, with another glare at his friends.

"You're seriously kicking us out?" The other girl's gaze slanted from Kate to Tyler and back again. "Come on, we're going to have some fun."

"Get out."

The harsh order stunned them all into silence. Kate slipped past Tyler and marched into the bedroom. Her hands shook as she retrieved her crumpled suit from the floor.

Old feelings of awkwardness and embarrassment crashed over her. She could only imagine what Tyler's "friends" would say about his new fuck buddy when she left.

Then again, why should she care? She wouldn't see any of them again after this affair was over. Tyler either.

"Kate, they're gone." Tyler came into the bedroom, frustration and anger still tightening his face. "I'm sorry. I didn't know they were coming."

"Do they often just show up like that?' She dressed quickly, crumpling up her stockings and shoving them in her bag. "I thought this was an apartment, not a frat house."

He compressed his mouth into a thin, rueful line. "I'm changing the locks. It won't happen again."

"They have a key?" Kate shook her head in disbelief.

"Kate." He stopped in front of her, blocking her path to the door. "I want you to stay."

Her breath hitched. She wanted to stay, too. But she wanted to stay because she and Tyler meant more to each other than just good sex. Because they were more than "a hook up." She wanted them to do all the things together that she'd imagined last night—travel, dinners, movies, adventures, curling up on the sofa to watch TV.

But while they were friends and having a good time together, they were also from totally different worlds. They could never succeed in an actual romantic relationship.

Self-disgust rose in her. She'd broken Unwritten Rule #1 of the fuck buddy relationship. *Don't let your heart get involved.*

Her heart was involved, all right. Deeply, painfully, irrevocably involved.

"Please stay," he said.

A sudden weight pressed down on her shoulders. She had two choices. Admit that she was head over heels for Tyler and break it off with him before she ended up flat on her face—which was the only feasible conclusion to falling in love with a fuck buddy. Or remember why she'd suggested this whole plan in the first place and try to keep her emotions in check.

Her intellect told her to do the former, while her heart begged for the latter.

She wasn't ready to give him up yet. And at Sugar Rush, she was a pro at concealing her emotions behind a wall of composure.

She could do that with Tyler, too. And if she was in love with him...well, that would be her own little secret. At least she'd know for the rest of her life what *love* felt like. Wild and exhilarating, but also warm and comforting. The heady anticipation of wanting to be with one person alone. Private jokes, teasing, trust, giving and taking, pancakes at 2:00 a.m. Bliss.

Maybe she'd already experienced more than most people had. And maybe she could make it last just a little bit longer.

"I'm going to go," she said.

Tyler's expression fell. Before he could open his mouth to protest, Kate held up her hand.

"I need to sleep at home, or I'll be a disaster at work tomorrow," she explained. "I'll try to come to the library before lunch, and we can keep working on putting books into the system."

The creases on his forehead cleared. She picked up her bag and walked toward the door. He caught her arm as she passed him, tugging her closer. The heat and scent of him filled her blood and expanded her heart.

"So we're still okay?" he asked, his dark gaze searching her face.

"Tyler, we were never *not* okay."

CHAPTER 22

"Kate? Kate."

The familiar voice sounded as if it were coming from a great distance. Kate jerked her head up.

Luke was looking at her expectantly. She sat up, pushing a stray lock of hair away from her forehead and trying to refocus her scattered brain on the fact that she was sitting at a meeting with the department heads of Alpine Chocolates, and her boss had apparently just asked her a question. About something.

"Er, excuse me?" she stammered.

"You have the trade reports with the new tariff regulations?" Luke asked.

"Yes, of course." Kate straightened, fumbling to distribute the reports she'd compiled a couple of weeks ago.

Before she'd gotten together with Tyler. Before he'd charmed her with his dance moves, made her laugh, kissed her, touched her, changed her whole world...

"Kate?" Luke repeated, his voice taking on an edge of impatience.

"Sorry." She shook her head as if to rid herself of her wayward thoughts. "If you'll open the reports to the first page, you'll see a summary of the regulations that will affect the import of chocolate from the Ivory Coast."

The executives all turned their attention to the paperwork. Kate struggled to maintain her focus for the next hour as they discussed tariffs and import fees. Under normal circumstances, she would have devoured all the information, but circumstances were far from normal. She didn't think they could ever be "normal" again.

When the meeting finally ended, she gathered her things and hurried back to her desk in the hopes of hiding behind work. Or the pretense of work.

She hadn't seen Tyler yet today. After last night, she was still feeling fragile, even a bit brittle, and she didn't want her façade to crack at work.

Her phone buzzed with a text.

T. STONE: Did you hear about the new library at the prison?
K. DARLING: No.
T. STONE: It's filled with prose and cons.

Before she could type a response, Luke strode to the desk, his face etched with a frown.

"You feeling okay, Kate?" he asked.

Much as she hated lying to him, even worse was the thought of telling him the truth.

Actually, I'm fuck buddies with your incredibly hot, sexy brother, but I desperately want more from him even though I'm not supposed to…

"I just have a slight headache," she assured him. "I'll be fine. Thanks for asking."

"Take off early," he suggested. "I'll handle my afternoon schedule." His eyebrows drew together as he studied her. "You look very nice, by the way. New haircut?"

"New everything." Kate gestured to her suit. "I asked your aunt Julia to help me improve my appearance. She knows what she's doing."

"She does, but for what it's worth, you didn't need improving."

"Thank you, sir." As much as she respected Luke, Tyler had told her the same thing. And it had meant so much more coming from him.

Luke headed into his office. "Email me the afternoon call list before you leave, please."

"Really, there's no need for me to leave early. I'm fine. I just took two aspirin."

"Kate, go home," he ordered. "No arguments."

She'd heard him use that commanding tone with any number of other employees.

This was terrible. She'd told herself—she'd told *Luke*—that she wouldn't let things with Tyler affect her performance at work. But ever since they'd gotten together, everything had changed.

With a sigh, she emailed him the list and packed up her briefcase. She took a folder from her filing cabinet, figuring she could make some use of the afternoon.

Outside, the morning coastal fog had burned off, leaving a blue sky and warm, glowing sun in its wake. Kate walked to the parking lot and saw Miles coming toward the main office, his blond head bent as he studied something attached to his ubiquitous clipboard.

A strange feeling rippled through Kate. Fear?

She shook her head. Silly.

As Miles drew closer, she couldn't help noticing how different he was from Tyler. Miles was so smooth and polished, utterly lacking Tyler's rakish charm and potent masculinity. Not to mention his good humor and his perceptive *noticing* of everything about her.

"Hello, Miles." She lifted a hand to shade her eyes from the sun. "Coming back from lunch?"

"Yes, I just met a friend downtown." His blue gaze focused on her face, but without that faintly indifferent quality with which he usually looked at her.

Downtown. She hoped the "friend" hadn't been Melanie McGuffin, though the hope was based less on jealousy and more on the fact that Melanie was a bitch. She didn't deserve a nice man like Miles.

"Did you go anywhere special?" she asked.

"Sushi at Takara. I had the salmon roll."

He liked sushi. Good to know. Unfortunately she didn't.

She took a step back, expecting him to do the same with his usual, "Have a nice day, Kate," but he didn't move. Instead he continued his intense scrutiny of her—almost like he was seeing her for the first time. She'd lost track of how many times she'd wished he would look at her that way, with actual interest sparking in his brown eyes.

"Did you do something to your hair?" Miles asked.

"Oh." Kate touched her hair, which she'd been wearing loose thanks to the new Julia-inspired style. "Yes, I had it cut recently."

"It looks nice."

Wow. A compliment from Miles Norwood. She might get excited any second now. Or not.

His gaze slid over her body clad in the Vera Wang suit. "Kate, would you like to have lunch with me on Monday? They're offering a new seaweed-tofu scramble at the Licorice Café."

Kate could only stare at him, shocked at the sudden realization of an event for which she had desperately hoped. Miles Norwood, her heartthrob crush, the brilliant data analyst who was her perfect soul mate, had just asked her to have lunch. How many times had she imagined this moment?

"Uh...okay," she said faintly, the words coming out almost of their own volition because in all her daydreams, not once had she ever imagined herself responding any other way.

"Great." He smiled, displaying a blindingly white set of teeth. "I'll meet you there around noon."

"Great," she echoed.

He nodded and walked back to the main building. Kate broke out of her stupor and continued on her way. She shook off the distressed feeling that she was being disloyal to Tyler. *This* had been the point of all these shenanigans.

Tyler was helping her be more romantically appealing to Miles. It was her own damned fault if the thought of dating Miles now held about as much appeal as...a seaweed-tofu scramble.

Not that this was a date. This was just lunch between colleagues. And maybe it would help her gain some emotional distance from Tyler.

She'd look forward to it soon enough—after all these months of pining for Miles and then getting overly caught up with Tyler, this *dream come true* had just caught her off guard. That was all.

She drove to downtown Indigo Bay and parked near the in-progress branch of Wild Child. A Knight Security truck sat by the curb, and the door was open to let the air circulate through the freshly painted interior.

Hannah and Polly both stood on ladders, painting a stenciled filigree border close to the ceiling. Gavin Knight was busy wiring something into the counter. And priming the wall on the other side of the room was...Tyler.

A mixture of both excitement and unease filled Kate—because as much as she wanted to be with him, her feelings were like a helium balloon, growing and expanding to immense proportions. Pressing against the walls of her heart. She wasn't at all certain she could keep so big a secret.

"Hi, Kate." Polly peered down from the ladder, pushing a lock of hair back under her bandana. "Wow, you look fantastic. Is that a new suit?"

Kate nodded, feeling Tyler looking at her as if he wanted to eat her.

"Courtesy of Julia Bennett," she told Polly.

Polly laughed. "She got her claws into you, huh? Good for her. Are you taking off early?"

"CEO's orders." Kate put the folder on a nearby table and tapped it with her forefinger. "Just wanted to drop these by on my way home. Placement permits for the dumpsters out back and the signage."

"Great, thanks."

Kate worked up the courage to look at Tyler, her whole body flushing with heat. He hadn't taken his eyes off her.

Her blood warmed. In a paint-splattered T-shirt and worn jeans, his hair-roughened arms corded with muscle, Tyler was the exact opposite of polished Miles. And there was no question that her body liked what Tyler could offer.

Heck. Her body *wanted* what he could offer. Craved it. Lusted for it.

"Hi, Tyler." She smiled weakly and gave him a little wave. "How are you?"

"I'm good, Kate. How are you?"

Wishing you'd come over here, haul me into your arms, and kiss me senseless.

"I'm fine," she squeaked. "Why aren't you at the library?"

"I took off early too. Came to help finish painting."

Polly glanced from her to Tyler and back again. "So, Kate, do you want anything to eat or drink? There are still some sandwiches in the back left from the lunch Evan brought over."

"No, thanks." She backed toward the door, her nerves humming. "I'm just going to head home. Thanks."

She turned and hurried out. She had almost reached her car when Tyler fell into step beside her. Every cell in her body lit up with pleasure.

"Come on, Darling." He indicated his Trans Am parked at the curb. "We'll get your car later. I want to talk to you about something."

She had to talk to him about "something," too. Namely, the fact that she was having lunch with Miles Norwood on Monday.

Though her chest tightened with misgiving, she got into the Trans Am and tried to work up the courage to tell him. He knew the point of all this had been for her to attract Miles. Technically, he should be happy about the fact that she was having lunch with the other man because that could lead to them actually dating.

But Kate couldn't bear the thought of Tyler being *happy* about her even having lunch with another man, much less dating him.

And what would happen if she did actually start seeing Miles? Surely that would be the end of her and Tyler, because even though he'd said that fuck buddies sometimes dated other people, she would never be able to date one man while being in lo... sleeping with another.

And she'd certainly never tell Miles about Tyler, which would mean she'd have to lie...so no. That would be it. Dating Miles meant her relationship with Tyler would end.

Except lunch at the corporate headquarters wasn't a *date.* Maybe Miles wanted to discuss the data analyst report she'd compiled for the next board meeting. There was no need for her to tell Tyler about a business lunch. If it turned out that Miles did intend for the lunch to be a prelude to a real date, then she had time to figure that out later.

Relieved at having come to that conclusion, Kate settled against the leather seat. Tyler drove through downtown and navigated back to her house. He pulled into the driveway and parked.

"What did you want to talk to me about?" she asked.

"I was going to tell you at the library, but you didn't show up this morning." He opened the trunk to take out a cardboard storage box. "So I was going to come over after work."

"Is that a box of library books?" Kate unlocked her front door and preceded him into the house.

"Yep. Take a look." He set the box on the coffee table and removed the lid. "I found a whole stack of them."

Kate leafed through one of the tattered leather-bound books, which contained pages of scrawled, handwritten notes, and drawings.

"Are these all recipes?" she asked.

"Some of them are also Stone Confectioners' history," Tyler said. "But there are a bunch of recipes, some with additional notes about what worked and what didn't. There are also drawings of candy and chocolate-making machines, and lists of what Edward Stone wanted to sell."

"These are amazing." Kate scanned a page filled with information about tempering chocolate. "How many are there?"

"A couple dozen, at least. They were shoved way in the back of the alcove. Remember when you said it would be fun to try to recreate the recipes? I asked Spencer if he could do that, but what if Sugar Rush put out a line of historical Stone Confectioners' chocolate and candy, like the kind Edward Stone sold in the nineteenth century? And based on the same recipes?"

Kate was struck by the eagerness in his eyes, the energy radiating from him. Like light.

"Tyler, that's an incredible idea," she said. "Have you mentioned it to Luke?"

He shook his head. "I wanted to talk to you first. I didn't tell Spence why I was interested in seeing if the recipes could still be made."

"The tech department is working on a revamp of the website and including a whole new section about the history of Sugar Rush. That would be a great thing to tie in with a proposal for a historical product line."

"You think we could do an actual proposal?"

We. Two tiny letters that contained a thousand possibilities. He studied one of the pages, a line of concentration between his dark eyebrows and a paint smudge on his forehead. The fragile book looked incongruous in his big hands, but he held it with infinite care, like he was holding his family's history.

Oh, I love you, Tyler Stone.

He glanced up and caught her staring at him. Kate jerked her attention back to the book she held.

"You should definitely write a proposal," she said.

"*We* should write a proposal."

"It's your idea, Tyler."

"No." He shook his head. "It's our idea. I wouldn't have thought of it if you hadn't brought it up. I won't do it without you. Hell, I *can't* do it without you. I don't know anything about business proposals."

Kate's insides softened with tenderness. "I'll help you with it. I know Luke would be interested in a project like this. I'm sure your father would be as well."

"So how do we start?"

She smiled. "With a notepad and a pencil."

She went into the bedroom to change out of her suit and into a pair of yoga pants and a pink T-shirt. For the next few hours, she and Tyler sat at her dining table, perusing all the books and taking notes about recipes, ingredients, techniques. Tyler did a lengthy internet search about historical candy products, and Kate dug into her files for information about marketing and the company customer base.

"Tomorrow, we can look for ads that show the original packaging," she suggested, lifting her arms above her head to stretch. "We can include a section in the proposal about retro packaging. Maybe include Stone Confectioners somewhere on the package to show it's the heritage of Sugar Rush."

Tyler sat back in his chair, surveying the clutter of books on the table and the notepads filled with scribbled notes.

"Thanks for doing this with me." He glanced at his watch. "Almost five. Come on, I'll repay you with an early dinner. I didn't eat lunch."

"I have a baked ziti in the fridge." Kate got to her feet. "I made it last night, so it just has to be heated up."

They went into the kitchen. She put the casserole in the oven, and Tyler uncorked a bottle of wine. After pouring, they clinked the glasses together.

"To great ideas," Kate said.

"And great friends." He winked at her and took a swallow of wine.

Friends. They were great friends. She could be happy with that alone. Again, it was more than a lot of people had.

After a dinner spent discussing everything from their favorite candy to the latest storyline in the *Batman* franchise, they sat in the living room finishing up bowls of chocolate-chip ice cream.

Tyler leaned over to put his empty plate on the coffee table. He picked up the DVD of *My Fair Lady*. "Were you watching this?"

"Re-watching," Kate corrected. "I had it on last night while I was working. I can't believe you've never seen it."

"Have you seen *My Bare Lady*?" He lifted an eyebrow in challenge.

"I have not." Kate took the disc from the box and slipped it into the DVD player.

"But you've seen porn, right?"

"Of course I've seen porn." She scoffed and sat beside him on the sofa with the TV remote. "I have an internet connection, for heaven's sake. Come on, let's rectify this lack in your education."

She hit the play button before he could stop her. Tyler let out a sigh of resignation, but settled back against the cushions. Five minutes in, he was yawning, but ten minutes in, he muttered something about the movie being "not horrible" and asked if she had any popcorn.

Kate left him watching the movie while she made popcorn. She returned and handed him the bowl, then settled beside him again. If she let herself, she could imagine so many more evenings like this, seated close to Tyler on the sofa after a day at work. Feeling the warmth of his strong thigh beside hers, the brush of his granite-hard arm, the rumbling sound of his snore...

Snore?

"Tyler." Kate pinched his arm lightly. "Really? You fell asleep?"

"Sorry." He pulled himself out of a doze, his eyes unfocused as he peered at the TV. "I'm awake. Is there still rain in Spain?"

"It's halfway over." Kate shook her head at him in amusement before turning off the DVD player. "I see you found it thrilling."

"It wasn't bad." He rubbed his eyes. "Higgins is kind of a dick, though, huh?"

"No more so than the Higgins in *My Bare Lady*, I assume," Kate replied dryly. "Especially if, as you said, there is spanking involved."

"Want to see for yourself?"

Kate's heart bumped against her chest. He wasn't serious...was he?

"Um...you carry the movie around with you?" she asked.

"No. But it's probably for rent." Tyler reached for the remote. He did a quick search and pulled the movie up on a channel. He hit the rent button, and a box appeared onscreen prompting him for a password.

He handed the remote to Kate. She hesitated for an instant, then punched in the password and confirmed the rental. Seconds later, the movie started.

With a bang.

CHAPTER 23

"*Oh, yeah...fuck me harder...I feel your cock so deep inside me... yeah...spank me...*"

Oh my God.

She wasn't doing this. She was not sitting here in her very own living room, watching a porn flick with Tyler Stone. She was not getting tingly and hot and intensely curious.

Except that she was.

"This is a bad idea," she said, her voice oddly squeaky.

Tyler shot her a grin. He was sprawled on the other side of the sofa, his feet planted on the floor and his long, muscular body relaxed. Watching explicit movies with a woman was likely no big deal to him.

Heck, he and his dates probably created their own movies in the bedroom. Based on what she'd seen of his girlfriends on social media, they all had bodies that would look amazing naked.

Not that she wanted to be thinking about his dates or girl-friends.

Him, on the other hand. That sculpted wall of muscle with hard, corded thighs and a ripped abdomen with a trail of hair leading right down to—

Was it okay to want to jump his bones because of a porn flick? Why did that feel so dirty? And so wildly exciting?

She shifted, folding her arms over her breasts and crossing her legs. She tore her gaze away from Tyler and refocused on the screen, where the movie had gotten right down to action with Higgins banging one of his students on his desk.

The girl was stretched out on her belly, gripping the other side of the desk with him thrusting into her from behind. They were both grunting and moaning so loudly that Kate hoped her neighbors didn't hear.

"I'm pretty sure that's against university rules," she remarked.

Tyler chuckled. "You don't ever break the rules, huh?"

"Not *that* rule."

She wiggled again and squeezed her thighs together, letting out her breath slowly. She was almost embarrassed by how wet she already was—though she wasn't sure if her arousal was from the movie or the sudden image of Tyler doing the same thing to her. On *her* desk.

She bit her lip to stifle a moan. If she were alone, she'd already have her hand down her panties.

She felt him looking at her, and she tore her attention from the screen to face him. A faint tension stretched through his body. His eyes gleamed with both curiosity and growing heat.

"So what rules have you broken, Darling?" he asked.

The one about not letting my heart get involved in a fuck buddy arrangement.

"Kissing you in the library is probably one of them," she said.

"We could do a lot more in the library, you know."

Kate made a *tsking* noise, even as her mind filled with images of Tyler fucking her against a library bookshelf. She shivered.

"Have you ever done something like that?" She gestured to the TV, where the actors were still going at it hot and heavy.

"Sure."

Her pulse sped up. "You've had sex with a woman on a desk?"

"I've had sex with women in a bunch of places." He turned his gaze back to the movie. "A desk has been one of the most ordinary."

She tried to scoff. "A bed isn't the most ordinary?"

"A bed can be the most extraordinary place for a good fuck."

He said the word *fuck* the way he'd said *Kate* when they'd first met. Like he was crunching into a piece of hard candy. Like he was about to lean across the sofa and kiss her, using his tongue to urge her lips open so he could slide the candy from his mouth into hers and deepen the kiss until they were lost in a wave of sweet, hot pressure and the taste of melting peppermint candy...

Her body throbbed. Onscreen, Higgins had already approached Eliza and was giving her her first acting lesson in masturbating for the camera. Eliza rubbed her round breasts and spread her legs as she started touching herself.

Kate blushed hotly. Too much more of this, and she'd come from the visual stimulation alone.

Was Tyler as aroused as she was? She shot a quick glance at him. Her breath caught, fresh heat spiraling into her core.

An unmistakable bulge pressed against the fly of his trousers —one he was making no effort to conceal. He had one arm behind his head, and a taut energy coiled through the long muscles of his torso and thighs.

He returned her gaze. Electricity charged the air. Kate's heartbeat hammered in her head. He took her hand and tugged her closer. Her whole body was primed, ready for him to kiss her, to take her...

The music of "Super Freak" burst through the room suddenly. Tyler muttered a curse and pulled away from her, grabbing his cell from the coffee table. He glanced at the screen and started to toss the phone aside, then stopped.

He hit the reply button. "Yeah?"

Seriously? He was answering the phone instead of kissing her?

"That's awesome, man, thanks. I'll be right over." He ended the call and pushed to his feet. "Sorry, sweetie, I gotta go."

"What?"

"Really sorry." He touched her hair, regret flashing over his expression before he started toward the door. "But I've been waiting for, like, months, and they're finally in."

"What are you talking about?"

He grabbed his keys from the foyer table. "You want to come with me?"

"Where?" With a grumble of irritation over the fact that he was choosing an errand over hot, porn-inspired sex with her, Kate picked up her bag and followed him to his car.

"Where are we going?" she asked again, when he reversed out of the driveway.

"You'll see."

Kate spent the drive into Rainsville attempting less-than-successfully to quell her lust. Evening sunlight slanted across the windshield of the Trans Am. Tyler bypassed Wild Child and the downtown shopping district before heading into a sparsely populated neighborhood.

After a few turns, he pulled up beside a somewhat rundown garage. Old cars sat in the grassy lot outside, their hoods flipped open to reveal the grimy innards.

"What are we doing here?" Kate got out of the car, reaching down to pet a black lab that bounded up in greeting.

"I'll show you."

Tyler tossed the dog a treat as they walked over a gravel-strewn path to the garage, where a grizzled man of about fifty held up a hand from the open bay.

"Hey, man, I put them on the worktable. Finally, huh?"

"You're not kidding. Charlie, this is Kate. Kate, my friend Charlie."

"Hi, Charlie." Kate extended her hand.

He grinned, wiping his greasy palm on his overalls before shaking her hand. "Nice to meet you. First girl Tyler's ever brought over here."

"Most girls aren't interested in cars." Tyler grasped Kate's elbow and guided her into the garage.

The familiar smells of engine oil and grease filled her head. Cars sat in several different bays, some perched on hydraulic lifts, and tools lined the tables and benches.

Her father's garage hadn't been anything like this—just an attachment to their little house—but the feel of it was the same. Two other men lounged in lawn chairs outside the garage, and they gave her and Tyler nods of greeting.

At the end of the garage, a car sat beneath a blue cover. Tyler stopped and tugged the cover up over the hood, then rolled it back over the windshield. Before he'd even gotten the cover halfway off, Kate was staring at the silvery blue car in astonishment.

"Is that a California Special?" she asked.

"'68." He shot her a grin across the hood. "I thought you'd appreciate it."

Kate ran her hand over the fender. "Where in the world did you get this?"

"A few years ago, a fellow over in Salinas called Charlie about a bunch of barn finds. You know, cars that've been found abandoned in old garages or barns." He patted the car. "This was one of them. I'd just dropped out of college and was spending all my time futzing with old cars, which my father didn't like.

"So when I heard about the barn finds, I figured I'd piss him off even more by spending his money on an old junk car. So I bought this car, had it towed over here, and told Charlie I wanted to learn how to restore it. After he finished laughing, we sat down and came up with a plan. I stripped the car down to the bones and have been working on rebuilding it from the floor pan up."

"It's beautiful." Kate walked around looking at the car from all angles. "How long has it taken you?"

"A few years. It's been hard to find all the original parts, so we've had to do a lot of searching and waiting." He went to a workbench, where two red lights sat. "The taillights just came in. That's what Charlie called about. I'm still looking for a '68 gas cap with the Mustang emblem, but we're close to being finished."

"What will you do with it when you're done?"

"Charlie wants me to take it to car shows." Tyler went around to the back of the car to study the tail section. "Mostly I just did it to see if I could."

"Why did your father not like you restoring old cars?"

"At the time, I was just hanging around the garage changing oil and whatnot," Tyler said. "It wasn't so much the car repair my father didn't like as the fact that I'd dropped out of college to do it. And it wasn't even a job…just something I did when I had nothing else to do. The president of Sugar Rush doesn't like it when you don't have anything else to do."

Kate could see the president's point, but Tyler was down-playing his accomplishments.

"Restoring a Mustang is no easy task," she said. "It takes serious dedication, commitment, attention to detail. Does your father still not realize that?"

Tyler shrugged. "He knows I'm into old cars and that I've been working on the Mustang, but he's never seen it. It's just a hobby."

"Would you stop putting yourself down?" Kate rounded the car and paused next to him, her ire rising at the discovery that no one, not even his family, not even Tyler himself, realized how much he had to offer. His *value*.

"I know about car restoration, Tyler." She poked him in the chest to emphasize her point. "It's an art. It's taking something that's been ruined and making it fresh and new again. It's about unearthing hidden beauty and bringing history to life. If your family doesn't understand that, that's one thing. But don't you dare try and tell yourself you're not doing something extraordinary here."

He didn't look at her, rubbing at a spot of dirt on the fender. Kate stepped back.

Uh oh, had she crossed a line? But hadn't they been doing that since the beginning? They'd been breaking all the fuck buddy rules.

Maybe *friends with benefits* had a different set of rules. Despite him telling her the terms meant the same thing, Kate didn't think so. Friends did things together. They talked, had dinner, shared interests, went to the movies. They let each other into their lives. Maybe when the *benefits* part between them was over, they'd still hold on to the *friends* part. Because her life would be very empty without Tyler in it.

Her chest constricted. She turned and started back out to the Trans Am.

"Hey." Tyler came up behind her, touching her arm. "What's going on?"

"I just think...I mean, you're better than everyone else seems to realize." Kate swallowed past the sudden tightness in her throat. "Even you. I get that your brothers are all mature and accomplished, but that doesn't mean they're better than you. And it doesn't mean you don't have something to offer. You've hidden behind this party-boy image for all these years because you've thought you'll never be like your brothers. But you've never realized that you don't have to be. Yeah, you've acted like a total ass... a speedboat, for God's sake...but you don't have to do stupid things like that for attention. All you have to do is be you, Tyler. That's more than enough."

The sunlight reflected off his thick hair, the ends glowing blond. His eyes were golden-brown, the color of topaz, his skin bronzed. Kate knew that at no time in the future would she ever again meet someone like him. A comet who had swooped into her path and set her life on fire.

Before she'd realized he'd moved, he was pulling her into his arms. She fell against the hard wall of his chest the instant his mouth came down on hers. The world dissolved to nothing except the pressure of his strong arms around her and the quest of his lips.

She put her arms around his waist and held on as if he were an anchor in a shifting sea. He slipped his tongue into her mouth, licked the corners of her lips. Through the thin material of his T-shirt, his heart beat faster, the thumping sound echoing through her and settling in her core.

Only when the whoops and cat-calls of the other men filtered through the haze of lust did they finally ease apart. Tyler smiled at her, moving to block her from sight as he flipped the men off.

Seconds later, they were driving the Trans Am back to her house. Kate thought they'd return to working on the historical candy proposal, but when they went inside, Tyler closed the door, spun her around, and backed her right up against it for a hot kiss. He pushed his hands under her pants and tugged them down her thighs.

"Oh...um..." Kate squirmed, breathless. "Should we go into the..."

"We will," he assured her.

He trailed his lips to her neck and bit gently at her collarbone while his hand wiggled into her underwear.

Kate's head spun. Before he'd even gotten a finger inside her, she was melting from the inside out. A sudden fire lit in the air, and then he was yanking impatiently at the rest of her clothes, his body lacing with tension.

His urgency fired her own. Kate shoved her hands under his T-shirt, stroking the slopes of his pecs as she jumped up to wrap her legs around his waist.

He grabbed her ass and stalked into the bedroom, where he lowered her onto the bed, stripped them both out of their clothes, and planted himself solidly on top of her. Kate lost all track of time, the surroundings, even her own name as he plunged inside her and started to thrust. To *fuck.*

God in heaven, she loved it—this stunning, delicious plunging in and out, the friction and heat flooding them both, the wet smacking sound of their bodies. She loved their sweat running together, the bite of his teeth on her neck, the flex of his shoulder muscles beneath her fingers. She loved the way he hooked her legs over his forearms to deepen his penetration, and she loved his raw, throaty whispers of encouragement when he sensed she was close to the edge.

She came over and over, with cries, screams, and whimpers, until Tyler spent himself inside her and they collapsed, exhausted, against the pillows.

She loved *him.* She only wished she could tell him that.

CHAPTER 24

"Dude, you're in my light." Spencer slanted Tyler an exasperated frown.

Tyler couldn't help it. He was almost jittery with anticipation.

Spencer's work in the lab had always seemed mystical to him —like his brother was some sort of wizard with his formulas and potions—but watching him recreate historic Sugar Rush recipes had been downright cool.

Spencer had walked Tyler through the processes of roasting and winnowing the cocoa beans, then grinding them into chocolate. Then he showed Tyler how to use the tempering machine, which formed the chocolate into bars.

He leaned closer to watch Spencer pull the chocolate from the candy mold. Shiny and a rich, earthy brown, the rough-hewn block almost glowed under the light.

"Is it staying together?" he asked.

"So far so good. And no mutton suet needed." Spencer extended his gloved hand to show Tyler the finished lump of chocolate. "Pure chocolate with only sugar, salt, and spices."

Tyler picked up a knife and broke two pieces off the block. He handed one to his brother before taking a bite. Though grainier in texture than modern chocolate due to the traditional process of stone-grinding, the chocolate was pretty good—semisweet with hints of pepper, nutmeg, and cinnamon.

"I think we got it." Spencer took another bite. "The brittleness is a result of the manufacturing technique. This kind of chocolate would probably have been grated and melted into milk to make hot cocoa. There's another recipe that includes musk, ambergris, and pistachios. I'm going to work on that next. After I figure out if musk and ambergris are even food safe."

"What about the Gold Rush bar?" Tyler asked.

"It's a more recent recipe, so it's smoother and sweeter. As close to the original as we can get."

Tyler broke another piece of chocolate off the block. "And the other candy recipes?"

"The honey candy isn't too different from what we've done recently," Spencer mused. "I'd like to give the lollipops a try, though based on the formula I think they might be too soft."

"They were supposed to be," Tyler said. "Edward Stone sold them in food carts on the street, and he put them on sticks because it was more convenient for people to eat on the go. So the candy itself had to be soft so it would be easier to fit onto the stick."

Spencer's eyebrows lifted. "Sounds like you're doing more than just shuffling books in the library. Good for you."

"It's neat, this whole history thing," Tyler said. "I never knew Stone Confectioners sold chocolates and candy that we don't even make anymore. Don't you think that stuff is an important part of the company's heritage?"

"Well, sure, but times change," Spencer said. "Maybe they didn't sell, or there was a problem with suppliers and the company had to cut back."

"Still, we have all the recipes." Tyler spread out his hand to indicate the digitized pages he'd given his brother. "Cream candy, molasses candy, vinegar candy. How many of them do you think you could recreate?"

"As many as we want." Spencer shook his head, amusement lighting his eyes. "Man, I've never seen you so into anything that doesn't have big tits and long legs. What's going on with you?"

Tyler was too excited to be insulted. He and Kate had come up with a *big idea* that could be even bigger, if he could get his brothers on board. And why wouldn't they want to be? This was Stone Confectioners and Sugar Rush's history all bundled up with shiny gold foil and ribbons.

"Text me when you finish the bar and the truffles," he told his brother. "When do you think you'll have them ready for tasting?"

"Soon as I can, man." Spencer still looked amused. "I'll let you know."

"Thanks."

Tyler left the lab and hurried across the campus. He was eager to get back to the library and see what else he could find about the Stone Confectioners' recipes.

As he approached the Gumdrop Bistro, the door opened. His father and Julia stepped out, their heads bent in conversation. With Warren in his tailored suit and tie patterned with candy hearts and Julia in a navy sheath dress, they looked like they should be holding court.

Julia saw him first and came to a stop. "Tyler, I sent you an email about a fundraiser for the Cocoa Bean Team. Don't forget to reply."

"I won't. Hey, thanks for helping Kate out. She looks great. I mean, she always looked great, but she's been wanting to get new clothes."

Julia blinked, as if she couldn't fathom why he was thanking her. "You know Kate?"

"Sure." Suddenly realizing he should have been less obvious,

Tyler shrugged. "I mean, she's helping with the tech stuff at the library."

"She's invaluable," Warren said. "Luke is lucky to have found her."

So was Tyler, but he wasn't about to confess that to his father and aunt. He switched the topic so he didn't inadvertently say something else to give himself away.

"We're well into getting the library resources installed in the system," he said. "And we're initiating proper handling procedures as well. Nothing has been stored right, but we're fixing it all now."

"Good." Warren nodded, a pleased gleam appearing in his eyes. "You seem to be doing well, Tyler. We'll get together this weekend, and I'll give you a check for your work so far. You can bring it over to Dan Corrigan, both as a first payment and a good faith gesture."

The reminder of *why* he was working at the library didn't bother Tyler nearly as much as it once would have. Yeah, he was being punished, but he deserved it. He'd fucked up. But he was fixing his fuck-up.

Though it would take him months to make all his payments, he was starting to find comfort in having a plan. He'd never had a plan before. For the first time in his life, he knew where he'd be tomorrow and the next day. The schedule didn't seem as confining as it did predictable.

And of course, there was always Kate.

"I'll text you," he told his father before moving past them into the bistro. "Hey, I also need to talk to you and Luke about digitizing the collection, especially the old recipes and handwritten journals. It would be great to have everything stored in a centralized database so anyone can access it."

Julia and Warren exchanged bemused glances.

"That's a great idea," Warren said. "We'll talk about it this weekend."

And Tyler would be ready. He'd learned more about digital collections in the past week than he'd known his entire life.

He ordered two smoothies, then headed back to the library to both work and wait for Kate.

CHAPTER 25

"So ultimately data analysis drives decision-making." Miles sliced a cherry tomato with his knife and slipped half of it into his mouth. "But first the company has to improve key metrics to reach its strategic objectives."

Kate nodded in agreement, though she was only half-listening. Miles ate the way she'd imagined he would—with careful precision and neatness. Not like Tyler, who dived into his food with ravenous pleasure, wolfing down bites and licking his fingers as if he'd never be able to satisfy his appetite.

He fucked the same way. Greedy, hungry, messy. Delicious.

She shivered.

"Are you cold?" Miles glanced up at the clear blue sky. "We can move more into the sun, if you'd like."

"I'm fine, thank you." Kate poked at her salad with her fork. "So have you seen any good movies lately?"

"Yes, I saw an excellent independent film at the San Francisco film festival last week." He patted his lips with his napkin and reached for his bottle of vitamin water. "It was by the German director Reinhold Werner Hollister, and it was a very provocative attack on the gestalt of German cinema."

Was Tyler in the library right now? Maybe he was grooving to "Hot Chocolate." She pictured his hips gyrating, his muscular body moving with easy fluidity...

Miles was still talking. Kate snapped her attention back to him. *Gestalt.* That was important, relevant stuff right there. Much more cultured than '70s disco music. She was enormously interested in topics like gestalt and zeitgeist.

"That sounds great," she said, half-wondering if she should get more dressing for her Chinese chicken salad. "What other films were at the festival?"

Miles went on about a few more movies from Russian and Spanish directors. Kate was glad that he didn't seem to notice she wasn't participating in the conversation very much.

When he started talking about the conceptual framework of modern cinema, she discreetly reached into her jacket for her cell phone to check the time. Her fingers touched the empty holster. She'd forgotten her cell phone. She never forgot her cell phone.

"Miles, I'm sorry." She gave an apologetic smile and rose to her feet. "It seems I've forgotten my phone. I should get back to my desk and check in with Luke."

"Oh, okay." He squinted at her. "This was a pleasure. Thank you for joining me."

"Thank you for asking me."

He stood respectfully as she collected her tray and crumpled napkin. Manners, indeed. Though for all his party-boy reputation, Tyler had manners too. He always opened doors for her, stepped aside to let her precede him, and made sure she came first.

Kate choked back a laugh. She had to stop comparing the two men. It was like comparing day and...quiche. The bright, blazing sun of Tyler Stone and the pleasant, if a bit bland, taste of Miles.

Her stomach twisted as she walked away. Much as she loved being warmed in Tyler's presence, she was fair-skinned and always ended up burning if she stayed in the sun too long.

She wasn't an outdoorsy type anyway, what with all the bugs and mosquitos. Not to mention, she didn't dance, didn't eat junk food, and she held a high-level, respectable position in an enormously successful company.

Serious, dedicated Miles, who would be perfectly content to sit at home on weekends, was her tribe. Not party boy Tyler, who'd be out painting the town red with his bros and at least half a dozen hot girls.

At least, she needed to convince herself of that.

With new resolve strengthening her spine, she returned to the office. She found her cell phone on her desk and sent Miles a text: *Thanks again for lunch. Let me know if you need any help with the reports.*

Her phone buzzed with an incoming text.

T. STONE: What kind of pastry comes with a thesaurus?

K. DARLING: ?

T. STONE: Synonym rolls.

K. DARLING: Cute.

T. STONE: C'mere. I have a large smoothie for you.

K. DARLING: Is that what you're calling it now?

"Kate?" The door to Luke's office opened.

She turned. "Yes, sir?"

"Could you come in for a moment, please?" Luke stepped aside and gestured for her to enter his office.

Kate's heart began a slow sink into her belly. Her boss's expression, as usual, gave nothing away but usually when he summoned her into his office, she had some idea of why she was needed. Now all she could think about was that between Tyler and the library, she'd somehow let one of her EA balls drop.

"Of course, sir." She reached for her notebook.

"You don't need that," Luke said.

Well, shit. Her notebook was her armor.

She smoothed the wrinkles from her skirt and preceded Luke into his office. Her heart sank a few more inches when she saw Evan Stone sitting in one of the leather chairs. Then it plummeted to her toes when Warren Stone—*Warren Freaking Stone*—turned from looking out the vast windows.

"Hello, Kate." Warren crossed the room to her, all corporate presidential in his tailored gray suit and silk tie patterned with candy hearts. "Nice to see you again."

Kate struggled not to start shaking. Under normal circumstances, she liked Warren and had a good relationship with him, but he could be unforgiving and even a little scary when something went wrong. Which seemed to be the case at the moment, though she had no idea why.

"Have a seat, Kate." Evan rose from his seat and extended a hand to the opposite chair.

A touch of panic rose in her. Was she about to get fired? How would she explain that to her father?

Don't cry, Kate. Whatever you do, don't cry.

She sat down and forced a smile. "Did I miss a memo?"

"No." Luke sat in the chair beside his brother, and Warren took the seat opposite him so they were all in a tidy little square seating arrangement. "We have something we want to discuss with you."

She'd made a mistake. A horrible one, if it meant two of the Stone brothers and their father had to "discuss" it with her.

Kate scoured her brain for what she might have done, but came up empty. Surely it couldn't have anything to do with Tyler because Luke would have asked her about that privately, if it were an issue—not ambush her like this.

"How do you like working here, Kate?" Warren asked.

"Very much so, sir." She gripped the arms of the chair. "I told Luke not long ago that I love my job. I think I'm good at it too."

"You're better than good," Luke agreed. "You're an exceptional assistant. I would hate to lose you."

Kate tried to smile. "Is there some reason you would?"

Evan and Luke exchanged knowing glances.

"We've been very impressed with the work you've done not only for me," Luke continued, "but for the other executives at Sugar Rush. Your work with Evan's Cocoa Bean Team has been invaluable, not to mention your help with the website content and reports for all the global divisions. As a former workaholic, even I'm amazed by how you manage to do it all without letting anything fall by the wayside."

"And you don't do it partway either," Evan added. "You complete all the tasks thoroughly and very well."

"I like to triple check things," Kate said, unsure if she should be relaxing a bit or getting more nervous. This didn't sound like the start of a reprimand, but maybe they were waiting to drop the bomb. "And I've enjoyed helping out wherever I'm needed. I've learned so much about the company and business in general."

"We've noticed that," Luke said. "And we've thought for a while now that we're underutilizing you by keeping you in an assistant position."

Tears sprang to Kate's eyes, and she couldn't keep the question in any longer. "Are you firing me?"

The three men stared at her in astonishment. Evan's mouth even dropped open.

"Firing you?" he repeated.

"What gave you that idea?" Luke asked.

"Well, it sounds like you're about to get rid of me." Kate sniffled and tried to discreetly wipe the corner of her eye. "Telling me everything I've been doing right before giving me a list of everything I've done wrong."

Luke laughed—not his humorless laugh or his mild chuckle, but his booming, genuine laugh that filled the room with warmth. In response, Kate smiled tentatively, though her stomach still roiled with nerves.

"Kate, we're not firing you." Warren picked some papers off

the table. "But we do think that at some point, you're going to realize that what Luke just told you is true. As excellent an assistant as you are, you're not being utilized to your full capacity."

"And that's what we want to change," Luke added, "before another company lures you away from us."

"Sir, I'd never leave Sugar Rush," Kate assured him emphatically. She was so relieved at hearing that she wasn't getting fired that she'd have accepted a demotion, if necessary. "I care too much about this company and everything it does."

"Which is why..." Luke took the papers from his father and handed them to Kate. "We'd like to offer you a promotion to the position of Vice President of our new Corporate Social Responsibility division."

Kate stared at him. His face faded in and out of her vision.

"Excuse me?" she squeaked.

"Sugar Rush has always had a strong mission toward sustainability and social responsibility," Warren explained. "But with the launch of the Cocoa Bean Team, we want to make it more a part of our corporate infrastructure. The CSR division will continue to ensure that all our candy is made with ethically sourced products, to work with sugar and coffee plantations toward sustainable farming methods, find ways to reduce the company's environmental footprint, and create education and employment opportunities. Evan is already doing all of that with the Cocoa Bean Team, but we want it to be the driving force behind the whole company."

"And we want you to spearhead the initiatives," Luke said. "You know our brand as well as we do, you've worked with every department, and you have a strong knowledge of our global strategies and best practices. Not to mention, no one in this company knows how to organize and deploy an agenda better than you do. We have no doubt you could do that very successfully on a global scale."

Kate was about to cry again, but this time for a very different reason. She blinked hard to keep the tears at bay and tried to scan the job description Luke had given her.

"We don't want an answer right away." Warren nodded at the folder she held. "Take your time. Look over all the paperwork, the mission statement. Consider what you like about it and what you don't like. Think about what strategies you'd use, what goals you'd want to achieve. Write a list of any questions you have. Then we'll set up a meeting to talk about it more."

"I don't know what..." Kate stopped and cleared her throat. These three men were among the most powerful corporate leaders in the country, if not the world.

And they wanted *her*. She'd always known she was good at her job, but to be told that she was meant for so much more, that she could *do* more...

All this time she'd thought she was so unnoticeable. That hadn't been the case at all. They had *noticed* her. Good lord, how they'd noticed.

"Thank you." A smile bloomed across her face, pride and happiness bubbling inside her. "I'm so honored and flattered. Thank you *so* much."

"We're honored to have you consider it." Luke stood, returning her smile. "Evan and I will always be available to help you and answer questions, if needed."

With another round of thanks, Kate shook their hands, resisting the urge to hug them all, before hurrying back to her desk.

Funny how sometimes opportunities dropped right into your lap when you least expected. Even if you didn't know you were ready for them, the universe believed you were.

And sometimes the universe was right.

CHAPTER 26

*K*ate forced herself to wait until the workday was over before going to the library. Regardless of the magnitude of the offer, she was still—for now, at least—Luke's EA, and she still had work to do.

At six, she collected her things, texted Luke that she'd see him in the morning, and hurried to the library. Her stomach knotted with anxiety.

She wanted Tyler to be happy for her, but his relationship with his family and Sugar Rush was a bit complicated. What if he didn't like the idea of her being offered a promotion?

She knocked at the library door and peeked inside. He was at the computer, inputting books into the system.

"Hey, Darling." He turned, giving her a wide heart-stopping grin. "You're late. I had to drink your smoothie."

"I'll forgive you." She entered the library and closed the door behind her.

"Check this out." He took a box from under the desk and opened it to reveal a lumpy brown brick. "Eighteenth-century chocolate, courtesy of Stone Confectioners' history and lab-nerd Spencer Stone."

"Really?" She peered into the box. "He was able to recreate the recipe?"

"Yeah." Tyler broke off a piece and handed it to her. "It's weird because it's so different from modern chocolate, but it's interesting."

Kate bit into the chocolate, intrigued by the gritty texture and spices. *Interesting* was the right word. But that was part of the whole process—educating people about the history and techniques of chocolate while giving them a chance to sample what it once might have tasted like.

"I also mentioned the idea of digitizing the collection to my father," Tyler continued. "We're going to talk more about it. I think all the handwritten stuff should be digitized, at the very least. Maybe we need to start a priority list."

He grabbed a notepad and started writing. Kate smiled. She loved how dedicated he was becoming to the company's history, despite her recollection earlier that day of him as a "party boy."

Shame rustled through her. She'd known for a while now that Tyler was so much more than a party boy. And if anyone was her tribe, it was *him*—a smart, funny, loyal, crazy-sexy young man with a love for Monty Python and the singular ability to teach her how to have a good time.

"I have some news," she said.

"Good news?"

"I think so." She took a breath, her heart rate increasing. "I had a meeting with Luke, Evan, and your father this afternoon."

Tyler's expression didn't change, but a faint tightness lined his mouth. "About?"

"Nothing to do with us." She went around to his chair and leaned against the desk. "They offered me a promotion. Vice President of the Corporate Social Responsibility division."

Tyler stared at her for an instant before a smile broke out on his face, lighting his eyes. "That's amazing, Kate. Congratulations."

"Thank you." Relief spilled through her. "They told me to think it over."

"What's to think about? Of course you're going to take it. They couldn't have offered it to a better candidate."

She smiled, sliding her fingers into his thick hair. "You would be okay with me being a VP?"

"Why wouldn't I be? I know how good you are."

Kate drew her hand down the side of his face. The VP offer had emboldened her, but she realized now that she had been building up her courage to tell him the truth about her feelings for several days now.

"Luke might also be more inclined to listen to a VP when we pitch the historic candy line idea," Tyler said.

"You still want to do that?"

"Sure." A crease appeared between his eyebrows. "Don't you?"

"Of course, but..."

"But what?"

"Tyler." Kate lowered her hand and gripped her fingers together. "I know I don't have any fuck buddy experience, but this...this feels as if we've not only broken all the rules, but gone beyond the kind of relationship you described."

His jaw tightened. "For what it's worth, I never thought of you as a fuck buddy. A friend with benefits, yes, but only because that's what you seemed to want. I've always wanted you to be more than that. I've always *thought* of you as more."

Her heart skipped. "Really?"

He stood, warmth rising to his eyes. He wrapped his arm around her waist and tugged her closer.

"Kate," he said. "From the second you fell into my arms, you've been so much more. More than a friend, a hell of a lot more than a fuck buddy, even more than just a girlfriend. You're something no other woman ever has been or will be to me."

Love and hope bubbled up inside her. "What's that?"

"You're my Darling."

She smiled. He moved his hand around to the back of her neck and their lips met in a warm, lovely kiss that felt like they'd kissed a thousand times before. Like they'd already experienced a lifetime of kisses together.

Kate moved away from him and went to the door. Without looking at him, she closed the door and locked it with a flick of her wrist. Her heart rate ratcheted up as she returned to the desk. Tyler was sitting by the computer again, eyeing her with both heat and a touch of wariness.

"We're at work," he reminded her, even as his gaze drifted to her breasts.

"I know. We're also off hours." She pushed his chair away from the desk and straddled his lap, pressing their groins together.

Tyler muttered something under his breath and settled his hands on her waist. "Really not a good idea."

"I've thought the same thing a few times since we made our little deal." Kate slipped her hands under his T-shirt and pressed a kiss against his neck. "Turns out being with you is one of the best ideas I've ever had."

His breathing increased. "And what if someone actually needs to use the library?"

"They'll come back." She pressed a line of kisses up his jaw to his lips. "Besides, the door is locked."

She wiggled on his lap, rubbing her ass against his thighs. She felt his capitulation in instant before his arms slid around her.

He lowered his head and pressed his lips against hers. Kate couldn't suppress a moan at the contact, loving the full pressure of him—his chest pressing against her breasts, his mouth on hers, his hands gripping her hips with firm possession.

He guided her backward, his lips still locked to hers, until her bottom hit the desk. Then he lifted her onto it and edged between her thighs, pushing her skirt up, the warm friction of his palms sending tingles through her blood.

Kate lifted her legs, wrapping them around his hips as his groin rubbed against the juncture of her thighs. She sighed with pleasure, shifting to get closer, feeling his heat even more powerfully through her thin silk panties.

Tyler gave a muffled grunt and trailed his fingers up the tender skin of her inner thigh. Before she realized what he was about to do, he grabbed the material of her sheer nylons and pulled, ripping a hole in her stockings.

Kate gasped. "Tyler!"

He grinned, pushing his fingers into the hole to find her panties. "Easier access. Ah shit, I knew you'd be wet already."

Kate groaned, her concern over her nylons slipping away when Tyler yanked them over her legs and tossed them onto the floor. Then he pressed her back to lie on the desk and moved his face between her legs.

Oh my God.

Kate almost shot off the desk at the touch of his tongue on her folds. She grabbed the edge, arching her body upward as heat flamed through her. She lifted her head, shocked and thrilled by the sight of his dark head buried between her thighs, his hands keeping her legs open. He licked and sucked her with leisurely expertise, as if he had all the time in the world to pleasure her.

And oh lord, was she pleasured. Sensations sparked and burst in her veins, urgent arousal coiling through her body. Her clothes suddenly felt stifling, and she quickly worked the buttons of her shirt and cast it and her bra aside. She felt Tyler's hot gaze as she rubbed and squeezed her breasts, rolling her nipples between her fingers.

He drove his tongue into her, working it back and forth. Kate fisted his hair, unable to believe what he was able to do to her. With a cry, she bucked upward, an orgasm exploding through her, her breath stopping in her throat.

Tyler worked the sensations from her before sliding his hands around her waist to unzip her skirt and toss it aside. His eyes burned hot with lust and need.

"Darling," he whispered, unfastening the fly of his jeans. "I need to fuck you."

"Oh, yes, please."

She stared hungrily at the thick ridge of his erection as he retrieved a condom from his wallet and rolled it on. He positioned himself between her legs, and she bowed her body upward to accept the heavy, immediate thrust of his cock.

A gasp tore from her throat, fresh heat sparking through her. He planted his hands on either side of her head, his shaft gliding with slick ease in and out of her. She was enthralled by the sight of him above her, his T-shirt dampening with sweat, his eyes lit with fire and his hair tousled from the desperate grip of her fingers.

She convulsed again, twisting her fingers frantically in his T-shirt. He groaned and plunged into her, his jaw tightening as his own body shuddered with release.

"Christ, you're amazing." Tyler rested his forehead against hers, his hot breath brushing her lips. "I'm not letting you go."

"Good. Because I don't want to be let go."

She pressed a kiss to his lips and wiggled to indicate she needed to get up. He moved away from her, pulling a hand through his hair.

Kate eased off the desk and reached for her bra, tugging it on over her swollen breasts, the skin reddened from whisker burn and the greedy clutch of Tyler's hands.

She loved the way he *marked* her during lovemaking, as if he wanted to imprint himself on her body. He'd already done that to her mind and heart.

She fastened the front clasp of the bra and stepped into her now-abominably wrinkled pencil skirt. As she was zipping it up, the doorknob to the library turned and rattled.

Alarm shot through her. Tyler grabbed her shirt from the

floor and tossed it to her. Kate hurried to turn the sleeves right-side out.

At least she'd had had foresight to lock the door. Still fumbling with the shirt, she started for the alcove.

The lock clicked. The knob turned. The door opened.

Luke stood in the doorway, his big frame almost filling the space. Kate's breath stopped. Tyler darted in front of her, shielding her from his brother's view, but it was too late.

With one sweeping glance, Luke assessed the scene—Kate in her bra and skirt, Tyler in unfastened jeans. The papers and books strewn on the floor, the empty surface of the desk.

A burn of humiliation crawled up Kate's neck. She wanted to die.

Luke's inscrutable expression registered nothing. Then he left, closing the door behind him.

A heavy silence fell. Tyler turned. Kate half expected him to make some flippant remark, or to flash his cocky grin and try to make light of the horrid situation.

He didn't. Instead he touched her hot cheek in a gesture that was painfully tender.

Instinctively, Kate jerked away. His expression darkened. An ache filled her chest, cracking through her bones. She pulled on her shirt and skirt, buttoning them with shaking fingers.

"Kate…"

"No, don't. Please."

She shoved her feet into her shoes, grabbed her briefcase, and hurried out the door without looking back.

CHAPTER 27

*T*yler had walked the road of shame numerous times in his life, usually a path right to his father's office door. But he'd never thrown himself on his oldest brother's mercy for the sake of a woman.

For Kate, he would. Hell, he'd wear a hair shirt and walk around flagellating himself, if that was what it took. He'd do anything for her.

The realization didn't surprise him. She'd gotten under his skin the minute he'd first locked his arms around her. What did surprise him was that his need to do anything for her—*anything* —wasn't based on his inability to say *no* to a pretty girl. Just the opposite, in fact.

There was no negativity where Kate was concerned, no battles with his conscience or struggles about doing the right thing. He didn't want to follow her around catering to her every whim—well, okay, sometimes he did—but more than that, he just wanted to be with her.

He wanted to hang out with her all the time—having sex, watching Monty Python, working on the Mustang, eating pizza. He wanted to show her his favorite hiking trails in Big Sur, to take her to clubs in the city, to travel. He wanted to dance all his dances with her.

A few times in the past, he thought he'd been in love. He'd been an idiot. Because *love* was all the things he'd heard about but never felt until Kate—a crazy, spinning happiness, the knowledge that he was a better person with her than alone, that she'd *made* him a better person.

It was the desire to be her hero because she deserved nothing less, not because she'd coerced him. She was everything he wasn't, and at the same time, everything he was.

For the first time in his life, he got it.

He punched the code into the gate control of Luke's driveway, then drove up to the massive Nordic mansion on a cliff overlooking the ocean. Polly's red hybrid—the only car she'd let Luke buy for her—sat next to his Porsche.

Tyler parked and approached the door. He'd never much liked the custom-made house with all its glass and straight lines, but he could appreciate how hard Luke had worked for it. He'd developed a whole new appreciation for hard work in recent days.

"Hi, Tyler." Polly opened the door and smiled, but worry shadowed her eyes. "Luke's in the kitchen. I was just heading over to Evan and Hannah's."

Tyler nodded. Polly squeezed his arm and slipped past him to walk to the driveway. How much had Luke told her?

His stomach knotted as he entered the kitchen. His brother sat at the black granite counter, his head bent over his tablet. The smell of something hot and floral filled the air.

"Hey." Tyler stopped, shoving his hands into his pockets.

Luke glanced up, his expression grave. For an instant, he looked so much like a younger version of their father that Tyler almost faltered.

Almost. Because he'd never falter when Kate was involved. Ever.

"You want some chamomile tea?" Luke indicated the teapot

sitting on the counter beside two mugs. "Polly just made it. She says it's very soothing."

"Uh, sure." Tyler hitched himself onto a stool at the counter while his brother poured the tea.

Luke pushed a mug across the counter to him. Tyler sipped the fragrant tea, which tasted like dirt.

"Kate," Luke said, "is my most valuable employee."

"I know."

"I guessed something was going on between you two when you lost it at the bakery," Luke continued. "I hoped you'd have enough sense to keep it private, but that was obviously hoping for too much. Sex in the workplace is a total violation of Sugar Rush's code of contact."

Old shame rose in Tyler's chest. He hadn't felt it in such a long time that it was almost a surprise.

"When did you start up with her?" Luke asked.

"Day one."

His brother's mouth twisted with derision. Tyler's shame intensified. He dragged a hand through his hair "She offered to help with the software and stuff, and we...got together."

Luke's eyes narrowed. "Don't you mean you hit on her?"

Irritation prickled Tyler's spine, even though the answer to that question was *yes*. At first. Then she'd turned the tables on him, and his entire world went up in flames.

"Kate is an adult," he said. "She doesn't need you protecting her from me."

"I know she's an adult," Luke said, anger threading his voice. "She's also smart, dedicated, and organized. We just asked her to consider a position as Vice President of the CSR division."

"She told me."

Luke shoved away from the counter in annoyance. "She told you, and still you messed with her at work? Come on, man. You can't fuck with her career potential just because you can't keep it in your pants."

Goddammit.

Tyler shouldn't have been surprised by the accusation. His reputation preceded him. It was his own damned fault. But it still hurt that his brother would never think better of him. Never believe he was capable of better.

"She hasn't slacked off on the job, has she?" he asked.

"Of course not," Luke said. "But she's been distracted these past few weeks, and now I know why. I can't have you messing with my employees."

Tyler's hands tightened on the mug. "I'm not *messing* with her, man. I care about her."

"That doesn't make it right."

"So you're telling me it's *wrong*? There's no law against us being together."

"Tyler, with all the shit this family has been through, didn't you stop to think it might be a bad idea to hook up with my assistant?" Luke snapped. "I know your relationships never last long, and that Kate isn't your usual type of woman. What happens when you end it?"

Tyler's blood fired with anger. "What makes you think I want to end it?"

Luke regarded him with that implacable calm that made him such a great CEO but not such a great confidante.

"Considering your past string of relationships, I don't want Kate to either get hurt personally or be caught in a situation that could be detrimental to her career."

Tyler looked at the mug. He knew exactly what his brother was saying and why he was saying it. Tyler had skirted the line for too long, and the crashed speedboat hadn't just been the final straw for him—it had been the culmination of years of irresponsible behavior.

Why would Luke believe that two weeks of working at the Sugar Rush library and an affair with Kate could change him?

Hell. Tyler hardly believed it himself. Waxing poetic to his older brother about being *in love* wouldn't change anything either.

"What business is this of yours anyway?" he muttered.

"It became my business when you and she started screwing around on company time in the company library." Luke took his mug to the sink, his shoulders tight with anger. "I've fired people for infractions a lot less severe than that. So give me one damned good reason why I shouldn't fire you for putting my assistant in a compromising position during work hours."

Shit. Shit. Shit.

A panicky feeling spread in Tyler's blood. What if his brother said the exact same thing to Kate? What if he not only rescinded the VP offer, but flat out fired her for violating the company's code of conduct?

He swallowed a mouthful of tea to give himself a second to think.

"What's going to happen to Kate?" he asked.

"You don't need to concern yourself with Kate right now," Luke said. "You're in enough trouble as it is. And I haven't even talked to Dad yet."

Oh fuck.

The past twenty-seven years crashed over Tyler like a steamroller, flattening him to the ground. Pretty soon everyone in the whole damned family would know that Tyler had "messed with" Luke's assistant.

He could almost see them rolling their eyes and nodding their heads, because of course they'd known all along that he'd somehow manage to fuck up his job at the library.

He pushed his mug aside and got to his feet.

"You don't have to fire me," he told Luke. "And you don't need to hash this out with Dad or anyone else. The only thing I'm asking is that you let Kate keep her job. She loves working at Sugar Rush. And you know you won't find anyone better than her. Just...don't hurt her, please. It was all my fault. You know me...can't say no to a pretty girl, right?"

Luke's expression darkened. "What do you want me to do then, man?"

"Nothing you haven't done already." Tyler held up his hands and backed toward the front door. "Let Kate do her job. Hire a new librarian. Because I quit."

Luke frowned. "What about your payments?"

Tyler shrugged. The deal had been that if he missed his payments to Dan Corrigan, he'd press charges. At first, that had been enough to get Tyler's ass in gear. Now he didn't much care.

"Guess I have to face the consequences," he said. "About time, huh?"

Before his brother could respond, Tyler turned and left the house.

CHAPTER 28

*K*ate was pretty sure that in all of history, no one had ever actually died of shame. But after spending the evening curled up in a ball on her sofa, she was getting close.

At least a million times, she reached for the phone to call Luke, but then the thought of talking to him and knowing what he knew had her throwing the phone against the sofa pillows.

Then there were the relentless questions burning through her mind. Should she quit? Would he fire her? Would he fire Tyler? Was her promotion in jeopardy? Would Luke tell Evan and his father what had happened? Would she be reported to HR?

Not to mention—what the *hell* had she been thinking?

She ignored a dozen calls from Tyler, but close to midnight, knowing the incident hadn't been his fault, she texted him. *I'll talk to you later. Just need to be alone right now.*

The next morning she hauled herself up and started to dress in one of her boxy old suits. She caught a glimpse of herself in the mirror—ratty hair, bags under her eyes, pale as a sheet—and frowned.

Was this what Tyler had done after he'd crashed the speedboat? No. He'd felt like an ass and he'd stumbled around before finding his footing, but in the end he'd buckled down to work. To fix his mistake.

"Grow the fuck up, Kate," she snapped at her reflection. "You made a mistake. Own up to it. Don't hide. You wanted to be noticed, right? Well, there you go. People will notice your successes as well as your failures, and you need to deal with it."

After that little come-to-Jesus, she put on her tweed, wool Chanel suit and leather pumps. She pulled her hair into a smooth chignon, carefully applied makeup, and headed to the Sugar Rush campus with her head high and her heart beating like a drum.

She approached the reception desk. The receptionist looked up with her usual smile. For an instant, Kate was startled before remembering that no one else knew what had happened. *Yet.*

"Hi, Kate. Luke's in his office."

"Thanks." Kate tightened her hand on her briefcase. "Nancy, is Tyler Stone in yet? I need a few resources from the library."

"Tyler?" Nancy lifted her eyebrows. "He left about half an hour ago."

Kate's heart stuttered. "What do you mean, he left? It's not even nine o'clock yet."

"He said he was done with the work he had to do, so he's gone."

Gone?

"Pity, huh?" Nancy gave her a conspiratorial smile. "He was a hottie. I loved watching him walk in here every day."

Kate didn't respond. She took the stairs to the basement level and hurried down the corridor to the library. The door was locked. A strange panic spread through her chest. She took out her phone and texted Tyler.

K. DARLING: Where are you?

No response. She went to the twelfth floor, noting that Luke's office door was half open. She set her briefcase on her desk, ran trembling hands over her skirt, and knocked on the door.

"Come in."

She stepped inside. "Good morning, sir. May I have a moment of your time?"

He looked up from his computer and nodded, gesturing for her to sit on a chair in front of his desk. Kate closed the door, hoping her skirt concealed the fact that her knees were shaking.

She sat and folded her hands, taking the opportunity to speak before he did.

"I'd like to apologize for my conduct yesterday," she said, glad that her voice was steady. "Obviously it was completely unprofessional and immoral, and I want to assure you that I've done nothing like that before, and I've no intention of doing so again. I disrespected my position with this company, and I utterly violated the code of conduct—"

"Kate." Luke held up a hand to stop her tirade. "Yes, that's all true. And if this were a situation in which your conduct affected the company negatively, we'd have to look at disciplinary proceedings."

"I'm sorry." She twisted her fingers together. "Is that what happened to Tyler? Nancy in reception told me that he was gone."

A frown creased his forehead. "Yes, he's gone. Because he quit."

"He *quit*?"

Luke nodded. "He took the blame for what happened, said it was his fault, and asked me not to fire you."

"Why would he do that?"

"Because he was afraid I would." Luke's mouth twisted. "Look, I know he talked you into what happened at the library. It's just the kind of thing he would do. God knows he—"

"*Sir.*" Outrage speared through her. She rose to her feet, unable to remain sitting any longer.

"Excuse me for speaking out of turn, but that is so...so wrong," Kate snapped. "He did not *talk me into* what happened. For your information, I seduced him. He was the one who said we shouldn't do that at work, and of course he was right.

"And more, for a man who started working without an ounce of library experience, he's done an incredible job. He's made an effort to learn the collections management system and how to organize resources, he's learned about proper handling of archival materials, and he's even started researching how to better store the more fragile items.

"Even more, he's increasingly dedicated to preserving and protecting Sugar Rush history, which quite frankly, no one else in your family has done before now. So don't you dare start thinking *'Well, that's just Tyler being Tyler, screwing my mousy little assistant at work,'* because that's not true."

She strode forward and put her hands flat on the surface of his desk, leaning forward to look him in the eye. Her heart jackhammered.

"Do you want to know what *Tyler being Tyler* really is?" she asked. "Tyler is dedicated, loyal, passionate, intelligent, creative. He's an amazing dancer. He would do anything for his friends, sometimes to a fault. He's always wanted to be valued in your family, but he hasn't known how because he's always been overshadowed by his older brothers.

"He knows he's screwed up a lot, but for once he was trying to fix things. To make them right. If you could *see* that instead of blaming him when things go wrong, then maybe you'll discover what an incredible part of this company he could be."

Not until she stopped did Kate realize she was shaking. Luke stared at her as if he'd never seen her before. She stepped back, drawing in a breath.

Luke was silent for so long that the moments seemed to stretch into eternity.

"First," he said, "I appreciate your defense of Tyler, though I've known him a lot longer than you have."

"You've known him longer, but I don't think you know him *better*." Kate no longer cared that she was overstepping her boundaries. "Maybe you just need to realize that his value is different from what you and your father expected. God knows *he* needs to realize that for himself."

She held up her hands to stop him from speaking. "I'm sorry. I know it's none of my business, and that I'm totally out of line. Given everything that's happened, I'd like to tender my resignation."

Luke's jaw tightened, but he didn't look surprised. He must have known there could be no other recourse for her.

"Do you want to leave Sugar Rush?" he asked.

"No."

"Then why resign?"

"Because I don't believe this situation is at all fair. And I've never seen you treat anyone at this company unfairly. And..." She swallowed past the tightness in her throat. "I behaved unconscionably."

He fell silent again, as if he were thinking very hard.

"If you don't want to leave, then I won't accept a letter of resignation from you," he said. "Only three of us know what happened. Considering your track record at Sugar Rush, I'm willing to forget the incident ever happened. I know it won't again."

Kate couldn't quite believe what she was hearing. She didn't deserve such altruism. "You mean I can keep my job?"

"I would like you to, yes. And the promotion offer still stands."

Her heart raced. "I...I can't accept that, sir. A proper VP doesn't make bad decisions, like I obviously do."

Luke sat back in his chair and studied her gravely. "I've got news for you, Kate. Proper VPs do make bad decisions. And when they do, they come clean and try to fix the problem. But more often than not, their job performance and successes far outweigh their mistakes. I believe that will be the case in your situation as well."

But she would have to prove it. Luke didn't need to tell her that.

Trust was a tricky thing—easily broken and painfully difficult to regain. She'd broken not only her boss's trust, but his high regard of her and probably his respect too. She had a great deal to earn back.

"I...I don't know what to say." Tears stung the backs of her eyes. She didn't know what to *do*. If her father ever found out about this...he would be so ashamed.

"Your mistake was significant," Luke said. "But I do appreciate your honesty and your apology. I'd expect no less from a potential VP. I'm also a believer in second chances, and I'm willing to give you one. It's up to you whether or not you want to take it."

Kate pulled a hard breath into her lungs. If she took what he was offering, she'd spend the rest of her career working to prove that she really was the model employee he'd always believed her to be.

And she'd prove to *herself* that a great career and a tidy life with a professional businessman had been the right path for her all along.

Tyler had just been a wild, exciting, unexpected detour. One she now had to leave behind.

"Thank you, sir." She took a step back, anxious to leave the office before her tears spilled over. "I accept and appreciate the second chance more than I can tell you."

She hurried to the door.

"Kate."

She turned.

"Don't make me regret this."

"Never, sir."

"And for God's sake." Amusement threaded his voice. "Please stop calling me *sir*."

"Yes, si...Luke."

She slipped out of the office and returned to her desk, burying the waves of emotion beneath a mask of efficiency. She took calls, organized the schedule, reviewed board meeting minutes, and ordered Luke a protein drink. On her lunch hour, she read over all the paperwork for the VP position.

Her phone buzzed with a text. Her heart stuttered with hope before disappointment took its place.

M. NORWOOD: Hello, Kate. Would you like to have coffee tomorrow morning? I can meet you at the Chocolate Café at ten.

She hesitated, her new resolve warring with emotions too deep, too powerful, to be easily shoved aside. And yet, she would have to do exactly that. She forced herself to respond.

K. DARLING: That would be fine. See you then.

She left the office at seven, an hour after the last employee had gone home. She gathered her things and walked to the parking lot. When she approached her car, her steps faltered.

Tyler was leaning against the side of her car, one hand shoved into the pocket of his jeans, his dark head bent over his phone. Kate slowed, her heels still clicking on the pavement.

He glanced up. Across the distance, an arc of electricity crackled between them. Her heart rate increased with that one look, even though she knew—she'd known, since the second Luke had walked in on them at the library—what she had to do. Not only would she never let Luke regret his decision, she would never allow herself to make another mistake like that one.

"Hey, Darling." Tyler straightened, his gaze roaming over her appreciatively. "I've been trying to reach you."

"I know." She stopped. Her insides twisted. "It's nice to see you."

"You too." A crease appeared between his eyebrows at her formal tone. "You okay?"

For a moment, she couldn't respond. In some ways—because of him—she was more than okay. She was better than she'd ever been.

And in other ways, she'd never felt worse. Because of her, Tyler had quit the job that was his chance at redemption, both financially and in the eyes of his family.

"Luke didn't fire me," she said. "In fact, he said he was willing to forget the whole incident ever happened."

"That's great." He gave her a somewhat uncertain smile. "So why do you look as if you're about to face an executioner?"

She looked past him. "You shouldn't have quit. I was the one who started the whole thing."

"Hey." He took hold of her chin, turning her face toward his. "I didn't try very hard to stop you, right?"

"That doesn't mean you should have taken all the blame. I told Luke it wasn't your fault."

"Kate, it doesn't matter. I'm used to being at fault."

She tightened her jaw against a wave of frustration. "But you *shouldn't* be used to it. Why can't you see that? Why don't you *know* it?"

"Because of you, I'm starting to." He tucked a lock of hair behind her ear. "Come on, Darling. Let's get some dinner and—"

"No."

He dropped his hand away from her. "No?"

Kate shook her head. A tremble coursed through her. She needed distance from him. Their relationship had happened so fast, and with such force, that if she let herself return to him again she'd find herself caught in the same whirlwind.

Now, of all times, she couldn't muddy her thoughts and feelings. She had to stay clear-headed, focused. On the fucking *path*.

She started to walk to the driver's side. He grabbed her arm.

"Where are you going?"

"Home."

"So give me the keys. I'll drive."

"No." Kate twisted her arm out of his grip, steeling herself against the confused look in his eyes. "Tyler, we can't see each other anymore."

"What?" He lowered his hand to his side. "Why not?"

"I'm sorry." Shame rose to the surface again. "I never...I'm a *professional*. Never once in my life have I done something embarrassing in the workplace, much less totally immoral and unethical. Kissing you in the library was bad enough, but having sex...? No. I can't forgive myself for that. And with Luke giving me a second chance, even with the VP position...I need to prove that he made the right decision. Even more, I need to prove that everything I've been is *true*. I can't do that with you."

He stepped back, darkness descending over his expression. "So that's it, then? We're done?"

"Tyler." Kate dug into her purse for her keys, her hand shaking. "We were never meant to be anything serious. We both knew that from the start. So this is as good a place as any to end it."

His mouth thinned. "It may not have started as anything serious, but it damned well ended up that way."

Kate's heart ached. She opened the car door, turning away from him as she got behind the wheel.

"No," she said. "It just ended."

CHAPTER 29

"*T*hanks, man." Paul extended his hand to Tyler. "I'll take good care of her."

"You'd better." Tyler patted the fender of the Mustang, trying to smother a stab of sorrow over having sold the car.

Over the past few years, he'd probably spent more time with the Mustang than he had with any single human being. But as much as he loved the car, he'd give it up a hundred times over if it meant he could finally find his place in the world.

Like Kate did. He couldn't stop thinking about her, even though she'd closed the door so hard he still heard the slam. According to Luke, after the debacle a week ago, Kate had taken a couple of personal days off before returning to Sugar Rush to start the VP position.

Good for her. She deserved it. And he had to figure out a way to keep going without her. A way that didn't mean going backward.

He dug into his pocket for the keys and handed them to Paul before walking back to the garage where Charlie was working. He lifted a hand in farewell and headed toward his Trans Am.

Worst case scenario, he'd have to sell this car, too. Hopefully it wouldn't come to that. He could live with selling the Mustang, but the Trans Am had been a gift from Evan and he really didn't want to let it go. Between the car sale and not renewing his apartment lease, he hoped he'd be able to set his plan into motion.

He returned to the apartment, which was as silent as a tomb. The living room was so sparkling clean it would impress even Martha Stewart. Tyler hadn't thought he'd miss the mess and noise created by his friends, but damned if he didn't wish they were around to distract him from his own misery.

He boxed up a few more of his belongings and spent a couple of hours scrubbing down the kitchen. He'd been cleaning and packing for the past week, though the exertion still hadn't rid him of his anger and frustration.

However, it *had* prevented him from driving over to Kate's and doing something stupid, like falling to his knees in front of her or holding up a boom box blaring a sappy love song.

A sharp knock came at the door. He opened it. Spencer stood on the doorstep.

"Hey, man." His brother held up a cardboard box. "You didn't come back to the lab, and Luke said you weren't at the library anymore. So I brought these over."

Tyler stepped aside to let him in. "What is it?"

"Take a look." Spencer put the box on the kitchen counter and opened the fridge.

Tyler unfolded the box top and removed a stack of chocolate bars wrapped in foil. Each one had the GOLD RUSH logo stamped on the top.

"The 49er truffles are in there too." Spencer popped the cap on a bottle of beer and took a swallow. "I'm still working on the exact recipe, but those are close. Better than the eighteen-century chocolate, too, since they used a more modern manufacturing process. The Gold Rush bars in silver foil have nuts."

"Thanks." Tyler set the bar back in the box. "Can I keep these?"

"Sure." Spencer eyed him perceptively. "So what did Dad have to say about your job?"

"Nothing, yet. I'm meeting him downtown for dinner. Probably also for a stern lecture. I guess he'll put me to work on the factory floor."

"Then what's happening with the library?"

"No idea. Luke had put out a call for applications for a librarian, so he'll have to step up the game." Tyler looked at the clock. "I gotta shower and get ready."

After his brother left, he headed into the shower. Thankfully their father had suggested a non-fancy restaurant to deliver yet another comeuppance, but the Dijon Bistro was upscale enough that Tyler dressed in slacks and a button-down shirt instead of his usual jeans.

When he arrived at the restaurant, his father was already waiting at a corner booth. Belatedly, he wished he'd asked Spencer to come along, as a buffer if nothing else, but he knew he had to do this alone. Kind of like Luke Skywalker facing down Darth Vader.

As Tyler sat, he started to apologize—then stopped. He was done with apologizing and feeling guilty. He didn't want to be a screw-up anymore, but he also had to put all his past transgressions behind him.

"Luke told me you won't return to the library," Warren remarked, nodding his thanks to the server as she poured them each a glass of wine.

"Did he tell you why?" Tyler asked.

"No. He did, however, assure me it had nothing to do with your work itself." Warren eyed him with more perception than Tyler was comfortable with. "In fact, both he and Spencer have been impressed with what you've accomplished in so short a time. So have other employees. Seems everyone is sorry to see you go."

Tyler shrugged. He was sorry to go too, but only because he'd known he could actually finish the job. He'd never be sorry for protecting Kate.

"So how do you plan to continue making the boat payments?" Warren asked.

Good question.

Though he was glad his father had cut right to the chase, Tyler didn't speak for a moment. He'd rehearsed this speech a few times, but now the words all jumbled in his head.

"I thought..." He paused and cleared his throat. "I sold the Mustang."

Warren raised an eyebrow. "You sold it? I thought you'd planned to exhibit it at car shows."

"The Fordwell show is off, and it's not like I'd make a living going to car shows. But Charlie is planning to retire, so I was thinking of using the money for a down payment on his garage."

The final words came out on a rush. He couldn't read his father's expression, but Warren didn't exactly jump out of his seat and start shouting about what a great idea that was.

"I figure it's one thing I can do," Tyler added hastily. "I mean, I'm a certified mechanic, and I'm good at it. I could start small and maybe work toward specializing in classic car restoration. I know it's not what you'd want, but I can do it."

"What I *want*," Warren said, picking up the menu, "is for you to do something you're good at and that you enjoy."

"Then why have you always thought my interest in cars is stupid?"

"I never thought it was stupid," Warren replied. "I didn't like that you'd gone through all that training and then weren't doing anything useful with it. And in the meantime, you were still getting into trouble and living off your trust. I wanted you to realize your *behavior* was stupid and that it was about time you grew up."

"Does that mean you'd be okay with having a son who's a mechanic?"

"Tyler." A pained expression crossed his father's face. "When I was fifteen, my father told me he wasn't going to hand the family company over to me until I knew what real, honest work was like. Until I could prove I'd be a success even if we didn't own Stone Confectioners. For my first job, I changed oil and pumped gas at an old Shell station on the corner of Wells Street in San Francisco. Worked there for three years."

"I didn't know that."

"Contrary to appearances, I haven't always lived and breathed the candy business," Warren said. "I've done yard maintenance, delivered newspapers, worked at a convenience store, drove a supply truck. My first job at Stone Confectioners was packaging lollipops in the factory. I didn't actually start making my way up the corporate ladder until I was in my thirties."

"Did you want to?" Tyler asked. "Or did you do it because your father wanted you to?"

"No, I always loved the idea of working at Stone Confectioners. That was why I worked so damned hard at everything else. I wanted to earn my way into the family company. And so I did. But your mother and I always knew that not all of our children would feel the same way. That was fine, as long as you all found another career path that fulfilled you."

Which Tyler never had. At least, not until now. Maybe.

"Charlie wants to get rid of the garage because it's not doing well," he said. "Competition, high cost of insurance. I don't know for sure I can do any better, but I know a lot of guys who'd bring their cars in for work. With some advertising, maybe I can make a go of it."

Warren's eyes narrowed slightly. "And what about your boat payments?"

"I don't know," Tyler admitted. "I won't make a profit for a while. I can maybe work part time in the library, though it will take a while to pay it off. Dan Corrigan might not want to wait that long."

Warren nodded, his forehead creasing.

"I don't want to use my trust fund money either." Tyler took a sip of water. The instant he said the words, a weight seemed to lift from his chest. "I know it's mine, and so is a share of Sugar Rush. But I want to save it for later...maybe one day I'll have kids or something. Or maybe we can use it to help fund the veteran's programs for the Rebecca Stone Foundation. Whatever we do with it, I don't want it now. I want to figure this out on my own."

Then prove I can do it.

"I'm not like Luke and Evan," he continued. "I never will be. I don't want to work at Sugar Rush. But I don't want to be the family disappointment anymore either."

Regret flickered in Warren's eyes. "I've been disappointed with your choices, Tyler. Not necessarily with you."

"Same difference."

"No. But to answer your question..." Warren reached for his wineglass. "Yes. I would be fine with having a son who's a mechanic. More, I'd be proud. I'm already proud of what you've done."

Tyler didn't respond. He was too busy trying to smother the weird feelings rising into his throat. He didn't think his father had ever before said he was actually *proud* of him.

"I'll talk to Dan Corrigan and renegotiate," Tyler said. "He might be okay with waiting until I start to make money."

"If not, the library is always open for you, if you want to come back."

Part of him did want to finish the library job, but another bigger part of him knew he could never do it without—

His heart crashed against his ribs. Disbelief filled him. He blinked, and his vision cleared.

She was there, seated at a table by the window. The reddish sun filtered through the glass and shone on her brown hair. She was focused on her plate, her eyelashes downcast as she sliced into a steak.

Tyler's pulse sped up, as if he hadn't seen her in weeks rather than days. Now that, for the first time in his life, he had his father's blessing, maybe he could find a way to win Kate back. If he wasn't at Sugar Rush anymore, there wouldn't be a workplace conflict, and—

Kate lifted her head and spoke to the person seated across from her.

Oh, fuck no.

His brief hope crashed and splintered like broken glass. Miles Norwood with his stupid styled hair and pale blue suit sat across from Kate, his jaw flapping in an apparently nonstop monologue. She was nodding in response, her perfect lips parting as she took a sip of wine.

No. No. *No.*

Before he could think, Tyler shot to his feet. He stalked across the room to Kate's table. Her eyes widened with shock and a deep, fiery emotion he could see but couldn't yet name.

"Tyler." Pain tightened her voice.

"Kate." He fixed Norwood with a hard stare, his hands clenching. "Norwood."

"Have we met?" The other man gave him a bland smile and extended a hand. "I don't recall."

"Yeah, I know. Because you're an arrogant dickwad who doesn't deserve her."

Kate gasped. Norwood blinked.

"Excuse me?"

"You heard me." Tyler lowered his head to look Norwood in the eye. "You. Don't. Deserve. Her."

"Tyler, please." Her hand closed around his arm.

He faced her, tension clawing at his chest. "Walk away with me."

She stared at him, her eyes bright and filled with despair. "I can't."

"*Please.*"

"Hey." Norwood stood so fast, his chair scraped backward. "Do you mind? We're on a date here."

"The fuck you are," Tyler snarled.

"Is there a problem?" A server and the house manager hurried over, both of them glancing warily from him to Miles.

"Yes, there's a problem." Norwood waved his napkin at Tyler. "This barbarian is disturbing us."

"He's not a barbarian, and he's not disturbing us." Kate got to her feet, still gripping his arm. She moved closer to him and lowered her voice. "You have to go."

He shook his head. The sweet scent of her filled his nose, warming his blood. The second he stepped away from her, he'd be cold again.

"Sir." The manager leveled him with a glare. "I need to ask you to leave this couple alone."

"They're not a fucking couple," Tyler snapped.

"Excuse me." Warren Stone's voice cut through the air.

"Mr. Stone." The manager smiled weakly, a sheen of sweat on his forehead. "I'm so sorry for the disturbance."

Warren silenced him with a lift of his hand. "Never mind. We're leaving. Put the bill on my tab, please."

"Oh, no need, sir," the manager said. "I do apologize."

Warren gripped Tyler's shoulder. "Come on, son."

Kate's face was pale, her eyes luminous. He wanted to grab her like a caveman, haul her over his shoulder, and take her back to his place where he would never let her go. He wanted to watch Monty Python marathons and eat pancakes at 2:00 a.m. with her. He wanted her to admit that she *belonged* to him. Just like he'd belonged to her the second she'd fallen into his arms.

"Please go away, Tyler," she said, her voice breaking on his name.

He stumbled back, only his father's grip keeping him upright. He pulled away and stalked to the door. The ocean air did nothing to cool the anger and misery boiling inside him. He stopped halfway down the sidewalk and inhaled a few hard breaths.

"I guess Julia was right." Warren came out of the restaurant, tugging on his suit jacket.

"About what?"

"She said you were in love with Kate. As much as I try not to admit she's right, I'm frequently forced to acknowledge that she usually is."

Tyler managed a hoarse laugh. "Women, huh?"

"Indeed." Warren retrieved his car keys from his pocket.

Tyler dragged a hand through his hair, forcing himself not to turn and look through the restaurant window at Kate. Even though everything inside him ached for one more glimpse of her.

"Come on," Warren said. "I have a cold six-pack in the fridge, and I'm sure there's a game on somewhere we can watch."

An invitation? Tyler couldn't remember the last time he'd done anything alone with his father—if he ever had. Growing up, his brothers had always been around, and as the youngest, he'd spent most of his time either trying to compete with them or fighting with them.

Warren was already walking down the sidewalk. A knot loosened inside Tyler, one that had been tied tight longer than he cared to think about. He hurried to catch up with his father, falling into step at his side.

CHAPTER 30

"The data hub would allow Sugar Rush to study consumer purchasing trends." Miles speared his fork into a soy veggie patty.

Overhead, a passing cloud briefly obscured the sun shining down on the outdoor seating terrace of the Licorice Café.

"Which in turn would inform the development and deployment of business strategies," he continued.

Kate bit into a greasy slice of pizza and almost moaned aloud as the gooey cheese and pepperoni flavors hit her tongue. She'd eaten more junk food in the past week than she'd eaten her entire life, trying to smother her painful emotions beneath layers of carbs and sugar.

Not to mention 2:00 a.m. pancakes, which, as it turned out, weren't nearly as good alone as they were with a certain hunky librarian.

Unfortunately, her junk food binge wasn't working. Neither was her attempt to rebound with Miles, who'd invited her to lunch the Monday after their interrupted dinner date.

"So when you combine analytics with consumer insights and trends…" His voice droned on.

While Kate still appreciated his knowledge and wanted to figure out herself how to make his analytics intersect with global trends, she could no longer muster even an ounce of interest in him personally. He was smart, yes, but about as bland and boring as unsweetened rice pudding.

Not to mention, she couldn't stop thinking about Tyler, which was definitely poor date etiquette. She'd replayed that scene at the Dijon Bistro countless times over the weekend, and part of her still desperately wished she'd taken him up on his offer.

Walk away with me. Just the memory of his deep voice, scraped with a plea, intensified the ache in her heart.

Walk away with him. Tyler would grab her hand and haul her off the *path* to run through wild fields and across sandy beaches. Then he'd pull her down with him onto the warm sand and kiss her until her head spun and her heart danced upward into the clouds.

Her eyes stung. She couldn't allow that. As the Vice-President of Corporate Social Responsibility, as *Kate Darling*, she'd made a commitment to both herself and her new position. A professional, well-ordered life in which there was no room for mistakes or messiness.

"So, Miles." She polished off her slice of pizza and grabbed a napkin. "Would you like to go dancing tonight?"

"Oh." He blanched a little. "I'm sorry. It's Monday night. Besides, I don't dance."

"I could teach you. I really get down with the Funky Chicken."

"No, thank you. I dislike dancing rather intensely."

Then you haven't had the right partner.

"What about a movie?" Kate asked. "Or I know of a great arcade we could go to."

"Arcade?" He lifted an eyebrow in faint confusion. "Do you mean video games?"

"Yes. They have a ton of classics like *Pac-Man* and *Space Invaders*. All set to free play, too, so it's unlimited."

"Er, that sounds a bit unsanitary." His mouth twisted as he gestured to his hand. "Germs and all."

Kate took a gulp of water, wishing it was wine.

"Miles." She set her glass down and straightened her spine. "You're a brilliant, very nice man, and I've enjoyed getting to know you. It's been wonderful working with you as well, but I'm afraid this social element isn't working for me."

He blinked, as if he couldn't believe what he was hearing.

"That is, I don't think we should start dating," Kate added gently.

Miles was silent for a long moment before he reached up to loosen his tie. He sat back in his chair, his shoulders slumping.

"Why does this keep happening to me?" He pinched the bridge of his nose and heaved a sigh. "Every. Single. Time."

Kate bit her lip and deflected a pang of regret. She reached across the table to pat his hand.

"I can relate," she admitted. "It took me a while to figure out that it really wasn't me. Sometimes people just don't mesh romantically. And frankly if a girl doesn't make your heart pound and your palms sweat, then she's probably not the one."

He gave a humorless laugh. "I want a woman who challenges me, not one who gives me cardiac arrest."

"I mean, you should feel all warm and tingly every time you look at her," Kate said. "And she should feel the same way about you. Like you can't get enough of each other."

"For heaven's sake." Miles rolled his eyes. "That kind of thing is for fairy tales and romance novels. I want a woman who will be my partner."

"Exactly. And your partner is a person you want to be with all the time. Someone who gets you right down to your core and gives you the things you've missed in life. Someone you can tell all your secrets to, who laughs at your jokes and knows how you like your coffee. Someone you can dance with."

"I told you, I don't dance."

"When you find the right person, you will."

Kate squeezed his hand and let go. She gathered her briefcase and cell phone, then walked slowly back to her office. She wasn't sorry to break things off with Miles—not that they'd really gotten started yet—but she was a little sad. She'd once had such high hopes for him. And if it hadn't been for Miles...she might never have experienced the brilliant, shooting star that was Tyler Stone.

She entered her new office, a spacious room with a fancy computer system and a wall of windows overlooking the coastal hillside. She even shared an assistant with another VP now, which was a switch in roles she was still getting used to.

A small package sat on her desk. Though she hadn't been expecting anything, Kate peeled off the paper. Two chocolate bars appeared, wrapped in gold and silver foil that bore the words GOLD RUSH.

What...?

"Kate." A knock came at the half-open door and Luke looked in. "Do you have a minute?"

"Of course." She set the bars down and moved around from behind the desk, still feeling weird about offering the CEO a seat in her office. "How can I help you, si...Luke?"

His expression unreadable, he extended several papers printed with slides from a presentation. The first sheet read STONE CONFECTIONERS' HISTORICAL CANDY.

Kate leafed through the pages, her shock deepening. This was the proposal she and Tyler had talked about, the one he'd wanted to present to Luke and the other board members.

He'd listed all his ideas for reviving the forgotten chocolate and candy upon which the Stone Confectioners and Sugar Rush empire had been built. Chocolate drops, lollipops, truffles, candy made with orange sugar, molasses, vinegar, fruit. Caramels, bonbons, pastilles, jujubes.

Kate lowered the pages. Her heart was suddenly racing.

"Did Tyler give this to you?" she asked.

"Yes. He said you'd gotten the idea when you were working with him in the library."

"*I'd* gotten the idea?"

"He also said Spencer has already been working on recreating the recipes," Luke continued, folding his arms across his chest. "When I agreed that you could help Tyler with the library database, I hadn't known you were concocting this kind of plan."

"I...I wasn't, sir...I mean, Luke." She swallowed, uncertain why he was being so stern. "Tyler found some old Stone Confectioners' recipe books, that was all. We thought it would be fun to see if they could be recreated in the lab, to find out what eighteenth and nineteenth-century candy actually tasted like."

"And the proposal about it becoming a new product line?" Luke asked.

Kate fidgeted with the papers. If he was upset about this, she didn't want to blame Tyler.

"What about it?" she finally said.

"It's one of the best ideas I've heard in a long time."

Kate jerked her head up. "Really?"

A smile broke out on his face. "Really. It's brilliant. I'm only irritated that someone hadn't thought of it before now."

"Luke, it wasn't my idea at all. Not even close." Relief filled her, sparking a wave of pure happiness. "It was Tyler's. We talked about the recipes, but he's the one who suggested it could be part of the Sugar Rush line, both as a viable product and an homage to the company's history. We did market research, too, and there's nothing like this out there. It would be a totally new avenue to explore."

"Which we're going to do," Luke said. "But why did Tyler tell me it was your idea and that you're the one who should spearhead the whole project?"

"I don't know."

Though she did know. Tyler wanted her to take the credit so

that she could erase the humiliation of her mistake. So that she could start off on the right foot in her new position.

Even now, even after she'd pushed him away both privately and in public...he wanted to help her. Because he had a heart that was bigger than the world.

"Ask Spencer," she said. "He'll confirm that Tyler was the one who came up with the idea. I'd encouraged him to write up a formal presentation to present to the board, but then..."

Her voice trailed off. *Shit happened.*

She certainly didn't have to tell Luke that.

"We need to talk about this." He nodded to the proposal. "I like it. A lot. My father will, too. I'll ask the new librarian about compiling information, and I want at least one or two historians on board to ensure we're getting it right. I'll have my assistant call you to set up a meeting."

"What about Tyler?"

"He says he's done with Sugar Rush." He took the papers back from her, regret tightening his mouth. "I told him he's always welcome to come back, but it doesn't sound like he wants to."

Because of me?

Lord in heaven, she didn't know how much more of this her heart could stand.

"What's he doing, then?" she asked.

"He's planning to take over the garage from his friend Charlie." Luke started toward the door. "I guess Charlie was ready to retire, so Tyler's going to run the place now, first doing general maintenance work and building up a clientele for classic car restoration. Seems to be happy about it too, so that's good to see."

This news eased a little of Kate's raw emotions, because there were few things she wanted more than Tyler's happiness. And the thought of him doing what he loved, putting an old car back together piece by piece, restoring it to its original beauty... nothing could have made *her* happier.

Well. Maybe there was one thing...

After Luke had gone, she sat back at her desk and looked at the Gold Rush bars. One plain and one nut, exactly like the ones her father had bought for her from Grenville's every Friday evening.

Love, fear, and hope swarmed inside her like butterflies. Tyler would do anything for her. She should have known—his loyalty to his friends, often to a fault, and his dedication to Charlie and the garage proved his willingness to put others before himself.

He'd fumbled and fallen in the process, of course, but his heart had always been in the right place. Funny how all the things she'd once derided about him—his spontaneity, his devil-may-care attitude, his drive for fun—were now qualities she admired the most.

He'd shown her the value of being with someone who strengthened the places where she was lacking, just as she did for him. Her organization and practicality had helped him succeed at a job he'd been convinced he couldn't do.

And he'd shown her that sometimes the *path* was in a place where you least expected. She just had to find the courage to take his hand and step onto that path with him.

She picked up her cell and hit the call button.

"Yup," responded a male voice.

"It's me." Kate pressed a hand over her pounding heart. "I have a favor to ask you."

CHAPTER 31

"This area is for the swap meet." John spread a map out on a table in the office and indicated a section of the field. "People drive in here, register at the gate, and park their show cars in the designated spot. Food trucks and booths here, stage and music tent here."

"Looks good." Tyler checked the list of action items. "I got two yeses from car dealerships for vendor booths. So that brings us to…three vendors so far."

John gave him a wry grin. "That's three more than we had last week."

"I'm hitting a bunch of places tomorrow. Auto parts stores, motorcycle shop, a few sporting goods stores. I just signed the lease for the field rental, so we're on for September 15. How many car entries do we have?"

"Four." Charlie peered at the registration form on the new computer. "One Paul Waters was first to register with a '68 California Special."

Tyler was pleased to think of the Mustang getting a well-deserved exhibit. He hadn't ruled out the hope that one day the garage—*his* garage—could focus exclusively on classic car restoration. If they started turning a profit and getting a reputation for restoration work, that hope could become a reality.

The desk phone rang, and Charlie picked it up. "Stone Garage and Restoration Services," he announced. "Charlie speaking."

Tyler turned back to his list. They had a ton of work to do in order to make the Fordwell Classic Car Show a success, but for the first time in his life, he was equal to the challenge.

Hell. He craved the challenge. Because he could do it.

He'd negotiated a new agreement with Dan Corrigan for the boat payments, which might not come as steadily as they would have had he still been working at the library. But Dan, a self-made multi-millionaire who'd started his own labeling company, had been willing to see both the change in Tyler and his efforts. So had Warren Stone.

"Guy says he found an old Pontiac at a repo sale." Charlie held the phone away from his ear. "He's thinking about restoring it, but doesn't know where to start. Want to talk over a plan with him?"

"Yeah, definitely."

"He can have it towed here this afternoon."

"Great." Tyler checked his watch. "I need to run over to Wild Child for a couple of hours, but I'll be back by three."

Charlie conveyed this info to the caller before hanging up. Tyler and John finished going over the updated Fordwell plans, then Tyler headed over to the bakery for a business session with Polly, who was helping him set up the P&L and expenses spreadsheets for the garage.

When he returned to the garage later in the afternoon, he eyed the rusted old Pontiac now sitting in the bay where the California Special had been.

He walked around the car, surveying the body and assessing all that would have to be done. Like his Mustang, this car would need to be rebuilt from the floor pan up. Dismantle the car bolt by bolt, rebuild the engine, reassemble the body.

"'67 Firebird." Charlie approached from the office. "Never had one here, huh?"

"No kidding." Tyler ran his hand over the fender, trying not to get too excited at the idea of starting a new project. "Any time frame or budget?"

"Not yet. Told the owner you'd work up a plan."

"Does he know I'm not a pro?"

Charlie shrugged and nodded toward the office. "Go sell yourself."

Figuring he had nothing to lose, Tyler returned to the office. He stopped in the doorway. His heart suddenly careened around his chest, as if it had just been freed from a cage.

"Kate?"

She turned from the window. His soul took flight. For a second, he almost couldn't breathe. If he'd thought two weeks apart would have changed his feelings for her, he couldn't have been more wrong. Love, wild and riotous, rose inside him with the power of a sea storm.

"Hi, Tyler." She gave him a tentative smile.

"What…" He couldn't stop himself from letting his gaze roam hungrily over her body in well-fitted jeans and a blue T-shirt that hugged her in all the right places. "What are you doing here?"

"I heard there was a new car restoration business in town." She tilted her head toward the door. "So I wanted to find out what you could do with that old junk heap."

"The Pontiac?" Tyler asked in disbelief. "That's your car?"

"I bought it, so yes."

"But…I thought the owner was a man."

"A man?" Her forehead creased in confusion. "No. Oh, my father called Charlie to make the transportation arrangements, but he's not the owner."

"Your father?" He couldn't seem to make his brain work. He was too busy struggling not to grab her, haul her against him, and kiss her senseless. He curled his hands into fists to prevent himself from surrendering to the urge.

"He's visiting from Wabash for the week." Kate gestured out the window to a tall, bearded man who was consulting with one of the mechanics. "He'd like to meet you, and for the record, he knows you're not a data analyst. He also knows you're incredibly smart, loyal, and dedicated, and he was really happy to hear that you're into restoring cars. Do you think you'd be interested in working on the Firebird?"

"Do you come with it?"

She shot him a mischievous grin. "I come with *you*. All the time."

He chuckled and started toward her, then stopped. Hope was bubbling inside him like hot springs, but he still didn't know if she was here for *them*.

"Thank you so much for the Gold Rush bars," she said. "You told me Spencer was recreating the historical recipes, but I had no idea you'd given him the one for Gold Rush bars."

"I wanted to surprise you," Tyler said. "You told me you were disappointed that Sugar Rush doesn't make them anymore. And God knows I never want you to be disappointed."

Kate's eyes grew suspiciously bright. "Why did you tell Luke the historical candy idea was mine?"

"Because you're the best person to run with the idea," he said. "The only person who can do it right."

"But I…I wouldn't want to do it without you." Kate closed the distance between them, resting her hand on his chest. The warmth of her palm burned through the material of his T-shirt and straight into his blood. "Will you come back to Sugar Rush?"

Tyler shook his head. He desperately wanted to come back to *her*, though.

"I'd like to visit the library again," he said. "Maybe even do a little more with the collection, but working at Sugar Rush was never what I wanted. For you, though...you're all kinds of amazing there."

She smiled. "I love you, Tyler Stone. You're bold and fearless, and you've shown me that the world can be so much bigger, so much *better*, than I've ever believed."

His entire soul squeezed tight, like she was hugging it. But he still refrained from touching her.

"What about Norwood?" he asked.

"Turns out I'm completely incompatible with a stick-in-the-mud," Kate said. "A sexy, rakish mechanic who loves pizza, disco music, family history, and whose kisses make my toes curl with delight, is far more my type. My *only* type."

Relief flooded him, fast and hard. Before he could respond, Kate stepped away and reached into her bag. She removed a small white box.

"I had a hard time finding this." She held the box out to him. "But finally I did."

He tugged the lid off. A nest of white tissue paper lay inside. He opened it up, and his heart gave a crazy leap. He stared at Kate in astonishment.

"Where did you find this?"

"My father has a friend at an old car parts store in Charleston. He asked around for me."

Tyler took the item out of the box. Etched with the emblem of a galloping horse corralled into a rectangle, the pop-off gas cap was unique to the '68 California Special Mustang. For three years, he'd been too late to the game when one became available for purchase or auction.

A strange emotion filled his chest—a combination of gratitude, pleasure, regret, and unbearable love. He closed his fingers around the gas cap.

"I sold the car." He looked at her, a laugh rising to his throat. "I sold the Mustang so I'd have enough money to buy the garage from Charlie."

Her lips parted with surprise. "Really?"

"Really. I don't want to use my trust fund money anymore, so I figured that was the only way I could start on my own. Got a good chunk of change for it, too. I'm also moving out to Rainsville because it's cheaper. See what a bad influence you've been on me? I'm acting like an actual adult now."

"Oh, Tyler." Her eyes warmed with a mixture of pride and sorrow. "I love what you've done and I'm so proud of you, but I know how much that car meant to you."

"It never meant nearly as much to me as you do."

Her smile almost brought him to his knees. He wasn't sure his heart could contain all the wild, happy emotions she was generating, as if she'd reached inside him and turned on a switch.

He held up the gas cap. "This is the best present I've ever gotten. I'm keeping it."

"I'm keeping the Gold Rush bars." She moved closer to him, her brown eyes filled with wary hope. "And I'd like to keep *you* too."

He couldn't wait any longer. He took hold of her shoulders and tugged her closer, letting his head fill with her sweet, flowery scent. Her body fit so damned perfectly against his, every curve molding to the planes of his chest until it felt as if a lost part of himself had been locked back into place.

"I love you, my Darling," he said.

Happiness radiated from her like light from the stars. She put her hand on his jaw and rubbed her thumb over his mouth.

"Maybe you could reconsider that move to Rainsville," she suggested. "I know of a secretly sexy, newly appointed VP who might have a room available at her house."

"Hmm." He cupped her face in his hands and drew her closer. "I'll bring my library card and come check that out."

"Your presence is long overdue."

"I'm going to give you a kiss now." Tyler lowered his head. "If you don't like it, you can just return it."

He covered her mouth with his. The rest of the world disappeared, fading into the touch of her lips, the press of her body, the beat of her heart in rhythm with his.

This was it. After being recklessly adrift for years, acting like a jackass, grabbing whatever he could find to escape his fears, it turned out that all he'd had to do was stop and reach out.

And everything he'd ever wanted had fallen right into his arms.

EPILOGUE

Six months later

*D*ozens of restored classic cars—Mustangs, Pontiacs, El Caminos, Thunderbirds, Camaros, Corvettes—sat in perfect rows across the field, their polished painted exteriors gleaming in the sun.

A banner proclaiming *Fordwell Classic Car Show: A Fundraiser for the Veterans' Association* hung at the entrance. Vendor booths and food trucks lined the opposite end of the field, along with a stage where a live band had been performing all morning.

Kate made her way through the crowd, which consisted of both local and visiting guests as well as plenty of volunteers. Gavin Knight and several other men staffed the Veterans' Association table. The scents of burgers, burritos, and fried chicken hung in the air as people wandered around sampling food and enjoying the cars and the music.

She waved at Polly and Luke, who were selling croissant sandwiches and Declairs at the Wild Child booth. Not far from them, Julia Bennett and Spencer Stone staffed the Sugar Rush Historical Confectionary booth—the first preview of Sugar

Rush's new line of historically authentic, small-batch artisan chocolate and candy.

Luke and Warren had insisted that Tyler be paid a substantial licensing fee and royalties for the idea, and after paying back Dan Corrigan, Tyler was putting the money into his trust fund and using it to upgrade the garage.

Kate stopped at the Smooth Moves truck and ordered a Mango Sunrise and a Blueberry Blast smoothie. She gathered two straws and walked to the display area, where Tyler was making the rounds among the rows of cars.

Dressed in cargo shorts and a *Fordwell Classic Car Show* T-shirt, walkie-talkie in hand, he looked both comfortable and entirely in his element as he stopped to discuss the vehicles with both guests and owners. People gravitated toward him as if he were a king holding court, reaching out to shake his hand and slap him on the back.

He was perfect for this role, smiling and laughing easily, eager to talk about the cars, thanking people for their support. His buddies—both the vets he'd hired to work at the garage and his college friends—patrolled the area as volunteers ensuring the program stayed on track.

Kate approached, and Tyler glanced in her direction as if he'd sensed her coming. A smile spread across his face, his gaze skimming her figure in shorts and a car show volunteer T-shirt.

"You need to go back there right now," he said, indicating the food booths.

Kate stopped. "Why?"

"So I can watch you walk toward me all over again."

She smiled, extending the Blueberry Blast smoothie. "How about I put on my red camisole tonight and walk across the bedroom toward you instead?"

His eyes darkened, and he leaned over to give her a swift kiss.

"That'll work," he murmured roughly.

Kate patted his chest, her heart bursting with pride over

everything he'd accomplished in recent months. Business at the garage had been steadily increasing, and he'd had three new classic vehicles come in as restoration projects. Not to mention, the car show was proving to be a huge success, with full-capacity registration and proceeds that would exceed their expectations.

"You did it." She stroked her hand over his chest. "Congratulations."

"*We* did it," he corrected, capturing her hand and pressing a kiss against her palm.

"Tyler."

They both looked up at the sound of Warren Stone's deep voice. Kate had never seen the Sugar Rush president dressed so casually—like everyone else, Warren wore shorts and a T-shirt, but even so he still conveyed the regal force that was such a part of him.

"I was talking to Brian Oldham, from the factory." Warren stopped beside them, nodding a greeting at Kate. "Says he knows a guy who has an old Model-T, like the kind Stone Confectioners once used as delivery trucks. We should contact him. A restored Model-T with our logo on the door would be a great marketing tool for the Historical Confectionary line. Your aunt Julia has all kinds of ideas about opening a shop downtown, in which case we could park it outside, maybe even offer deliveries."

"That's a great idea, Dad."

Warren extended a business card. "Give him a call, see what you can work out."

Tyler glanced at the card and slipped it into his pocket. "Does Julia know you're considering her shop idea?"

"Not yet." Warren's forehead furrowed, though amusement lit in his eyes. "Once I tell her, she'll charge into it full-force. Julia is nothing if not passionate about her ideas."

"I'm going to assume that's a compliment," Julia said, her tone dry.

They all looked up. She walked toward them, a vision of loveliness in khaki capris and a well-fitted car show T-shirt. She stopped beside Kate and arched an eyebrow at Warren, who responded with a faintly abashed smile.

"Have I ever given you anything but compliments?" he asked.

"Unfortunately not." Julia muttered the response under her breath, so softly that Kate was sure she was the only one who heard it.

She glanced from Julia to Warren. Was there really a sizzle of heat arcing between them or was it just the sun? Tyler seemed utterly oblivious, his attention focused on an incoming call on his walkie-talkie.

"Spencer is going on a lunch break," Julia told Warren. "Can you come and help out at the booth? We have a line of about a dozen people."

"Let's not make them wait longer than necessary," Warren replied.

The two of them headed back to the Sugar Rush booth. Tyler spoke into the walkie-talkie, then cut the connection and pressed a kiss to Kate's forehead.

"You need anything?" he asked.

"Just you."

He smiled and pulled her into his arms, the place she loved most in the world. The past few months of living and working together had been a combination of everything that made her and Tyler so good as a couple.

Their lives were both a whirlwind of pleasure and a steady routine—work days broken up by spontaneous weekend trips, dirty hot sex mitigated by gentle flirtations, dinners of chicken and kale salad varied by takeout pizza.

And through it all, everything they did either together or separately, ran a strong unbroken thread of love and loyalty. Not a second passed that Kate wasn't aware of Tyler in the world, his presence as strong and timeless as the stone of a quarry, his devotion to her as deep as the sea. She was no longer alone or homesick. In fact, she'd found her home the moment she'd fallen into his arms.

Finally, she understood. Love wasn't about finding someone who shared all your qualities. That would be far too boring. Love was about finding someone who fit you perfectly because of your differences. Like eggs and bacon. Sun and moon. Heart and soul. Tyler and Kate.

ABOUT THE AUTHOR

New York Times & USA Today bestselling author Nina Lane
writes hot, sexy romances about professors, bad boys, candy
makers, and protective alpha males who find themselves
consumed with love for one woman alone. Originally from
California, Nina holds a PhD in Art History and an MA in
Library and Information Studies, which means she loves both
research and organization. She also enjoys traveling and thinks
St. Petersburg, Russia is a city everyone should visit at least once.
Although Nina would go back to college for another degree
because she's that much of a bookworm and a perpetual student,
she now lives the happy life of a full-time writer.

www.ninalane.com

ALSO BY NINA LANE

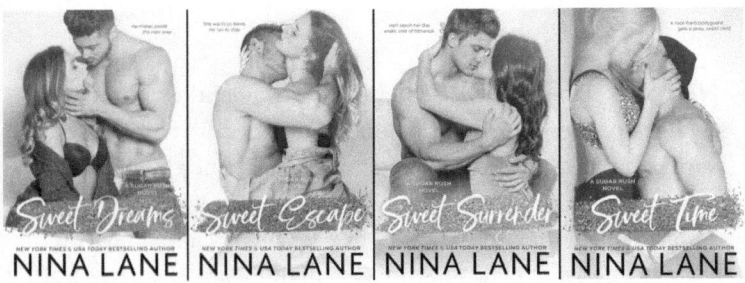

THE SUGAR RUSH SERIES
Sweet is the new sexy.

From the Stone family patriarch down to the youngest
bad boy, follow the lives and loves of the Sugar Rush men and the
women who bring them to their knees.

THE SPIRAL OF BLISS SERIES

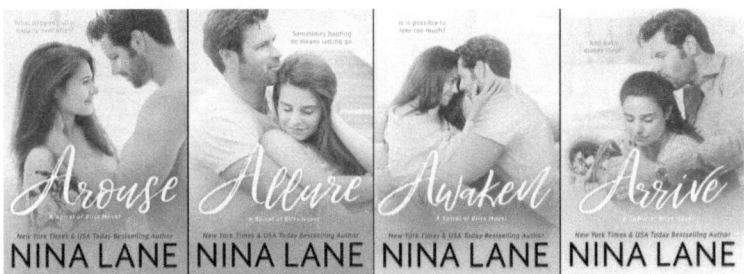

"Give me a kiss, beauty."

From an exhilarating crush to the intensities of marriage, Liv and Dean West embark on a passionate lifelong journey together. As the medieval history professor and his beloved wife face both personal challenges and painful battles, they never lose sight of the hope, humor, and devotion that belong only to them.

Liv and Dean's everlasting romance will melt your heart, turn you on, and enchant you with the power of a love to end all loves.

First we fell in love. Then we fell apart.

Shattered by tragedy a decade ago, two lovers fight the secrets that could destroy them.

"This book is a work of art."

A woman fleeing scandal. A town's mysterious recluse.

Lust and secrets collide in this provocative romance.